Applause for L.L. Raand's

The Midnigh...
RWA 2012 VCRW Laurel Wr... ...ы..t Blood Hunt
Night Hunt
The Lone Hunt

"Raand has built a complex world inhabited by werewolves, vampires, and other paranormal beings...Raand has given her readers a complex plot filled with wonderful characters as well as insight into the hierarchy of Sylvan's pack and vampire clans. There are many plot twists and turns, as well as erotic sex scenes in this riveting novel that keep the pages flying until its satisfying conclusion."—*Just About Write*

"Once again, I am amazed at the storytelling ability of L.L. Raand aka Radclyffe. In *Blood Hunt*, she mixes high levels of sheer eroticism that will leave you squirming in your seat with an impeccable multi-character storyline all streaming together to form one great read." —*Queer Magazine Online*

"*The Midnight Hunt* has a gripping story to tell, and while there are also some truly erotic sex scenes, the story always takes precedence. This is a great read which is not easily put down nor easily forgotten."—*Just About Write*

"Are you sick of the same old hetero vampire / werewolf story plastered in every bookstore and at every movie theater? Well, I've got the cure to your werewolf fever. *The Midnight Hunt* is first in, what I hope is, a long-running series of fantasy erotica for L.L. Raand (aka Radclyffe)."—*Queer Magazine Online*

"Any reader familiar with Radclyffe's writing will recognize the author's style within *The Midnight Hunt*, yet at the same time it is most definitely a new direction. The author delivers an excellent story here, one that is engrossing from the very beginning. Raand has pieced together an intricate world, and provided just enough details for the reader to become enmeshed in the new world. The action moves quickly throughout the book and it's hard to put down."—*Three Dollar Bill Reviews*

Acclaim for Radcly*ff*e's Fiction

2013 RWA/New England Bean Pot award winner for contemporary romance *Crossroads* "will draw the reader in and make her heart ache, willing the two main characters to find love and a life together. It's a story that lingers long after coming to 'the end.'"—*Lambda Literary*

In **2012 RWA/FTHRW Lories and RWA HODRW Aspen Gold award winner** *Firestorm* "Radclyffe brings another hot lesbian romance for her readers."—*The Lesbrary*

Foreword Review Book of the Year finalist and IPPY silver medalist *Trauma Alert* "is hard to put down and it will sizzle in the reader's hands. The characters are hot, the sex scenes explicit and explosive, and the book is moved along by an interesting plot with well drawn secondary characters. The real star of this show is the attraction between the two characters, both of whom resist and then fall head over heels." —*Lambda Literary Reviews*

Lambda Literary Award Finalist *Best Lesbian Romance 2010* features "stories [that] are diverse in tone, style, and subject, making for more variety than in many, similar anthologies…well written, each containing a satisfying, surprising twist. Best Lesbian Romance series editor Radclyffe has assembled a respectable crop of 17 authors for this year's offering."—*Curve Magazine*

2010 Prism award winner and ForeWord Review Book of the Year Award finalist *Secrets in the Stone* is "so powerfully [written] that the worlds of these three women shimmer between reality and dreams...A strong, must read novel that will linger in the minds of readers long after the last page is turned."—*Just About Write*

In **Benjamin Franklin Award finalist** *Desire by Starlight* "Radclyffe writes romance with such heart and her down-to-earth characters not only come to life but leap off the page until you feel like you know them. What Jenna and Gard feel for each other is not only a spark but an inferno and, as a reader, you will be washed away in this tumultuous romance until you can do nothing but succumb to it."—*Queer Magazine Online*

Lambda Literary Award winner *Stolen Moments* "is a collection of steamy stories about women who just couldn't wait. It's sex when desire overrides reason, and it's incredibly hot!"—*On Our Backs*

Lambda Literary Award winner *Distant Shores, Silent Thunder* "weaves an intricate tapestry about passion and commitment between lovers. The story explores the fragile nature of trust and the sanctuary provided by loving relationships."—*Sapphic Reader*

Lambda Literary Award Finalist *Justice Served* delivers a "crisply written, fast-paced story with twists and turns and keeps us guessing until the final explosive ending." —*Independent Gay Writer*

Lambda Literary Award finalist *Turn Back Time* "is filled with wonderful love scenes, which are both tender and hot." —*MegaScene*

By Radclyﬀe

Romances

Innocent Hearts
Promising Hearts
Love's Melody Lost
Love's Tender Warriors
Tomorrow's Promise
Love's Masquerade
shadowland
Passion's Bright Fury
Fated Love
Turn Back Time

When Dreams Tremble
The Lonely Hearts Club
Night Call
Secrets in the Stone
Desire by Starlight
Crossroads
Homestead
Against Doctor's Orders
Prescription for Love

Honor Series

Above All, Honor
Honor Bound
Love & Honor
Honor Guards
Honor Reclaimed
Honor Under Siege
Word of Honor
Code of Honor
Price of Honor

Justice Series

A Matter of Trust (prequel)
Shield of Justice
In Pursuit of Justice
Justice in the Shadows
Justice Served
Justice for All

The Provincetown Tales

Safe Harbor
Beyond the Breakwater
Distant Shores, Silent Thunder
Storms of Change

Winds of Fortune
Returning Tides
Sheltering Dunes

Visit us at www.boldstrokesbooks.com

PRESCRIPTION FOR LOVE

by

RADCLY*f*FE

2015

This Trade Paperback Original Is Published By
Bold Strokes Books, Inc.
P.O. Box 249
Valley Falls, NY 12185

First Edition: November 2015

CREDITS
Editors: Ruth Sternglantz and Stacia Seaman
Production Design: Stacia Seaman
Cover Design by Sheri (graphicartist2020@hotmail.com)

Acknowledgments

Like a lot of teenagers (especially those who don't quite fit for one reason or another), I couldn't wait to leave home, get to college, and be myself. That road took me a few states away from my small upstate New York village to Philadelphia and a busy career in surgery I enjoyed (mostly). I've been back almost ten years this December, thirty miles from where I grew up—living on a farm, no less. Last night I went a few miles down the road to the county fair, the very same one my parents took me to every single summer when I was a kid. The fair is still one of my favorite summer events and I still eat too much awful wonderful fair food. I just finished this book a few weeks ago, and everything I love about living here is in it—the sights, the sounds, the unpredictable weather, the beauty, and quite a few of the people. Nowhere is perfect, and every community has problems, but I wouldn't want to live or work anywhere else. I do wish sometimes I could have been a doctor at the Rivers back when it was first built in the early 1900s—but for that there's always fiction. I hope you enjoy the Rivers community as much as I have enjoyed creating it.

Many thanks go to: senior editor Sandy Lowe for shouldering much of the important daily BSB work so I can stay on deadline, editor Ruth Sternglantz for a keen ear and knowing eye, editor Stacia Seaman for amazing "catches" books after book, Sheri Halal for a super cover, and my first readers Paula, Eva, and Connie for encouragement and inspiration.

And as always, thanks to Lee for being her. *Amo te.*

Radclyffe, 2015

To Lee, for making life a surprise

CHAPTER ONE

Abby studied Blake's brooding profile and feared she'd made the biggest mistake of her life. A week ago they'd been living in New York City, and now she'd uprooted them from friends and community and transplanted them to a rural town in upstate New York. She might as well have teleported them to another planet. "I've got to get to the hospital. Are you going to be all right here alone today?"

Blake turned from the window, his blue eyes stormy. "Sure."

She'd gotten used to monosyllabic responses, ever since she'd told him about the new job and what that meant. She hadn't expected him to take well to the news, and to be fair, their conversations had dwindled to quick exchanges about schedules and appointments ever since Blake's fourteenth birthday. He'd been having a tough time at school the past year, but that didn't mean he was eager to leave his classmates and the excitement of Manhattan. She'd hoped this new place would be safer for him, but maybe physical safety wasn't the only thing that mattered. And she'd be late if she didn't hurry, but she couldn't just leave him looking so lost. Maybe he was fifteen and hugs were history, but he needed to know he was not alone. "What are you going to do today?"

"I guess walk around, check the place out." He smiled, more a grimace than anything else. "That ought to take me an hour or so."

"The movers will be here with the rest of the boxes and the big pieces this afternoon. You can get your room set up."

"We're going to get cable, right?"

"I sincerely hope so," Abby breathed. "We're not exactly in a third-world country."

"Are you certain?" Blake looked out the window again and Abby pictured their backyard, a sweeping expanse of green, more a meadow than a lawn, that meandered down to a clear-water creek. The creek twisted through stands of oak and evergreens and separated their property from a cornfield, at least she thought it was corn. Right now all she could see were rows and rows of five-inch-high green stalks. She imagined in the summer they'd be surrounded by whatever was growing out there, like shipwrecked sailors marooned on a desert island. Still, she'd been happy they'd been able to get anything on such short notice, and the renovated old schoolhouse had a quirky charm she liked.

"We'll get used to it," she said, fervently hoping that was true.

"Sure," Blake repeated with a lift of his shoulder.

"I'll call you. Keep your phone with you." Abby kissed his cheek. His face was so smooth, almost baby soft still, but that would change soon too. Abby firmly reminded herself they'd cross those bridges when the time came. All children changed, and she could handle it. She'd survived when he'd cut his hair without telling her. Now she was used to the short sides and long floppy top with the dark strands always falling into his eyes. He was a beautiful boy. Her boy. "There's money in the cookie jar if you need it."

"Sure." Blake didn't look over as she walked out the door, but just as the screen closed behind her, she heard his soft "Thanks, Mom."

Good enough for starters.

Abby started down the short gravel drive, past the picket fence in need of a coat of paint that marked their front yard, and headed into town. The two-lane through the village was divided by a fading yellow line and bordered on both sides by three- and four-story buildings with ornate cornices, tall narrow windows, and deep porches fronting the stores. One out of three of those storefronts was shuttered and empty. Ten minutes later, she turned in between two stone pillars, one bearing a brass plaque reading *Argyle Community Hospital*, and drove up a winding road between groves of apple trees. She slowed as an ivy-covered red brick building with a white colonnaded entrance and two symmetrical wings extending out in a lazy U came into view on the hillside above the village. A rolling grassy lawn studded with shrubs and flower beds edged the circular drive in front. A pretty place with tall, gracious windows and an air of peace and tranquility. Not the feelings she usually associated with a hospital, but then this was nothing like NYU Medical Center—or any hospital she'd ever trained at.

Following the signs to the visitors' lot, she drove around the front oval and parked. The lot was mostly empty at seven in the morning. She pulled on the navy blazer she'd stowed in the passenger seat, grabbed her briefcase, and walked the short distance to the main entrance. The expansive lobby with its high-domed ceiling, dark walnut paneling, and rows of oil paintings of solemn-faced men looked as if it hadn't changed in two hundred years. It probably hadn't.

No one manned the reception desk at the moment, but a discreet sign saying *ER* pointed to a doorway set into an alcove. She walked through and was immediately ensconced in the familiar sights and sounds of a busy hospital. The hallway was lit with overhead fluorescents and the walls were painted the familiar institutional beige, although surprisingly adorned with carved wainscoting and, here and there, an honest-to-God oil painting. The speckled gray-tiled floors were worn in two parallel rows from decades of stretchers and wheelchairs traveling down them.

She nodded to transport attendants pushing patients in wheelchairs and gurneys toward the service elevators on their way to the operating room or patient floors or radiology. She followed the noise, the conversation level rising as she approached the ER waiting room where a few patients waited in the rows of plastic chairs, the sight the same the world over. Entering the ER proper through the double doors announcing *Hospital Personnel Only* in big red letters, she approached the nurses' station just inside. A dark-haired woman about her age in navy blue scrubs sat at the counter organizing charts. She looked up and smiled. Her name tag read *Susan O'Connell, RN.*

"Can I help you?" Susan said in a welcoming tone.

"Yes," Abby said, extending her hand over the counter. "I'm Dr. Remy."

"New hire?"

Abby half laughed. "Yes, I'm—"

A red phone on the counter rang and Susan said, "Hold on," and picked it up. She stood quickly. "I'm sorry, got an ambulance coming into the bay right now. If you want to get started, we could probably use a hand. The PA on duty just headed up to the ICU to see someone with ARDS."

"Of course." Abby slid her briefcase over the top of the counter onto a shelf and tossed her blazer after it. "What is it?"

"Tractor versus motorcycle. One patient—the motorcyclist." Susan dialed the phone and spoke as she waited. "Head trauma, probable internal injuries…Mary Kate, it's Susan. We've got incoming."

A second later the overhead blared.

Code Blue, STAT, ER. Code Blue, STAT, ER.

Abby frowned. "No trauma alert?"

"No trauma team." Susan came out from behind the counter and motioned to Abby. "Follow me, Doc."

No trauma team. Welcome to small-town medicine, USA. Abby hurried after her, passing cubicles along both sides of the hall, most standing open, a few with the curtains pulled closed, presumably with patients inside. Susan pointed to a metal rack next to two swinging double doors, and Abby paused to pull on booties, a green cover gown, and a paper cap. Beyond the doors, the trauma bay was twice the size of the cubicles they'd passed, with a treatment table akin to an OR table occupying the center. Equipment cabinets filled two walls, and a long counter for charting and paperwork filled a third. The shelves were piled high with stacks of IV bags, dressings, cutdown trays, and the usual paraphernalia of a mini operating room. A red crash cart with drawers resembling a carpenter's tool chest, only this one filled with drugs, stood ready. At least *this* looked like they might be equipped to handle an emergency.

Susan quickly spread a clean sheet over the thick gel mattress pad on the table and checked that the adjustable foot- and headrests were locked. Abby spied a wall switch and flicked on the big round light hanging down from the ceiling on a flexible arm.

"Respiratory?" Abby checked the drawers on the crash cart to familiarize herself with the equipment. All neat and orderly and well-stocked. She pulled out a laryngoscope and several sizes of breathing tubes.

"They'll respond to the code," Susan said, briskly and efficiently checking the IV bags that hung ready from the poles on either side of the bed. Normal saline and Ringers lactate, already attached to sterile tubing.

"Right." Abby hadn't been in the position of not knowing the routine since she'd been a first-year resident. She was used to being in charge. When Presley had called to say she needed someone to take over and expand their emergency services department, she'd jumped at the job. She'd had offers to stay in the city, but many of the other parents advised that Blake would do best if he could start fresh. She'd hoped to have a little more time to settle in, but here she was. "Surgery?"

"I saw Flann's car in the lot. She'll be here."

Susan's casual assurance didn't quell Abby's rising anxiety. Where she had trained, the surgeons were always available 24/7, and by now the trauma bay would be teeming with nurses, residents, trauma fellows, and technicians. And here she stood with a nurse and no idea where to find anything. She'd spent the last year as the senior fellow in a level one trauma unit. This hospital was far from that. She braced herself for the coming chaos. Hopefully, they'd have the personnel to handle a serious trauma.

"What have you got, beautiful," a husky female voice called from the doorway.

Abby stepped aside as a sandy-haired woman in green scrubs barreled into the room. Even though she was average height and size, she seemed to fill the space. Maybe it was the energy pouring off her that electrified the air.

Susan responded. "Motorcycle versus tractor. Motorcycle lost."

"Don't they always?" The woman shook her head and pulled on booties. "ETA?"

"Ought to be pulling in right about now."

"Perfect. I'll be able to get my eight o'clock started on time, then."

The woman glanced in Abby's direction and shot her a cocky smile. "New nurse?"

Abigail forced a smile. And so it began. Surgeons never changed. Always swaggering, often condescending, and, unfortunately, necessary. She held out her hand. "Doctor. Abigail Remy."

A smooth, firm hand enclosed hers. The dark gaze slid over her face, and a slow smile formed on a broad, shapely mouth. Good-looking and she knew it. Abby suspected this was the point where most women surrendered their panties. She tried not to swoon.

"Flannery Rivers. I guess the new residency program is starting a little bit early."

Abigail kept her smile in place with effort and withdrew her hand. "Actually, no. I would be the ER chief."

The playful warmth in the brown eyes chilled. "Really. And here I thought that was my job. I guess I missed the memo."

Abby hesitated, considering whether to take up the gauntlet. Susan appeared to be watching them with the avid interest of a spectator at the US Open, her head swinging back and forth between them. Abby had no desire to be the talk of the entire hospital by lunchtime, although she probably couldn't change anything at this point. Still, this was no place and no time to butt heads over who was going to be in charge. She planned to be, but she'd just have to update Dr. Rivers on the details later. "I'm sorry if communications have gotten twisted. I gather a lot has been happening pretty quickly here."

"You might say that." Flannery reached for her cap, as if to pull it off. "I guess you don't need me here, then."

"Actually," Abby said, "I don't know the code team. You should lead it."

Flannery looked surprised and maybe a little chagrined. "Right, sorry. Sometimes I trip over my ego."

Abby was just as surprised at the admission. Points to Rivers for good sportsmanship. Not many surgeons had the confidence to laugh at themselves, or admit their egos often outweighed their body mass. "Comes with the territory, doesn't it?"

Flannery laughed and the cocky light returned to her eyes. "Absolutely."

"Here they come," Susan announced at the same time as a heavyset redhead pushed a portable X-ray machine into the room.

"Thought you might need me," the X-ray technician said, puffing slightly.

"Thanks, Kevin," Flannery said.

On his heels, two paramedics steered a stretcher through the open bay doors. A thin blonde in her forties balanced on the side of the gurney, bagging the patient, while a wiry Hispanic man guided them up to the bed, calling out, "Twenty-year-old white female. Unresponsive at the scene, vital signs erratic. Present BP 80/40, heart rate 130, Glasgow 10. Second liter of saline running in now, fractured right leg, right temporal contusion, breath sounds decreased on the right."

"Meds in the field?" Susan called, jotting notes on a chart.

"Two milligrams of IV morphine."

"I'll get bloods for type and cross and labs," Susan said, tying a tourniquet around the patient's right arm.

Abby edged up to the left side of the gurney across from Flannery, who had a stethoscope pressed to the girl's chest. She felt the trachea—midline—and visually assessed her torso and limbs. Her left arm was angled unnaturally in the midforearm, and her hand was gray and blue.

"Get ortho," Abby directed, and then stopped herself. She glanced at Flannery. "Fractured left humerus, possible compression syndrome. We need an ortho guy and possibly a vascular surgeon."

Flann nodded. "That would be me."

"Which?"

"Both for now."

Abby pressed her lips together. No orthopedist in-house. No vascular surgeon. Probably no specialists of *any* kind in-house. One surgeon to rule them all. God, what had she stepped into?

CHAPTER TWO

Flann ran through the routine of assessing the patient, the steps so familiar she could do them in her sleep. There had been a few times during her residency when she had. All the same, in the back of her mind, her father's voice reminded her to always expect the unexpected. Every case was unique, no matter how many times she had seen the battered bodies, the traumatized tissues, the unforgiving march of disease. Routine was her biggest ally and her most dangerous enemy, the sword with two edges she wielded in her daily battles. She checked pupils, reflexes, breathing, and heart rate. She palpated the abdomen, percussed for fluid, searched for signs of rupture and internal bleeding. Ran her hands down the extremities, over the pulses in the groin and behind the knees and feet. As she worked, so did the others, monitoring vital signs, throwing X-ray films up on the light box, regulating the respirator, and monitoring blood gases. Everyone did their part, that's what made them a team. *Her* team. Her domain.

As she worked, she was aware that the team had subtly changed. Abigail Remy worked across from her, their hands nearly touching at times—inserting IVs, catheters, and tubes; checking and rechecking the minute-to-minute vital signs for instability or improvement. They'd barely spoken, but she already knew so much about the new ER chief— her focus, her sure movements, her calm and purposeful directions spoke of confidence and intelligence and control. Still, Remy was no surgeon, and a stranger. And she was undoubtedly the harbinger of change. She was taking one of Flann's jobs, after all, or so it appeared.

Under other circumstances, she'd have been more than happy to make Dr. Remy's acquaintance. She'd only had a few minutes before entering crisis mode to assess her, but those few seconds had been enough to deliver a one-two punch. Abigail projected a lethal combination of beauty and power in a captivating female package that Flann had never been able to resist. Shoulder-length golden hair, wavy and thick, that could only be completely natural; green eyes so pure Flann could almost smell the spring leaves; and a body even the loose cover gown couldn't quite conceal, full and curved in all the right places. Anywhere else, any other time, and she would already be thinking about the first date.

Fuck it all. Not this time.

Flann strode to the light box and scanned the row of X-rays: skull, C-spine, chest, belly, arms, legs. Abigail appeared beside her, tilting her head as she studied each one. Even her silence vibrated with cool confidence.

Abigail extended a finger toward the chest X-ray, her subtly manicured nail gleaming with clear polish. "Blunting of the costophrenic angle right there."

"Yeah, I see it," Flann said. "Lung fields are clear, but that could be blood."

"You have ultrasound, don't you?" Abigail asked.

Flann cut her a glance. "We are operating in the twenty-first century here."

"I'm very glad to hear that." Abigail's smile was thin. So far the resuscitation had gone well, everyone doing their part and all the critical bases being covered. Still, the absence of in-house specialists, especially neurosurg and ortho, was a potential disaster waiting to happen. "Want to get ultrasound to check the belly?"

"Would be quicker if I did a cutdown."

"If she's ruptured her diaphragm above the liver, there might not be free blood in the cavity."

Flann upgraded her opinion of the new ER chief. The term rankled, but she set her irritation aside for now, even if taking orders from a medical doctor was not in her makeup. "Good point." She looked over her shoulder. "Susie, honey, can you get Terry down here super quick."

"Sure thing, Flann," Susan called, and reached for the phone.

"Honey?" Abby murmured.

Flann grinned, perversely glad she'd irritated her just a little bit. "Part of my Southern charm."

"I didn't realize you were Southern."

"Through and through, on my mama's side."

Abby blew out a breath. "The charm might be open to question."

"Give it time."

Abby laughed reluctantly. "MRI?"

"CAT scan. We've been trying to get an MRI suite for a couple of years. You know what they cost."

"I'll let Presley know it's a priority."

"Presley?" Flann knew exactly who Presley was—her soon-to-be sister-in-law and the new CEO of the SunView Regional Medical Center-New York Division. She wondered how well Abigail knew her.

Abigail gave her a long look. "Presley Worth. I understand she's marrying your sister."

"I've heard that rumor." Flann shook her head, still checking the films. "Unless Harper comes to her senses."

Abigail stiffened. Really, could she be more of an ass? "You don't approve?"

Flann grinned. Got her again. Remy was fun to tease. "Actually, I do. Harper is really happy, so not for me to point out the error of her ways. How do you know Presley?"

"We're sorority sisters."

"Ah. That's some kind of lifelong secret society kind of thing, right?"

Abigail didn't bother pointing out she and Presley came from different worlds and had formed a friendship despite that. The ultrasound tech appeared in the doorway, giving her an excuse to escape Flannery's uniquely irritating company. She'd rarely met anyone so irreverent, arrogant, and she would've said insufferable, if there hadn't been those moments every now and then when Flannery acted against type. When the conceit dropped away, something genuine and surprisingly intuitive snuck through. And now was not the time to be thinking about Flannery Rivers. In fact, anytime would probably be dangerous.

Abby focused on the ultrasound monitor as the tech coated the probe in clear gel and ran it over the young woman's abdomen.

"Got something here," the young Hispanic woman noted. She slowed the movement of her probe and gently pressed in small circles over the right upper quadrant of the abdomen.

Abigail pointed. "Right there. Is that a fluid collection above the right lobe of the liver?"

"Mmm," the tech said absently, outlining the extent of the abnormality with swift, careful strokes of the probe.

She was good.

"What's your name?" Abigail murmured.

"Teresa Santiago."

"I'm Dr. Remy—Abby. That's nice work."

The tech smiled. "Thank you."

Flann loomed over Abby's shoulder. "Probably a small tear in the liver capsule. Fluid in the chest could be an effusion."

"There might be a rupture," Abby said. "That might be blood."

"Terry," Flann said, "can you get the diaphragm any clearer?"

"I don't see a tear," Terry said after a second. "But if it's small…" She hunched a shoulder. "No, nada."

"What do you think?" Abigail said. "Wait and watch?"

Flann mulled it over. Her first instinct was to explore the abdomen. She was a surgeon. She always wanted to operate, and in this case, there was good reason. Blunt trauma severe enough to rupture a lobe of the liver could have torn the intestine free from the abdominal wall or ruptured a kidney or the bladder, or lacerated a blood vessel. In the operating room with the belly open, she could check visually, get a look at the diaphragm, and take care of any minor damage before it became life-threatening. If they waited, continued bleeding into the chest could compromise the patient's respiratory system, and she was already at risk of developing adult respiratory distress syndrome.

"If she's bleeding," Flann said, "she could go downhill fast."

Abby nodded. "Agreed. But an incision in her belly means a longer hospital stay, *and*"—she went on when Flann made a disparaging snort—"a belly incision is going to make it harder to wean her off the respirator."

Flann wasn't used to consulting with anyone other than Harper or her father on medical care. She trusted their judgment as much as her own. She didn't know Abigail Remy, but everything about her said she was sharp, and Flann's ego didn't extend to endangering the patient's welfare because she couldn't listen to someone else's opinion. Compromising, she said, "Let's get her down to CAT scan, and we can get her belly done after we take a look at her head. As long as her vitals are stable, I'm happy to wait a little while."

"Good, I agree."

"Susie," Flann said, "have you got the CT tech in yet?"

"He just texted from the parking lot. He'll be waiting."

"All right," Flann announced to the room in general, "let's roll her down."

Another nurse had joined the team sometime in the midst of the action, and he and Susan prepared the patient for transport.

Abby glanced at the clock. Twenty to eight. "Don't you have a case?"

"Yeah." Flann sighed. She hated delaying a patient who'd been waiting days, possibly weeks for surgery. Ira Durkee was already in the holding area, expecting to go to surgery any minute, and now he'd be sitting there for a few more hours. "A colon resection."

"I can take the patient down," Abigail said. "If there's any change, I'll call up and let you know."

Flann shook her head. "Can't do it. If I'm in the middle of my case, I can't leave."

"Do you have a resident who can—" Abby took a breath. She really wasn't in NYC any longer. "Right. No residents. Partner?"

Flann grinned. "I've got a great first assistant. But there's no one else with the hands to handle this if we need to explore."

"Well, then," Abby said, "I guess you better let the OR know you're going to be late."

❖

"Thanks, Mrs. Lattimere," Margie called, grabbing the stack of books from the checkout desk.

The librarian waved to her from behind her big oak desk tucked into the little alcove behind the counter and smiled. "Enjoy them. See you at the reading circle on Saturday."

"Sure thing!"

Outside, Margie headed down the flagstone sidewalk toward the bike rack on the other side of the white board fence surrounding the grassy lawn. The town library, a white clapboard building with its square steeple and big, tall windows, was just about her favorite place in town, and she stopped by almost every other day. Her mother had warned her it was going to rain when she'd biked out after breakfast, but the sky looked clear to her. Besides, she'd run out of things to read and had already passed her Kindle allowance for the month, with ten days still to go.

She didn't really mind the six-mile trip to the library, not when it meant she'd get first dibs on any new books that came in over the weekend. And she liked looking at the books, even the ones she'd already read. There was just something cool about seeing the shelves and shelves of spines, and discovering one she hadn't read, like unearthing a buried treasure. Mrs. Lattimere had stopped censoring her reading from the adult section a year ago when her father had paid a visit to assure her Margie was capable of choosing her own reading material, including what Mrs. L termed racy titles. Margie smiled, remembering that discussion, especially since she mostly liked the economics and business books. Although she always managed to grab a thriller or a romance that she guessed Mrs. Lattimere considered racy.

A boy slouched on a green park bench just inside the fence under one of the big weeping willow trees, watching her as she drew near but pretending he wasn't. He looked about her age, skinny like most of the boys in tenth grade—eleventh grade, she reminded herself—with a big loose T-shirt and tan ripcord shorts that came to his knees. His haircut was cool, short on the sides and kind of wild on top, and a pretty shade of dark brown. He was cute. She didn't know him, and that was kind of strange, seeing as how it wasn't really tourist season yet and strangers in the village were unusual. She waved when he kept staring. "Hey."

He looked surprised and blushed, like he'd been caught at something, and smiled almost tentatively. "Hey."

"How's it going?"

"Okay, I guess," he said, but it didn't sound as if he meant it. His voice was soft and a little bored sounding, with the slightest hint of sweetness to it.

Margie stopped in front of him and balanced her books on her hip. He was cuter than she thought at first. His eyes were a really neat shade of blue, a lot like Harper's and her mother's, really dark until you got close and realized they weren't brown but more like navy. "So, are you visiting?"

"No, I live here."

"Yeah?" Margie plopped her books on the end of the bench, sat down, and drew one knee up onto the wooden slats. Wrapping her arms around her leg, she faced him. "You just moved in, then."

He fidgeted a little, as if trying to think of what to say, and nodded. The sunlight cut across his face, and up this close, his skin appeared smooth and pale, his jaw softly tapered, his upper lip full and curved. Huh. Interesting. "That's cool." She held out her hand. "I'm Margie Rivers."

He looked at her hand for a second as if it were a foreign object. Then he took it. His hand was firm and warm. "Blake Remy. Hi."

"So, you'll be in school this fall."

He sighed. "I guess so."

She laughed. "You mean you're trying to figure some way not to be?"

He laughed too, and his eyes lightened as if a storm had passed through and the sun had started to come out again. "Not really. It's just weird, you know. I'm already halfway through high school, and now…" He shrugged. "You know. New guy."

"I've gone to school with the same kids since kindergarten, but I think it would be kind of neat to meet some new people. After a while, you know everyone."

He looked away. "Yeah, I guess."

"So I'll be a junior. How about you?"

"Me too." He straightened a little. "That's cool."

"Where do you live?"

He pointed off to the left. "At the end of town. The old schoolhouse."

"Oh, yeah. That's where the Weatherbys lived before their dad got transferred. When did you move in?"

"We got here this weekend, but we're not really moved in yet. The truck is supposed to come this afternoon with the rest of our things."

"Where did you live before?"

"Manhattan." He said it as if it were on the other side of the world, and a place he never expected he'd see again.

"Wow, that's different."

He stared at her a second and grinned. "Too right. So what's it like around here? I mean, what do you do?"

"Well, it's almost summer." Margie rolled her eyes. "I guess you figured that out already."

Blake laughed again. "I noticed."

"So there's not as much going on as there is during school, when, you know, there's band and soccer and school clubs. In the summer, though…" She stopped, considered. "I bet you don't have much experience with livestock, do you."

"Uh, no," Blake said. "I don't know anything about farms and animals and things like that." He toed his sneaker into the grass. "I'm so not going to fit in."

"Not everyone is a farmer," Margie said quickly. "My sisters are doctors—well, two of them—and so is my dad."

"Yeah?" Blake's face lightened. "So's my mom."

"She'll probably know my sisters, then." Margie knew a little bit about not fitting in. She had plenty of friends, but she knew she was different too. She didn't mind being alone, for one thing, and when she said she wasn't all that interested in dating anyone, even her best friends stared at her as if she was strange. Being different in a totally new place had to suck. "But you could still come to some of the 4-H stuff. You might like it. And a lot of us do it. There's also a summer softball league, with games two or three nights a week at least. Everybody goes there. And barbecues pretty regularly."

A look of panic crossed his face.

Margie grinned. "It's better than it sounds. And you know, you're less than an hour from Albany. There's good shopping closer than that, and movies not far away. The ice cream stand at the other end of town serves food, and a lot of us hang out there, you know, just to hang. You'll find plenty to do."

He looked away. "I guess."

"Listen, why don't you call me after you move in. I can take you around, meet some of the kids."

"Okay."

He didn't sound like he meant it, and maybe he didn't want to hang with her. "You know, if you want to."

Blake hesitated. "I do, yeah. I will. Call."

Margie rose and scooped up her books. "Okay, then I'll see you."

"Wait! Your number?"

She walked backward, calling out the numbers while he punched them into his phone.

He stood up when she reached the gate. He wasn't as tall as he looked sitting down, about her height with long legs. She bet he'd be great at soccer. He was watching her as if waiting for something.

She pushed through the gate, stopped. "Hey, I really like your haircut."

Blake smiled, and Margie thought again how really cute he was.

CHAPTER THREE

A bby stood behind the CT tech, watching the digital cuts show up on the monitor, scanning the images of the brain as they appeared in cross section, looking for evidence of bleeding or other trauma. Flannery crowded close to her, their shoulders touching. She caught a hint of a woodsy scent that reminded her of long-ago autumn nights and bonfires and crisp cool air. She missed the mountains and hadn't thought about them in years. So much she hadn't thought about in the rush to manage a baby and college and everything that came after in one long, exhausting blur. And now was not the time to be thinking about it. She concentrated on the scan again.

The door behind them opened and a lanky dark-haired woman in a pale blue shirt and khakis came in. She was a slightly taller carbon copy of Flannery—their coloring was different, but the resemblance was unmistakable. This must be Presley's soon-to-be spouse.

"Hey," the newcomer said to Flannery. "I heard you had something going."

"Hi, Harp," Flannery said. "Motorcycle. She's got some bleeding in the belly, we think. Just getting to the scans now."

Harper glanced at Abby, her brows rising slightly.

Abby extended her hand. "Abigail Remy."

Recognition flared in Harper's eyes. "You're Presley's friend and our new ER chief." Her grip was an extension of her easy confidence, sure and firm. "Harper Rivers. Good to have you aboard. Presley mentioned you'd gotten here early."

"Presley said the sooner the better. I had time coming, the house up here was empty, and I'd done all the paperwork by email." She glanced at Flannery, whose jaw had tightened. She probably should have checked with Presley before dropping by the ER, but that ship had sailed. "I'm afraid we took your sister by surprise."

"Not a problem," Flann muttered.

Harper glanced at Flannery and shrugged. "I think Presley was planning to catch you up after your first case."

"Well, we're all caught up now." Flann had had enough of hospital politics for the morning. They all knew Presley—aka SunView— would be making sweeping changes to keep the hospital afloat. One of those changes was establishing an independent ER group with a separate financial structure and its own staff to capture patients who might otherwise use urgent-care centers. Abby Remy was Presley's point person, and Flann's new opposite number. She'd live with it. "It looks like the liver is okay. Maybe a small hematoma that will bear watching."

Harper leaned a hand on the desk to get closer, studied the images, and nodded. "Pretty banged up. How's she doing otherwise?"

"She's stable," Abby said, aware that the two sisters were a tight unit personally and professionally. She needed to establish herself as an equal player right away. "But the closed head injury could be an issue. With that effusion in the chest cavity, her respiratory status is questionable too."

Flann said, "We can repeat the chest and abdominal CT in a few hours."

"I suggest that we transfer her to a level one. Then if she needs an intracranial bolt or prolonged ventilator therapy, they'll be able to handle it."

"We ought to watch her here for a few hours," Flann said. "If she deteriorates in transit, that's going to be a bigger problem than what might happen in the next few days. Harp?"

"Transfer will take at least a few hours. We'll have to send her to the ICU until then. If she remains stable, no reason to move her. But it's Abby's call."

Abby appreciated Harper backing her up and considered the compromise. Right now, the patient showed no signs of requiring urgent neurosurgical intervention, but if she did, they would not have very much time to transfer or treat. "You must have some kind of neurosurgical backup here."

Harper said, "We do. We'll call a consult now and get someone in here within the hour. If they're worried about her head, we can transfer then."

Abby blew out a breath. "All right, that sounds like a plan." She paused, looked at Flann. "Dr. Rivers? Are you comfortable with that?"

Flann nodded. "I'll be in the OR. I can break if I absolutely have to." She spoke to Harper, more out of routine than anything else. Abigail had been right in all of her assessments, and Flann didn't doubt she would keep an eye on the patient. All the same, her sister had been her backup in everything her whole life—when they were kids, in college, in med school. Even sometimes when she'd gotten herself into a relationship problem. Harper had always been there to talk her through or talk her out of trouble.

Harper said to Abby, "I'm going to make rounds now, but I'll stop down to the ICU as soon as she's settled and keep an eye on her all morning."

"Good enough," Abby said.

"The nurses will get her settled in the ICU," Harper said.

"I'm going to check in with Presley," Abby said. "Hopefully I'll have a beeper before long, in case anyone needs me."

"Oh, you don't need to worry about that," Harper said. "The page operators can always find you."

"How?" Abby asked.

"Welcome to Small Town, USA." Harper grinned.

Abby must have looked a little panicked because Harper and Flannery laughed at the same time. For just an instant, Abby was jealous of their camaraderie and their obvious affection. She had done so many things alone in her life. True, David had helped her when he could with the baby, but mostly she'd been a single mom, a commuter student the last two years of college, and a med student who didn't have time for the end-of-rotation parties that bonded everyone else. She had Blake, but Blake was her child and needed her to be strong, now more than ever. It would be good to see Presley again. A friend was exactly what she needed.

She followed Harper and Flannery into the hall. Flann pointed to the left. "Administration is that way. Presley has the big office with the big sign that says *President*."

Abby laughed. "I always knew she would be someday."

"As long as she isn't interested in DC." Harper's pride was obvious. She sketched a wave and headed away.

An awkward silence descended and Abby met Flann's dark, penetrating stare. She held the gaze, realizing she hadn't been on the receiving end of a woman's appraisal in a very long time. She felt heat creep into her cheeks. Damn it. Not a woman, a colleague, and one not so happy to meet her.

"Welcome to the Rivers, Dr. Remy," Flann finally said.

She turned and jogged away, leaving Abby wondering what Flann had seen in her face and praying her uneasy attraction hadn't been obvious. Because she wasn't really—attracted, that is. Flannery Rivers was easy on the eyes and sexy in an all-too-knowing way, but even under ideal circumstances, not Abby's type.

As it was, she had to figure out how they could work together without rubbing up against the sharp edges of competition between them. And she had no plans to start anything with anyone while she and Blake were still getting settled in a whole new chapter of their lives. One thing was for certain, even if she were desperate for company, Flannery Rivers would be dead last on her list of candidates.

Satisfied she'd put *that* distracting issue to bed, Abby set off to find her once-best friend, who, like so many things in her life, she'd let slip away. The administrative wing was deserted except for a few of the offices where doors stood open and early arrivals worked at desks, sorting papers and checking computer screens. The contrast to the seething energy of the medical wing was momentarily disorienting, a lot like her life these days—swinging from high to low with the sweep of the minute hand. Hopefully, she and Blake would find a little stability here.

At the very end of the carpeted hall, a redhead occupied a sleek L-shaped salt oak desk in a spacious alcove with an oriental rug, several plush waiting chairs, a coffeemaker on a credenza tucked into a corner, and a large window with a breathtaking view of the valley and village below. The vivacious-appearing late-twentysomething with bright green eyes and cover-girl complexion smiled at her. She wore tailored earth-toned pants and a pale green silk shirt. A square-cut emerald glinted on her right hand and a small diamond pendant matched studs in her ears. Understated and classy. "Morning. Can I help you?"

"I was hoping to catch Presley," Abby said, extending her hand. "Abigail Remy. I just started—"

The redhead jumped up, her smile widening, and grasped Abby's hand. "Oh! Of course. I'm Carrie, Presley's admin. It's great to meet you other than in email."

Some of the strangeness fell away with the warm welcome. Abby said, "You too. Thanks so much for making the whole process so easy. Is there anything else I need to do?"

"You ought to drop by personnel sometime today for a photo and get your ID card and a parking pass to the staff lot." As she spoke, Carrie pulled open the right-hand drawer of her desk, withdrew a glossy brochure, and handed it to Abby. "Here's a map of the grounds, and inside you'll find a key to all the important internal areas. You're all set with payroll."

Abby glanced at the brochure, a sweeping panoramic view with the hospital at its center. Beneath it were the words *SunView Medical Center—the Community's Hospital*. "Thanks. Things are moving fast, I gather."

"Presley is very efficient."

Abby laughed. "Oh, I remember that from when she was the sorority president. Can I get in to see her sometime this morning?"

"Hold on, let me check." Carrie sat behind her computer and typed. A second later a message alert chimed. "She says now is good, and she's ready for coffee and something to eat. Can I get you anything?"

"You know, I could do with a bagel or something, but you really don't have to—"

"I always go about this time to grab something myself. It's no problem."

"Then I'll take advantage and say yes."

"Great. Go on in. I'll drop off supplies in a few minutes."

"It's great to meet you in person," Abby said as she crossed to the door bearing a simple brass plaque with the words *Presley A. Worth, President* in etched block letters. She knocked and the door opened almost immediately.

"Abby!" Presley grabbed her into a huge hug. "I'm so glad to see you." Presley relaxed her grip and kept both hands on Abby's shoulders. Her gaze swept down and back up. "You look great. I can't believe it's been five years. How did we manage to let that much time pass with just cards?"

"I don't know." Abby swallowed around an unexpected lump in her throat. She'd forgotten how comforting real friendship could be, how the instant acceptance and sense of belonging could make any problem seem solvable. Sure, she'd been close to her fellow residents, but that was more out of mutual preservation rather than anything else. She'd never shared herself with them. Presley hadn't changed. Her blond hair was a little shorter, but her blue eyes were just as sharp and appraising as ever. No one could ever hide anything from Presley. She wasn't sure how deeply she wanted to be seen just yet. She stepped back, squeezed Presley's hands as they parted. "It's great to see you. I believe you're actually glowing. I didn't realize that was physically possible."

Presley's color rose. "I think it's sunburn."

"Well, country living seems to agree with you."

"You have no idea." Presley slid an arm around Abby's waist and led her into the room. The suite was spacious with windows on two sides and bookcases on the other two. A sitting area with an oval oriental rug, a beige leather sofa, two chairs, and a coffee table occupied one corner. An open door led to an adjoining conference room with a large table surrounded by a cluster of chairs. Presley's traditional dark wood desk sat in front of one wall of windows through which Abby saw clusters of lilac trees in full bloom. "How do you get any work done in here?"

"It took me a while to get used to it." Presley gestured to one of the chairs in the sitting area and took one of the others. "At first I felt hopelessly out of place, but it didn't take long to begin to feel at home."

"I hope you're right, because I'm feeling a little displaced myself."

Presley smiled gently. "I feel really lucky to get you here so quickly, but I hope I didn't rush you too much." .

"My fellowship was up in another few weeks, and I hadn't had any vacation time this year. I needed to make a final decision about a job"—Abby shrugged—"and frankly, none of them really appealed to me."

"I'm glad I caught you at the right time."

A double knock sounded at the door and Presley rose. "Come on in, Carrie." She helped Carrie distribute containers of coffee and a tray with bagels and spreads on the coffee table. "Thanks."

"You're welcome." Carrie paused on her way out. "Hey, Abby, do you play softball?"

"I—" Abby laughed at the unexpected question. "Not since high school. Sorry."

"That's great. I'll be in touch."

The door closed and Abby glanced at Presley. "Softball?"

"A local passion. There's a hospital team. You can run, but you can't hide."

Abby laughed again. "I might have to try. I was never all that good."

Presley shook her head. "Carrie is the new team captain and she's relentless. I only escaped by threatening to fire her if she kept nagging me to play."

The affection in Presley's tone belied her words. Abby envied the easy camaraderie. "She seems great. She really handled everything for me."

"Good. I know you're used to a big city hospital, but our ER is very busy. Probably not what you're used to, but—"

"Actually I just came from there. I walked into a trauma call."

"I heard the code," Presley said. "Everything all right?"

"So far."

"You must have met Harper, then." Presley's expression softened, as if the thought of Harper took her somewhere else for a second. "She was headed that way."

"I did. And Flannery. She wasn't expecting me. Sorry if I jumped the gun. I wanted to introduce myself to the night shift before they left, and one thing led to another."

"Ah." Presley sighed. "Damn it. I'm sorry you walked into that. My fault entirely. Harper and I were away for the weekend, but I should have called Flann to tell her you were on your way."

"That's fine. We made our introductions." Abby didn't plan on using her friendship with Presley to smooth out bumps with staff, even if—*especially* since—one of the bumps was with Presley's family. "We'll work it out. Transitions are tough on everyone."

"Flann is a great surgeon and a sweetheart, really," Presley said. "But you know, she's a surgeon."

Abby laughed. "I noticed. Harper seems terrific, by the way."

"We'll have to get together so I can gush," Presley said. "In fact, come to dinner this Saturday. We're buying the house I've been renting, and I'd love for you to see it and meet Harper."

"I—" Abby could make her own schedule now, and she'd just work Sunday to make up for the weekend day off. And Blake needed to meet people—meet their friends. "All right, yes. Thanks."

"Good. We didn't get much chance to catch up on the phone," Presley said. "I was too busy trying to sell you on this job. How is Blake? And David—do you see him much?"

"We talk pretty regularly, but he and Matt are living in Arizona now. They have a real estate development business out there. Blake has visited a few times but doesn't really press for more time with David."

"How did Blake react to the move?"

Abby suppressed the swell of words rising in a rush. She hadn't realized how much she wanted to talk to someone when she didn't have to pretend to be totally in control of everything. "About that. I was thrilled when you offered me this job—it's great to be close to a friend after all these years, and professionally, it's an amazing opportunity. But another big part of the reason I took the job is Blake. The last year has been hard."

Presley leaned forward. "What's happening? Not something medical, I hope?"

"No, not at all." Abby took a breath. "About a year ago, right before Blake's fifteenth birthday, Blake explained to me he was quite certain he was not a girl."

CHAPTER FOUR

Flann finished her colon resection in record time and had at least an hour free before her next case. She waited until her first assistant Glenn had the patient off the table and on the way to recovery before leaving the OR to speak to the family. She pulled on a white lab coat over her green scrubs, ditched her cap and booties in the trash, and after updating the patient's wife and daughter, took the stairs down to the first floor for a decent cup of coffee from the cafeteria. Sipping as she went, she strode through the main building and down the administrative wing. Carrie was at her desk typing rapidly, a half-eaten bagel on a paper plate by her right hand and her eyes glued to the monitor.

"Hey, beautiful," Flann said. "How's your morning?"

Carrie looked up and grinned. "It's Monday, so it's hell. How's yours?"

"The usual dragons to slay."

"I heard it started out with a trauma." Carrie's brow furrowed. "Patient doing okay?"

"As far as I know. Harper picked up the ball and has been keeping an eye on her in the ICU. I'm going to stop by there in just a few minutes."

"I heard the new ER chief was there too."

Flann considered her answer. Carrie was smart enough to be running the hospital on her own, and she was a staunch Presley supporter, not that that bothered Flann in the least. She liked Presley—as much as she liked any administrator, on a professional level. Personally, she liked her a whole lot more. Presley was a good match for her sister, and she was happy that Harper was happy, even if she wasn't exactly certain how she felt about having her almost-twin suddenly part of a couple. That hadn't ever really happened for them before. They'd both had girlfriends over the years, but neither of them had ever really gotten serious. They were so close in age they'd ended up in the same class in high school and med school, so everything they'd experienced, they'd done as a team. That stopped at the bedroom door, but short of that, they were each other's best friend and about as tight as two people could be. Now the person she trusted most in the world was about to have someone else to share her life with.

Presley and Carrie were a team too, inside and outside the hospital. Flann couldn't blame Carrie for fishing for a little insider information about how things had gone with her and Abby Remy. Carrie'd hear soon enough, but not from her. "We bumped into each other just before the code. I already knew her résumé, and she proved she's got the creds in the ER this morning. Presley made a good call recruiting her."

"So you're okay about handing off control of the ER to her?"

Flann laughed. "You think I'm okay about handing off control to anybody over anything?"

Carrie colored. "I wouldn't have said so, no."

"Bingo." Flann tossed her coffee cup into the trash. "Let's just say the two of us have agreed to coexist. Give us a little time to work out the ground rules."

"That sounds fair." Carrie smiled again, revealing a tiny gap between her front teeth.

Flann noticed, not for the first time, she was beyond cute—she was also smart and sexy and a great softball pitcher. She could give as good as she got with verbal jibes on the field, feisty and flirty in a non-gamey way. Flann had a feeling she'd be feisty and fun in bed too. She'd been thinking about asking her out since the first time she'd seen her, but she usually tried to stay clear of entanglements at the hospital, mostly because the place was a gossip mill and anything anybody did was fair game for lunchtime conversation, especially if it involved one of the doctors. Plus there was the added complication of Presley about to be her sister-in-law. If things got messy—not that she'd let things go that far—she didn't want her family involved.

For some reason she couldn't quite decipher, those reasons didn't seem particularly important just now. Since news of the hospital changing ownership, Presley arriving, Harper falling head-over-heels, and now Abby Remy moving in on the ER, her world was just slightly off-kilter. Since she couldn't do a damn thing to change any of it, she needed a diversion, and some downtime with a cute, sexy, smart woman was just what the doctor ordered. Thinking about a night with Carrie would definitely take her mind off the morning's meeting with Abby.

Abigail Remy unsettled her, something that rarely ever happened. Every time she replayed their first encounter, which she'd been doing pretty much constantly except for the ninety minutes she'd been scrubbed in the OR, she got sideswiped with a weird mix of irritation and intrigue. She didn't usually obsess over a woman, and this one was completely not her type—too serious, too controlling, and not in the least susceptible to being charmed. Abby's immunity to being charmed wouldn't have been annoying at all if Flann hadn't had the persistent, irrational, inexplicable urge to do just that. And there she was, getting sidetracked by images of Abby's cool, composed, admittedly beautiful face again. Flann pushed the image aside and leaned a hip on Carrie's desk. She turned the paper plate with her index finger, spinning the bagel with it. "What do you say we go out after a game some night."

"We always go out after the games," Carrie said. "Beer and pizza. It's tradition."

Flann shook her head. "I don't mean with the rest of the team. I mean you and me. We can grab a quick shower at my place and drive down to the city. Have a late dinner in a real restaurant. You know, the kind where they use cloth napkins and serve the food on dishes instead of paper plates."

Carrie stilled. "You mean, like a date."

"That would be the general definition, yes." Flann stopped the spinning plate and moved her hand a few inches until it touched Carrie's.

"I need to think about it." Carrie slowly moved her hand away.

Flann straightened. "Is your schedule full all summer?"

"Not quite yet," Carrie said slowly. "I'm just not sure it would be a good idea."

"It would be a great idea. You know we're a good combination." Flann leaned in again, just a little. Carrie'd been looking at her with interest for a while too. She didn't mistake those kinds of signals. "I know you feel it, same as I do."

"Maybe," Carrie said quietly. "But we're a pretty good combination right now."

"And we'd only get better. Why don't you think about it and let me know. The offer is open."

"I…I'll call you."

"I'll be waiting."

Abby rounded the corner and stopped abruptly, her gaze traveling from Flann, perched on Carrie's desk, to Carrie.

"Oh, sorry," Abby said quickly. She hurriedly handed several papers to Carrie. "They told me in personnel that Presley needed to sign these. I thought I'd just walk them back."

Carrie straightened and took the forms. "Of course. I'll see that they're completed and get them down there before lunch."

"Thanks." Abby turned to Flann. "Nicole Fisher—that's the patient from the motorcycle accident—is stable. Neurosurg should be reviewing her repeat CT about now. I'll give you a call when they're done."

"I'll be up in a few."

"Of course." Abby glanced from Flann to Carrie again, her face smooth and cool. "I'll see you there, then."

She turned and quickly disappeared.

"Did you want to see Presley?" Carrie said, sounding oddly formal all of a sudden.

"For a minute," Flann said contemplatively, wondering how much Abby had heard of her and Carrie's bantering date talk. Not that she should have cared. Oddly, though, she did. Pushing that irrational reaction aside, she slid off the desk and tilted her head toward the door to the inner sanctum. "Can I go in?"

"I think she's got a few minutes before a conference call. Let me check." Carrie typed and a second later said, "Go ahead."

"Don't forget to call me." Flann knocked once on the door, stepped inside, and closed it.

Presley was behind her desk, making notes on a pad.

Flann flopped into a chair in front of Presley's big desk—the one that used to be her father's and everyone expected to one day be Harper's—and crossed her ankle over her knee. "Morning."

"Flann." Presley smiled. "I was just about to call you."

"I had a few minutes between cases, so I thought I might as well drop over and save you from tracking me down."

"I hear you met Abby."

"I did. You didn't waste any time getting her here."

"There's no point in wasting time. Every day we are losing money. I know you and Harper and Edward aren't happy about the changes that are coming, but they're coming, and we've all agreed."

Flann blew out a breath. "I know, and I know you're right. It's just hard."

"I mean to do everything I can to see that the Rivers stays a community hospital, with community doctors and nurses and staff serving the community. But we don't have enough qualified physicians to expand our facilities, and an independent ER will bring revenue to SunView that I can funnel into the hospital, as well as referrals that we would have lost otherwise."

Flann grunted. In this she and Harper were attuned. They didn't care about money, they cared about practicing medicine. Her father was the same, and his before him. Unfortunately, doctors were often terrible at business, and the doctors who had been influential in running the hospital for 150 years hadn't moved fast enough with the times. She got it. She knew Presley was their best chance. But she also knew when the ER residency program started and new blood started moving in, the dynamics within the hospital would shift. Trainees who hadn't grown up here, who had no roots here, would be treating patients they hadn't grown up knowing. The personal touch would disappear, and with it, some degree of the personal responsibility that got her and Harper and their father up out of a warm bed at night to see that a patient got the best care possible.

The changes had already started, and it'd only been a few weeks since the takeover. The ER was no longer under the control of the department of surgery. Abby Remy was now in charge, but a good 50 percent of Flann's practice was ER based. She saw all the trauma patients and all the acute med-surg problems, and she was used to being the one to call the shots. "Remy is young," Flann said. "She just finished her fellowship, right?"

"She's not young in age or experience," Presley said. "She missed a few years and it took her longer to finish med school than it might have, so she came out of her residency a little bit later."

"Why the delay?" Flann said. "She certainly seems smart enough."

"She had a young child, and she was raising he—him pretty much on her own until her mom could relocate and help out."

Flann sat up straighter. "She's married with a kid?"

"No, she's a single mom."

"How old's the kid?"

"Blake is almost sixteen."

"Wow." Flann whistled. "She doesn't look old enough to have a fifteen-year-old."

"We were in college."

"And she made it through college and med school and an ER fellowship with a kid. Okay, I'm impressed."

Presley laughed. "That's what it took to impress you?"

"I don't doubt your MBA from Wharton was tough to come by, but you have no idea what it's like being a resident, especially when you're female with kids. Nobody has room for a resident who leaves early because a kid is sick or has an after-school event. That's what wives are for."

Presley stared. "I don't believe you just said that. You might be a surgeon, but you've never struck me as chauvinistic."

"It's not about being chauvinistic, it's just the way it is. Any medical resident has a tough time having a family, and surgery is longer and tougher. But a woman has it even harder. And a single mom?" She shook her head. "Your friend Abby must have a spine of steel."

"She's one of the strongest people I know," Presley said. "So try to give her a break, will you?"

"I'm not planning to give her a hard time."

"Thanks." Presley hesitated. "So we're good? You're not mad at me anymore?"

Flann grinned. "You're hard to stay mad at. Even if you didn't make my sister stupid happy, you'd still be hard to stay mad at."

Presley pulled her lip between her teeth. "Is she, really? Stupid happy, I mean?"

Flann cocked her head, studied her. Presley was a confident, aggressive woman and, rumor had it, a total ballbuster in the boardroom. She'd never seen her uncertain. "You're not serious, are you? She's crazy about you. Why, is there a problem?"

"No, it's just…she's so special, you know?" Presley grimaced. "And I don't have a lot of practice at this kind of thing."

"You mean love?"

Presley nodded.

"Well," Flann said, "I'm certainly not one to talk, but Harper knows what she wants and she wants you. That should be it, right?"

Presley let out a long breath. "You're right. I've just got jitters, I guess."

"Family coming in for the wedding?"

Presley looked pained for a second and her jaw tightened, her expression suddenly reflecting the Valkyrie she was, unafraid to battle to the death. "No. My parents are too busy and my brother—let's just say he's not happy with the way things turned out here. He got outmaneuvered, and his ego hasn't recovered."

"He sounds like an ass. Sorry for saying it."

"That's okay. Abby's here, and Carrie. I'll have friends here, and that's enough."

Flann circled the desk and kissed her cheek. "You've got lots of friends here. And a family."

"Thanks, it means a lot to me that you're okay with me and Harper. Because Harper would never be happy if you weren't."

Flann worked up a grin. "Hey. You and Harp don't have to worry about me. I'm good."

"If anything changes—"

"Just enjoy the wedding planning, and don't worry about anything else." Flann hurried out before Presley could start probing any deeper into her relationship status, or lack thereof. She wasn't like Harper. She wasn't looking for a relationship. Harper was the heir—the one who'd be carrying on the family name, the family legacy, the Rivers dynasty. She wasn't even a spare. All she wanted was a little uncomplicated companionship.

"See you at the game," Carrie called.

"I'll be waiting," Flann tossed back as she jogged out down the hall and back toward the hospital, her domain. She took the stairs to the second floor and the ICU, wondering if Abby Remy would still be there. Trying *not* to wonder why a shot of adrenaline hit her in the gut when she thought about it.

CHAPTER FIVE

F lann pulled down the drive at the homestead and parked behind Harper's pickup under the porte cochere. As she got out of her Jeep, the smell of supper mixed with fresh-mown grass enveloped her. The wafting scents carried her back to the hot summer days of her youth, and a tug in her chest made her long for simpler times. Shrugging away the whimsy, she strode around the back of the house and leapt up the two stairs onto the back porch.

Her mother called, "Shoes!"

"They're clean," Flann called back.

"Use the mat."

Grinning, she scraped her soles on the worn straw mat by the screen door. Most of the family was already congregated around the big trestle table in the middle of her mother's kitchen. The weather was too warm for a fire in the deep brick hearth at the far end, and the windows above the counters along one wall were all open, letting in the aroma of honeysuckle and lilacs. Platters of baked chicken, potatoes, roasted vegetables, and biscuits filled the center of the table. Her father sat at the end closest to her in his white shirt and dark trousers, and her mother, in a cotton boat-necked floral print dress, sat at the opposite end, as it'd always been all Flann's childhood. Harper sat on the left across from Margie, who was pretending not to read from the eReader propped against the table in her lap as she ate. Carson and the baby were missing, and she'd likely not be seen until Sunday dinner. Her husband Bill had finally come home from Afghanistan, and after the family met him at the airport, he and Carson had stayed close to home to reconnect.

Flann flopped into her chair next to Harper, grabbed an empty plate, and filled it with food. "This looks great, Mama."

"Long case?" her father asked, buttering a flaky biscuit. "I thought you just had a hernia repair this afternoon."

"Fractured wrist came in about five." Flann filled a glass with fresh milk. Her father always seemed to know what she and Harper, and most other docs at the Rivers, had going on. "Jimmy Hawkins."

"Damn," Harper said. "I just saw him last week in the office for a work physical. He got that summer job lifeguarding at the lake. I hope he doesn't lose it."

"Trying to keep the cast on him is going to be a major challenge." Flann grinned. "But if he follows orders, he'll only miss the first week of the season."

"Was his mama there?" Ida asked.

"Yep."

"Then he'll mind."

"I was out of the hospital most of the day," Edward said. "I didn't get a chance to meet the new ER chief." He looked pointedly at Flann. "I heard you did, though."

Flann turned slicing and buttering her baked potato into a work of art while she considered her answer. Parsing her words at the family table was something new, but Harper was sitting right next to her, and now, by extension, Presley was too. She guessed Harper and Presley would share everything, the way her mother and father did. The family, the concept of their unity that had been with her all her life, seemed blurry now. When Carson had married Bill, they'd welcomed him into the family, but he'd been deployed for a large part of their marriage. Now that he was home, and Harper and Presley were getting married, the core of the family would be changing. Something else she needed to get used to.

"Abigail handled things well. She looks to be well-trained," Flann finally said.

Edward regarded her silently.

Her mother passed her a bowl of green beans. "Vegetables."

"You know I don't really like—" At a sharp look from her mother, Flann let that battle go and took some of the steamed beans.

Ida said, "I think we can assume that anyone Presley hired would be well-qualified. How did the two of you get on?"

Flann gritted her teeth. Of course her mother would get to the point. She always did. "We got along fine. Dealing with her is the same as with any other consultant."

"Mmm," Ida said. "Except, in this case, you are the consultant."

Flann put her knife and fork down. "That's true."

"And you're used to being at the top of the food chain," Ida remarked casually.

Edward coughed on a laugh. "Those of us in medicine wouldn't necessarily agree with that, my dear."

"Nor do I, necessarily," Ida said with a hint of Southern sweetness. "But I wager that's not the way Flannery looks at it."

"There's not going to be a problem," Flann said, more for Harper's benefit than anyone else's. She was tired of the subject already and wanted to put it to rest. Hoping to divert the attention from her feelings about Abigail, she tried for a change in topics. "Presley tells me she has a teenager."

"Oh hey," Margie said, looking up from the eReader, "I met him today. At the library. Blake."

"Did you invite him to supper?" Ida asked.

"No, but I offered to show him around town. He seems kinda shy. You know, he's a city kid, so I guess everything here seems weird."

"All the more reason to invite him and his parents to dinner so they'll feel welcome."

"Okay, the next time I see him, I will." Margie went back to her reading, instantly absorbed.

"There's just Abby and Blake," Harper said. "Presley invited them over to her place on Saturday."

"As she should," Ida said, "but that doesn't mean that we shouldn't also."

"I'll see to it," Harper said, and Ida nodded.

Edward said, "How are things coming along with the purchase of the White place?"

"Good," Harper said. "The grandsons have been wanting to sell that place since old Mrs. White died. It's the right size, got the right amount of land, and Presley already feels comfortable there."

"So, Carrie's going to move into your place," Flann said.

"Seems like a good solution," Harper said. "The caretaker's place is move-in ready and I'm leaving most of the furniture. She won't have much to do and she'll be close by all of us."

Flann considered the possibility of spending the night with Carrie at the old caretaker's house on her parents' homestead—if they got further than one date. Assuming Carrie called her. She supposed she could put her Jeep in the barn if she didn't want to advertise her personal comings and goings. She could work it out if and when the time came.

"It's a pretty big place," Ida said casually. "What's it got—four, five bedrooms?"

Harper grinned. "Four besides the master, which we figure will be about right. I guess it's a good time to let you know we're thinking about adopting as soon as we can."

Everyone at the table stopped eating and stared at her.

"Well," Ida said finally. "That's welcome news. The sooner the better, because you can never have enough grandchildren."

Flann looked away before Harper got a look at the shock in her eyes. Harper married with kids. The picture had never occurred to her before, although why not, she couldn't imagine. Harper was practically a carbon copy of their dad. A family physician who made house calls and always would. Rooted in the community, born to head a family. Of course Harp would want her own family as soon as she could, now she'd found the woman she would make a life with.

"That's a splendid idea," Edward said. "How long do they expect the process will take?"

"Cool," Margie added. "Can you get two at once?"

"Yes, possibly," Harper said, laughing. "As to how long, I don't know. The agency says the average time is a year to two, but we could get lucky." Harper lifted a shoulder. "We're flexible about things like age or ethnicity, as long as we have a healthy child. The rest will be up to us, then, right?"

"All a child needs," Ida said, "is love. You let us know if there's anything we can do, and when the time comes, with the two of you working, I expect to be lending a hand in that child's care."

"Thank you, Mama," Harper said softly.

When dinner was finished, Flann helped Harper and Margie clear the table while her mother and father retired to the back porch with a glass of wine.

As soon as the last dish was dried, Margie said, "I'm going into the village for a while. See you."

"See you," Flann said.

"Be careful on your bike," Harper called as the back door slammed.

Alone in the kitchen, Flann searched for a neutral topic of conversation, something she'd never had to do with her sister before. The silence drew on until it felt awkward.

"So what do you think?" Harper said finally.

"What do you mean?"

"About the kids thing."

"I think the two of you will be great parents." Flann meant every word from the bottom of her heart.

"Big change, though, huh?"

Flann grabbed a beer out of the refrigerator, flicked off the top on an old bottle opener screwed to the undersurface of the wooden counter, and handed it to Harper. She opened one for herself. "It's about time. You probably should've been married five years ago. You were made for it."

Harper laughed. "It feels now like that's the truth, but I didn't know how much I wanted it until I met Presley."

"Then I guess that's a sign you found the right woman."

"So about the wedding," Harper said. "We're going to have it here, of course, and we both want pretty traditional."

Flannery laughed. "No surprise there either."

"So you're going to stand up with me, right?"

Flann's chest tightened. "Harp, I'll always stand with you. No matter what."

"Thanks."

"That's a dumb-ass thing to say. You don't thank me for being your sister."

"How about for being my friend?"

"Not that either." Flann scrubbed her face. She hadn't been doing a very good job of letting Harper know she was happy for her. Too busy feeling sorry for herself. "Is falling in love and getting married turning your brain to mush?"

"Only sometimes."

"I think Presley is great, and the two of you are going to be super together." Flann grinned. "As for the kids thing? Bring 'em on. We need new blood for the softball league, and we can get started training them up."

Laughing, looking younger by a decade, Harper took a long pull on her beer. "So, how do you really feel about Abby?"

Flann tensed. Had Harper read something in her face earlier? Because Abby Remy kept intruding on her thoughts. A lot more than a new professional colleague, even one who'd effortlessly moved in on her territory, should have. She kept remembering the quick sure movements of her hands as she examined the patient, the steady certain tone in her voice, the focus in her eyes. She was a strong woman, attractive just for that. And then there was the elegant curve of her cheekbones and the sensuous lift of her lips, on the rare occasions when she smiled, and the dynamite shape in a tight, curvy-in-all-the right-places body. Thinking about Abby's body was a really bad idea, since heading down that path would only lead to disaster. She only had to spend five minutes with Abby to know she wasn't the kind of woman to cut loose for a night and then walk away with a smile and a wave. And those were the only kind of women Flann wanted to think about—fun-loving, field-playing women just like her. "Presley made a good call. Having someone competent in the ER so we don't have to worry when we can't get there right away will take a load off us all."

"I'm glad you're okay with it," Harper said. "Presley really likes her. They were pretty tight in college and then—well, you know how it is when you get to med school. You have a tough time keeping any kind of relationship going with anyone most of the time, and they haven't really seen each other for a while. But the connection is still there."

"Yeah, I got that when I talked to Presley earlier. She told me a little about when she and Abby were in college—pretty impressive," Flann said, "that Abby made it through college and med school and residency while raising a kid."

That was another really good reason to keep her distance. Single women with kids were like mama bears—protective and reluctant to let anyone close. Rightly so, but not for her.

"Dad did it," Harper said, "but he had Mama. I don't see how he could've done it and set up his practice without her."

Flann glanced toward the back porch where her parents were

spending a rare few minutes alone together. Even now a lot of the people in the area wanted her father when they had a medical emergency, and he was often called out at night or came home after dinner was long over. Always, her mother had been there for all of them. Her father was Harper's hero, but her mother was hers. Harper would be the best of both of them, but Flann had always known she wasn't cut out to be a family woman. She hadn't even been able to hang in there when Katie was dying. The loss cut her heart out and she'd barely managed to say good-bye, let alone stand strong. She swallowed down the familiar guilt. "I'm sure things will work out fine. Abby has handled a lot tougher situations than relocating, it seems to me."

Harper set the empty bottle on the drain board. "It's going to be a challenging transition for her and her son. Moving from the city up here is just part of it."

"Well, Abby's got Presley, and that will help a lot."

"I don't know…"

"What?" Flann had never known Harper to be reluctant to discuss anything. "What's going on?"

Harper blew out a breath. "Abby told Presley a big part of the reason that she moved up here was to give her son a new environment, a new place to finish high school."

"Teenager troubles? Drugs or something?"

"No, nothing like that. Apparently, Blake identifies as trans. He had some trouble with the transition at his old school and Abby thinks a fresh start with new kids will help."

"Whoa," Flann said. "That's got to be a challenge for both of them. Is this the kid Margie met today?"

"Yeah."

"She didn't say anything."

"Maybe she didn't think anything of it—or doesn't think it's her place to say. A lot of kids their age are cool with different gender identities, even up here where being out about differences isn't as common as in the city. I haven't had a single kid in my practice talk about gender issues, and I'm sure some have questions."

"Neither have I," Flann said, and suddenly, she wanted to know a whole lot more. "You know, it's about time we did a few repairs to that barn at the Whites' place, don't you think?"

"There's a lot of things that need repairing," Harper said, seeming not to notice the change in topic.

"How about Saturday afternoon?"

Harper gave her a long look. "I'll tell Lila to make sure she leaves plenty of extra food for supper."

CHAPTER SIX

A bby pulled into the drive at sunset. Her commute had taken less than ten minutes. Amazingly, she'd saved an entire hour of travel that she'd usually spent on the subway in a haze of fatigue. Now she actually had a few hours to spend with Blake when she wasn't so tired all she wanted was to stretch out and not think about work or finances or what might lie ahead for her child. She left her bag by the front door and walked through the big living room, scanning the loft at the top of the staircase that was Blake's new bedroom. No lights up there, and a silent house. "Blake?"

"Out here," Blake called from the back porch.

Abby stopped to pour a glass of iced tea she'd made in the morning, carried it outside, and sat down next to him on the top step. From here any sound from the street was muffled and the only thing to see was pastureland. The stillness was unnerving and suspiciously restful. She wondered if she'd ever get used to the absence of the barely controlled energy that defined city life. "What are you doing?"

He held up his cell phone with a futile expression. "Trying to get a signal."

"Huh. Dead zone?"

He gave her a look. "I think the whole town might be a dead zone."

She tried to hide her horror. She wasn't *that* much into a calmer lifestyle that she could do without the Internet. Or her phone. "Really? That can't be right. There must be a cell tower around here somewhere."

"I walked just about everywhere, and most of the time I couldn't connect."

"What about in the house?" She imagined her son rambling

through town with his phone held up in front of him, like a displaced time traveler. He was, in a way, and not of his own choice. God, having a child was hard. Wonderful, but so damn hard. "Can we text inside?"

"It's sketchy."

"Let's see what happens when we get cable." She blew out a breath. "We need to have some kind of phone service in an emergency."

"Or if the hospital needs you," Blake said glumly.

"That's not going to happen as often as when I was a fellow. My hours will be a lot more regular."

"You're the boss, right?"

"Yes." The reality of that had sunk in by midday when she'd had to meet with the ER staff to review schedules, evaluate treatment protocols, confirm state-required documentation procedures, and a dozen other things she hadn't had to worry about a week before—in between seeing patients and supervising the PAs who made up the rest of the non-nursing staff. Most of the staff had been friendly and helpful. A few, as she'd expected, had been reserved, as if waiting to see what changes she intended to make. She hadn't seen Flannery after their morning conference with the neurosurgeon regarding Nicole Fisher's status. As busy as she'd been, she'd still had time to second-guess her initial meeting with the surgical chief. Flann was the single most important medical contact for her in the hospital, with Harper being a close second. Between them, they'd be consulted on almost every critical patient in the ER. Once she had the residency program in place and pushed Presley to apply for a primary care residency as well, she'd have a buffer zone where she'd be able to direct patient care much more actively. If the ER was to stand alone within the SunView system, she needed to sever the dependency on Rivers physicians. Flann would fight it.

Tomorrow would be time enough to worry about her battle with the Rivers MDs. Tonight was family time.

Blake regarded her suspiciously. "You called them, right?"

"Hmm? Sorry—called who?"

"The Internet people." Blake looked pained.

Abby crossed her heart. "I swear I did. They said they'd be here tomorrow. You can live until then without Facebook."

He made an exasperated sound and pushed his phone into the pocket of his khaki shorts. "Like I have a choice. About anything."

"What did you do today?" Abby wasn't going to try to convince him everything would be easy. It might not be. But they weren't turning back.

He hunched his shoulders. "Not much. Walked around."

"Did you eat?"

"Yeah."

"Define eating."

"Come on."

"Seriously."

"Cereal."

"For breakfast?"

"And lunch," he said reluctantly.

"Why didn't you go shopping and get something for sandwiches or something like that?"

He shifted on the stairs and gave her his what-planet-are-you-from look. "Mom. Have you looked around this place? There's no supermarket. Where am I supposed to get sandwich stuff?"

"Well, there must be somewhere to get food in town. Maybe one of the restaurants has a deli section or something."

"I didn't feel like going into every one, okay?"

He'd at least ventured out and explored. She'd count that as a win for the day. "What do you say we go find a pizza place. I'm starving."

"You think they have one?"

"I don't think any town could survive without a pizza place. Of course, if you don't want pizza—"

Blake jumped up. "Hell, yeah."

Smiling, she rose. "Give me five minutes to change into something more comfortable."

"Okay. I'll wait out front."

She wanted to give him a hug, but she knew it wouldn't be welcome. She squeezed his shoulder. "It's going to be okay. Food first, then we'll explore."

"Yeah, right," he muttered, but his expression had lightened.

Abby would do anything to keep him safe and help him be happy. She just hoped she'd know what needed doing when the time came. Step-by-step, they'd chart the waters together. After changing into jeans, a mint-green T-shirt, and flip-flops, she joined Blake where he sat on a board swing hanging by thick ropes from a big oak on the front lawn. Impulsively, she gave him a push and he swung forward.

"Jeez, Mom," he yelled, jumping down and landing in a small puff of dust. His big grin belied his outrage.

Abby's heart caught as it often did when she looked at the almost-adult and remembered the child. His hair had been lighter then, sun-kissed and curling around an oval face so unblemished and innocent, she'd believed somewhere angels truly flew. From the time he could talk he'd insisted on he, not she, choosing to be called by his middle name, not his more feminine first; and then for a time, a long frightening time, he'd gone quiet, and the beautiful child had grown joyless and solitary. Until he'd come to her at last, insistent and sure despite the plea in his eyes. And here he was, so different now, and yet at the heart, always the same. Hers to nurture and protect.

"Fine—you push, then." Abby plunked down on the seat and wrapped her arms around the ropes, the scratch of the frayed fibers and the sultry heat rising from the ground drawing her back to a childhood she rarely paused long enough to remember. Blake gave her a push and she extended her legs, leaning back and letting her hair fly out behind her. The freedom was exhilarating and she reveled for a few more swoops before slowing herself with a foot and jumping off.

"Okay." She threaded her arm through Blake's. "Lead on, my man."

Blake pressed against her for a brief, beautiful moment before letting go. The main street through the village was mostly quiet, a few cars and trucks passing now and then and the occasional dog walker, strolling couple, or clutch of teens passing by. Most of the businesses were closed, and the air, heavy with heat and dusk, felt more like mid-August than barely summer. The parking lot in front of Clark's pizzeria was full, however. Most of the vehicles were pickups. A bike rack along one side was nearly filled.

"This must be about the only place to eat at night," Abby said.

"Except for the bars."

"Well, that lets you out for a couple more years."

He snorted and paused on the sidewalk in front of the pizza place, a one-story cement-block building painted Day-Glo orange that looked like a converted garage. Two big plate-glass windows framed a red door. An old-fashioned white glass sign, lit by flickering bulbs, hung over it, with *Clark's* in red script. Teens and a few older patrons were visible through the windows.

"What do you say?" Abby said. Probably having pizza with his mom was the last thing on Blake's to-do list, and the first foray into the social life of the town would be even more of a challenge. The group she'd joined for parents of trans teens had stressed the importance of letting Blake lead the way in defining what was comfortable for him and what wasn't. If he wanted to tell his teachers and friends he was trans, she supported that. If he didn't want to be out or chose to be more selective and only tell a few friends, she supported that as well. The only absolute was that *she* supported him in all ways in all situations with all comers. She resisted the urge to ruffle his short hair. He was her child, of course she supported him.

"I'm starving," he said at last. "Pepperoni?"

"Mushrooms?"

He made a face.

Abby laughed. "Half pepperoni, half mushrooms?"

He grinned, and for just an instant she saw the child he had once been, filled with joy and expectation and trust. She wanted to see that smile dominate his life again.

"After you," she said.

With an almost perceptible squaring of his shoulders, he strode forward and she followed.

The place was one big room with a counter at the back, noisy, smelling of tomato sauce and cheese and, of all things, hay. Three booths occupied one side and the rest of the space was filled with five or six rickety Formica tables surrounded by chairs that looked like they'd been there since the 1950s, aluminum legs and vinyl seats, cracked and patched in places. Pizza boxes, paper plates, and sweating cardboard cups of soda covered every surface. A dozen teenagers lounged around the room in groups of twos and threes. Some glanced their way and then went back to their conversations. Blake ordered for them while Abby grabbed a booth vacated by three high-school-age girls. The girls smiled at Blake as he returned. He colored slightly and slid into the booth. Abby sat across from him.

"Presley invited us to dinner Saturday afternoon," Abby said.

"Do I have to go?" Blake said.

"Presley is an old friend and the head of the hospital. She used to help babysit when you were small."

"I don't remember." Blake picked at the edge of a paper plate.

"I know. But we live here now and I'd like us to meet people as a family."

"Yeah, okay."

He didn't sound particularly enthused. Meeting new people was always a challenge for them both. Sometimes there were questions, sometimes only curious looks. Fortunately, they'd rarely run into overt bias or hostility, but she lived with the expectation that could happen at any time, and she knew he did too. All they could do was deal with whatever came, together.

"The hospital's not far," Abby said. "Probably a fifteen- or twenty-minute walk if you want to have lunch when I'm on the day shift."

"I'd rather get a bicycle," Blake said.

"Really? Okay. First thing." The city hadn't really been conducive to biking, the traffic too dangerous and the subway too convenient. They hadn't lived all that far from his school, so he'd been able to walk or bus in inclement weather. He'd be ready for his driver's license soon, but he hadn't brought it up and she was in no hurry to have him on the roads. "I'll try to get off early one afternoon and we can drive"—she laughed—"somewhere to get one."

"I could probably get one on Craigslist."

"I think we can spring for a new bike."

The guy behind the pizza counter called out Blake's name. As he rose to get the pizza, a girl called, "Hey, Blake!"

A teenager with blond curls to her shoulders, brilliant blue eyes, and the graceful gait of an athlete crossed the room to Blake, a big smile on her face. That was interesting. Somehow Blake had made the acquaintance of a girl he hadn't mentioned. Blake picked up the pizza and gestured toward the booth. A moment later the two teenagers crowded into the booth across from her with the pizza pan in the middle of the table.

The girl held out her hand to Abby. "Hi, Dr. Remy. I'm Margie Rivers. Flann and Harper's sister."

"Hi," Abby said, hiding her surprise. "I didn't realize you two had met."

"Yeah," Margie said. "At the library today."

Avoiding Abby's gaze, Blake said to Margie, "Pepperoni or mushroom?"

"Oh, that's okay. I already had supper."

"Go ahead," Abby said, sliding a mushroom slice onto her plate. "I suspect there's probably still room for more."

"Well, maybe one." Margie glanced at Blake. "Pepperoni."

Blake eased a slice onto a paper plate and passed it to Margie.

"Thanks," Margie said.

Abby said cautiously, "I haven't had a chance to see the school, Margie. Presley said it's a regional high school, with a pretty big class. How do you like it?"

"It's fine. The teachers are mostly all pretty good. Our school graduating class has a seventy-five percent college acceptance rate, which is slightly better than the state average. We score okay on the SATs too, and if you select for just the college applicants, we do even better."

Abby put her pizza down and regarded Margie, suppressing a smile. "You seem to be somewhat of a statistician."

"No, not really. My sister Carson is the MBA. She's head of admissions at the hospital. I'm interested in economics, but I'll probably end up in medicine like the rest of the family."

"I take it that's something of a family legacy."

"Yeah. It's not required or anything." Margie shrugged. "But I guess it's kind of in the genes."

"I hope not," Blake muttered.

Abby laughed. "Maybe not in our family."

Margie looked at Blake. "So what are you planning on doing?"

"Oh. Well. I'm going to be a writer."

"That's cool. Novels, or what?"

"Fiction, yeah." Blake looked nonchalant, but his eyes had brightened.

"So, are you writing anything now?"

"I've got a couple things started."

"That's really cool. Do you think you'll go to college or just start out writing?"

Blake cut a look at Abby. "I think my mom would have a heart attack if I didn't go to college."

"Something along those lines," Abby said dryly.

Margie laughed. "Yeah, I know how that is."

"I don't mind," Blake said. "I think studying writing and literature will be good."

"Me too. I love books."

"Me too," Blake said softly.

When the pizza was done, they all walked out together. Abby held back a little while Blake and Margie walked ahead, discussing a book she'd never heard of. Margie stopped by the bike rack.

"I'll see you," Margie said to Blake. "Nice meeting you, Dr. Remy."

"Call me Abby. And you too."

Margie waved and biked away. Abby chose her words carefully. *Don't push. Don't pry. Leave the door open.* God, it was hard sometimes. She wanted to ask a million things—are you going to tell her? Do you like her—girls—that way? What do you want that will make you happy?

"She seems nice," Abby finally ventured.

"Yeah." Blake stuffed his hands in his pockets. "She is."

Small beginnings. Abby breathed the fragrant air and listened to the sounds of the night coming to life. One step at a time.

Chapter Seven

Abby glanced at the GPS, which had suddenly decided to send her in a completely opposite direction from the one in which they'd been driving. "That doesn't look right."

Blake leaned forward to study the map and then out the window. "None of this looks right either. I can't see anything. I don't think anybody lives out here."

"I'm quite sure they do," Abby said, laughing. "These are just farms."

"Yeah, but there aren't any houses."

"There's one right up on that hill over there."

Blake sat back with an undisguised huff of disgust. "Okay. *One.*"

Still laughing, Abby slowed to check the number on a mailbox coming up. She slowed further and turned in to a one-lane dirt driveway. "This is it."

"How long do we have to stay?"

"Until I've had a chance to talk to my friend, have a decent dinner, and find you a boarding school in another country."

"Ha-ha. Which country?"

"I hear Switzerland is nice."

"At least I could ski."

"I'm quite sure there'll be plenty of skiing around here in a few more months."

Blake perked up. "Can I get lessons?"

"Yes, if you think you can survive that long."

Grinning, Blake said, "I'll try."

"There's the house. Oh, it's really nice."

"Can we have a dog?"

"Do you really want one?" Abby pulled into a wide space between a big white clapboard house with a porch running along the front and a weathered red barn that was twice as big as the house. Come to think of it, the barns they'd passed were always bigger than the houses, a subtle sign of the priorities of farming life. "A dog is a big responsibility for a long time."

"Yeah," Blake said. "But it'd be nice to have someone around."

He didn't have to say *when you aren't there*, but she heard it clearly enough. Her mother had stopped living with them when Blake was old enough to come home from school and be by himself for a few hours until Abby got back from the hospital. With just the two of them, the apartment had seemed too big and too quiet, but she couldn't begrudge her mother a move to Florida after she'd given up more than a decade to live with her and look after Blake. She couldn't have managed without her, and even though her mother had insisted she was happy to do it and wouldn't have missed Blake's childhood for anything, living in New York City had been a sacrifice. Abby's father had died in a car accident while Abby had been in her last year of high school, and her mother had barely begun thinking about what she'd do with her life when Abby had gotten pregnant in her second year of college. Her mother had never wanted to live in the city. She'd grown up in the foothills of the Adirondacks, where Abby had spent some idyllic summers as a child with her grandparents. Living in the Syracuse suburbs where Abby had grown up, her mother had always talked of retiring somewhere warm without snow.

No, she didn't begrudge her mother a single day in the sun. She stopped the car and turned to Blake. "Yes, we can get a dog if you really want one. Just give it a while and think about what it means. You'll be the primary caretaker. If you're sure, then we will."

Blake nodded. "Okay, but I'm sure."

He probably was. He rarely changed his mind once he voiced a desire. She wouldn't mind a dog either, especially at night. She was discovering the quiet country nights under the vastness of a sky filled with a million stars she hadn't seen in almost twenty years made her feel small and inconsequential. Added to that, the nights were so deep, dark, and still, she almost wished for the sound of traffic outside her bedroom window. Almost.

A screen door banged and Presley raced across the porch and down the stone path toward them. Abby got out just in time to be caught up in a big hug.

"Have any trouble finding the place?" Presley looked relaxed in a yellow sleeveless top and dark green capris.

"No." Abby turned slowly, taking in the rolling fields and woods in the distance. "It's gorgeous out here."

"Isn't it?"

Blake got out and stood by the side of the car. He'd worn a black T-shirt with a stylized dragon breathing fire made from red and silver sequins, skinny blue jeans, and bright blue sneakers with no laces. He'd done something to his hair with gel that made it look spiky. He'd also grown another inch, Abby realized. David was over six feet, and it looked like Blake might come within a few inches of that.

"Hi, Blake," Presley called easily before Abby could make introductions. "I'm Presley. You probably don't remember me."

Blake shook his head. "No, I'm sorry."

"Don't be. It was ages ago." Presley looped an arm around Abby's waist. "Come on out back, you two. Carrie's there. She's staying on here until the wedding and then moving to Harper's place."

Another porch stretched the width of the back of the house, where Carrie waited in one of the white wood rockers lined up by the railing. Her crop top, cut-off denim shorts, and flip-flops made her look considerably younger than when Abby had seen her at work. A low bench served as a table and held a pitcher of lemonade, glasses, and a plate of cookies.

"You've met Carrie," Presley said.

"Yes, hi again," Abby said. "Carrie, my son, Blake."

"Hey, Blake," Carrie said, holding out her hand.

"Hi," Blake said quietly.

"Go ahead," Presley said. "Help yourselves to something to drink. And be sure to try the cookies."

Abby poured lemonade for herself and Blake, handing him a glass. "These cookies look fabulous. It smells like they were just baked. I'm impressed, Pres."

"Don't be," Presley said with a laugh. "I have the most amazing housekeeper, Lila. She cooks, bakes, shops, and pretty much keeps me alive. She made the cookies this afternoon before she left. She also put a pot roast in the oven along with the rest of dinner."

"I think we might need a Lila, Mom," Blake said, munching a cookie and dropping down on the top stair of the wide plank steps.

"Maybe you could just learn to cook," she said mildly.

"Yeah, right." He paused with the half-eaten cookie in his hand. "Hey, I think there's something wrong with that chicken."

Abby followed his gaze as a black bird with iridescent tail feathers stumbled around the corner and toward the porch. One leg was clearly damaged in some way.

"Oh, that's Rooster," Presley said. "He's fine. I mean, he obviously isn't, but it doesn't seem to bother him at all." She broke off a piece of chocolate-chip cookie and tossed it out onto the lawn.

The bird made an ungodly screeching sound and attacked the morsel with a series of ferocious pecks. Blake watched with a widening grin. "He's pretty cool. Do you have more?"

"No chickens, but there are some kittens in the barn. If you want to take a look, you're welcome to walk around. The kittens are only a few months old and really friendly."

"Sure, if you don't mind." Blake jumped up as if his pants were on fire, obviously anxious to be free of their company.

"Go," Abby said.

He strode off in the direction of the barn. Abby was aware of both Presley and Carrie watching him, but they didn't ask anything so she didn't comment.

"Thanks for inviting us," Abby said. "We both needed a break from unpacking, and a chance to put a little space between us. Moving is not a lot of fun."

"Unless you're like me," Carrie said, "and you just throw everything into one suitcase, sublease your apartment, and buy a plane ticket. That's pretty much what I did when Presley told me about this job. Of course, I didn't realize I'd be staying when I headed out here."

"How are you liking it?" Abby asked.

"I love it." Carrie grabbed a cookie. "The hospital is beautiful and the people are all pretty great to work with. And I love waking up every morning to sunshine and the green. I love the green."

"There is that." Abby looked off toward the barn. She couldn't see

Blake. "I hope Blake adjusts—I at least had summers in the mountains, but he's a city kid through and through."

"It's not nearly as provincial as it first seems," Presley said. "You'll find after a while everything you need is here."

Carrie laughed. "Well, your experience isn't exactly anything to go by. You've only been here a little while and you're suddenly engaged and about to be married."

Presley pushed a foot on the floor and set her chair rocking. "I know. It's so crazy, every time I think of it, I'm afraid I might be dreaming."

"If you are," Carrie said, "I am too. So don't wake any of us up."

"When is the big day?" Abby asked.

"We just decided last night," Presley said, a blush tinting her cheeks. "The last Saturday in July."

Carrie coughed and sat up straight. "That's a month away!"

"Yes, but—"

"Oh my God! We have to go shopping, we have to start planning, we—"

"Carrie, it's just going to be a small—"

"Oh, bullshit to that!" Carrie grabbed another cookie and took a big bite. "I'll start on the lists."

Presley held up her hands in surrender. "Okay—you're the official wedding planner."

"Of course."

"And you'll both be in the bride's party—the bride being me. Harper says she can't quite see herself as a bride, but bridegroom works."

"Mmm, that's kind of sexy," Carrie said.

"Well, consider the source," Presley said, and they all laughed.

"Harper seems terrific," Abby said. She meant it personally and professionally. She'd had a busy first week in the ER, and Harper had been down half a dozen times to evaluate patients, never complaining when she'd been called, always arriving as soon as she reasonably could, and offering excellent clinical advice. She was great with patients and staff too. A doctor's doctor. If Abby was sick, she'd want Harper to be the one answering the call. Unless she needed surgery, and then she'd want Flannery Rivers.

Presley glanced at her watch at the sound of a vehicle crunching across the gravel. "Somebody's early for dinner." She walked to the far end of the porch, leaned out, and scanned the driveway. She waved and turned back with a big smile. "Apparently Harper and Company are planning on doing a little construction work in exchange for supper."

"Convenient timing," Carrie said. "Who're the other handy hands?"

"Flann and Glenn are with her."

"Have you met Glenn yet?" Presley asked Abby.

"Yes, last night, as a matter of fact." Abby had called for a surgery consult on a farm worker with a swollen hand, and Glenn had responded. The surgical physician assistant covered the house on rotation with Flann and several of the other local surgeons. Abby wasn't used to PAs being first call, but she'd worked with residents her entire career and knew they had more experienced backup if needed. What she hadn't counted on was how very good Glenn was all on her own. Abby'd had only to discuss the case with Glenn and sign off after Glenn spoke briefly with Flann by telephone to ensure everyone was covered legally. "She's really good."

"She was an Army medic in Iraq," Carrie said. "Three tours, I think."

"It shows," Abby said.

"I think Flann prefers working with her over anyone else," Carrie said.

"She's the calm to Flann's storm," Presley said with a laugh.

Abby smiled. "You said it, I didn't."

"Sometimes I think Flann just likes to talk a good game," Carrie said.

"Sometimes," Presley agreed. "At least she's honest about who she is."

"She is." Carrie blew out a breath. "She asked me out."

"Oho," Presley said with a whistle in her tone. "Stepping into deep waters, huh?"

"I don't know," Carrie mused. "I'm not sure it's a good idea."

"Looking for something a little more serious?" Presley asked.

"Not necessarily. I don't really know, actually. But Flann and I get along fine right now, and with you and Harper being so close, I don't want to confuse things."

"Carrie," Presley said. "If you want to go out with Flann, it's perfectly fine. She's a big girl and so are you, and whatever happens or doesn't happen isn't going to affect our friendship or our working relationship."

"Maybe," Carrie said, sounding anything but certain. "I told her I'd think about it."

Abby listened without comment. She didn't know Carrie or Flann well enough to even have an opinion, other than the fact that she agreed with Carrie. Getting involved with Flannery Rivers was not something to take lightly. The woman had the potential for being a serious heartbreaker. Fortunately, she didn't have to worry about anything in that regard. The little twinge of envy was only a reminder she hadn't had a date in years. Maybe someday—with someone a lot safer than a surgeon with a God complex, no matter how gorgeous she might be.

Flannery grabbed one end of a stack of two-by-fours from the truck and slid them out of the bed. Glenn grabbed the other, and together they carried them around behind the barn. Harper followed with toolboxes and a cooler with beer for later.

"Where's the chicken wire?" Flann asked.

"In the barn," Harper called.

"I'll get it." Flann jogged around the side of the barn, noting the other vehicle in the drive. Abby must be here already. She'd seen Presley when they pulled up. The women must be on the back porch, probably talking about them. She grinned. She hoped so. Carrie had said no to a private dinner after the game the night before, but there was no rush. She'd seen Abby a time or two in passing during the week, but they'd been headed in opposite directions. Abby had been polite, and nothing else. Not even a second's extra smile suggesting she might welcome a conversation sometime. The dismissal irked more than Flann expected.

The sliding barn door was partly open and she slipped through into the cool, dim, sweet-scented air and walked down the main aisle. The stalls on one side stood open, waiting for the return of horses who hadn't been in residence for a long time. She wouldn't be surprised if Harp filled those stalls before long. Harp was a farmer by heritage as much as she was a doctor. Flann slowed at the sound of soft murmuring.

A teenager knelt by a pile of hay, stroking a black and white kitten.

"Hey," Flannery said softly.

The teen turned, and Flann saw the resemblance to Abby in the angle of the cheekbones and the curve of the jaw. This must be Blake. He was of the age where gender was often hard to tell at first glance with arms and legs that seemed too long and thin and a slender body that hadn't filled out yet. From a distance he might've been a boy or girl. Up close, it was still a coin toss. She wondered how he handled the confusion that must arise from time to time. Even more so for him. "I'm Flann Rivers."

"Blake Remy," the teen said in a melodic tenor. "Presley said it was okay if I came in here."

"Sure, why not. How are the kittens doing?"

"They're all really cute," Blake said. "I didn't see the mother, though."

"She's probably taking a snooze someplace cool. Come sundown, she'll go hunting."

"For what?"

"Most anything. Bird, mole, rabbit."

"No. Rabbit?"

Flann laughed. "The other day she dragged one back through the cat door for the kittens."

Blake grimaced. "They eat them?"

"They do. These are barn cats, friendly because they've been around people since they were born, but their hunting instincts aren't blunted. They kill to eat, and hunting is instinctual for them. The kittens will be going out with her before long."

"I guess it's okay, hunting to eat."

"Natural."

"They're not meant to be pets, are they?" His tone held regret.

"You looking for a cat?"

"I was thinking more dog."

"There's a shelter in the next village, about eight miles away."

Blake stuffed his hands in his pockets and straightened up. "Yeah?"

"I can tell you how to get there, if, you know, your mom is up for it."

"I'm working on that."

Flann laughed. "I know how that is. So what're you doing now?"

Blake made a face. "Hanging out while my mom talks to her friends."

"You feel like building a chicken coop?"

"Sure, I guess. But I don't really know anything about construction."

"No better time than now to learn."

CHAPTER EIGHT

Abby listened with half an ear to Presley and Carrie, mostly Carrie, discussing wedding plans—contingencies for the outdoor ceremony in case it rained, menu choices for the reception, music, traditional or individualized vows, floral arrangements, decorations, and a multitude of other details—and, with the other half of her mind, concentrated on the hammering, sawing, and occasional shouts from the direction of the barn. Blake hadn't returned from his explorations, and she suspected he'd volunteered for or been conscripted into Harper's construction company. She tried not to worry about how he was getting along or what he might be getting into. He had to be able to make his way in the world without her running interference, as much as she wanted to. All the same, he was still a teenager, and teens were not known for their best judgment. Added to that, Blake had had more than his share of disappointment and shattered dreams in the last year. Her instincts told her the adults could be trusted to be sensitive and responsible, but he was still hers to protect.

"I think I ought to check on the roast," Presley said when Carrie flipped a page in the notebook she'd been filling with wedding to-do lists. "Or at least look at the instructions Lila left as to when to take the cover off and brown it."

"You think we should eat inside"—Carrie put her pen and notepad aside—"or set up out here? The weather called for thunderstorms."

Several wooden picnic tables sat in a shady corner of the yard beneath two big oak trees. The nearly cloudless sky was clear and blue, the temperature warm enough for a T-shirt, at least until the sun went down.

"I think we should eat outside if we can," Presley said.

"I'll hunt around for a tablecloth," Carrie said.

"What can I do to help?" Abby said.

Presley shook her head. "Not a thing. Relax, I'm sure you need it after this crazy week."

"Sitting out here has done more for my mental health than anything I can think of in a long time," Abby said. "If you don't need me for a few minutes, though, I think I'll take a walk."

"Go ahead," Presley said. "There are no rules or have-tos out here."

Abby laughed. "That is definitely unique and different."

When Presley and Carrie disappeared inside, Abby strolled across the yard to the driveway and down a gentle slope toward the barn. Fenced pastures surrounded it, empty of animals now, but she could imagine animals grazing in them sometime in the not too distant past and imagined it wouldn't be long before some did again. The fences were still in reasonable repair, although here and there a post had tilted and a horizontal crosspiece had fallen out. The barn itself was weathered, with peeling red paint, but still sturdy looking. A section of the slate roof spelled out 1896 in various contrasting colors. NYC was the palace of the new and shiny. Out here, it seemed, history infused everything, from the hospital to the homes. She'd spent most of her life in the city, Blake all of his. Would they forever be outsiders here?

Abby reminded herself Presley and Carrie were newcomers, and they'd found their places. She and Blake would do the same.

She followed the sounds of construction around the back to the barn. Harper, Flannery, Glenn, and Blake were surrounded by sheets of plywood, coils of chicken wire, a plethora of tools, and a pair of sawhorses piled with lumber. Blake wore a pair of leather work gloves and plastic goggles someone must've lent him and a fierce look of concentration as he held a board in place while Flannery drove nails into it with a power gun. The pop-pop of the nails shooting into wood had Abby's stomach flipping in a rapid somersault. She told herself not to create disaster scenarios and waited until they had the board secured in place before advancing into the construction zone. She didn't want to distract anyone at a critical moment.

"How's it going?" she asked brightly.

Activity stopped and everyone looked at her as if she were an alien who had just landed in a great big silver spaceship.

"Fine."

"Good."

"Okay."

"Super."

Apparently she should be able to tell the state of affairs by looking. She studied the tall rectangular structure that Blake and Flann were attaching to the back side of the barn while the others waited with expectant expressions. Harper and Glenn appeared to be the design engineers, measuring, cutting, and directing where various pieces would go. She cocked her head and studied it. "It looks like a giant birdcage."

Blake grinned. "It's a chicken coop, Mom."

Abby frowned, seeing only a big empty space. "Where's the coop part?"

"Once we get the enclosure predator-proof, we'll bring over one of the old coops," Harper said. "With a little work, the coop will be fine. What's important is that the flock is protected at night while they're sleeping."

Abby glanced around. On a small knoll fifty feet away, the gimpy rooster strutted around, pecking at the ground. "Flock?"

"Patience," Glenn said slowly, her voice slow and sensuous.

Abby could imagine her singing the blues, spinning tales of heartbreak and betrayal. Something about Glenn spoke of sadness and sorrow, but perhaps she just misread her reserved nature for something more. Abby smiled. "Aha. I see chickens in the future. Hence the need for the coop."

Harper grinned. "It's a surprise."

"I'm sure." Abby was certain the surprise would be welcome. Presley seemed very fond of the rooster, of all things. "I'll get out of your way, but at the risk of sounding like an overly protective mother, I don't want Blake using power tools."

Blake groaned. His expression suggested he'd never seen her before and couldn't possibly be the person in question.

Abby shrugged. She could tolerate being temporarily disowned if it kept him safe.

"You don't have to worry about that," Flann said. "I never use power saws and I'm the only one manning the nail gun."

"Yeah," Blake said. "I'm just the grunt."

Just a grunt. Blake didn't seem the least bit upset by that prospect. In fact, he looked like he was having more fun than she'd seen in weeks, possibly months. A glimmer of hope surged. Maybe this move would be all right after all.

"All right—everybody be careful and have fun." Abby waved and headed back toward the house, slowing when she heard footsteps behind her. She turned as Flann jogged toward her.

"Blake is the youngest on the job," Flann said. "That means all the scut work and the grunt work."

"I understand. There's a hierarchy." Abby brushed a lock from her eyes as the breeze picked up and played havoc with her hair.

Flann nodded. "Yep. You have to be an apprentice before you can get to the good stuff."

"How is he doing?" Abby didn't want to say Blake had never done anything like this before. Life was filled with first times now.

"Studying everything like it's brain surgery and he'll be operating alone tomorrow."

She smiled. "He rarely does anything lightly."

"He's doing fine. And he isn't doing anything that's dangerous. I didn't want you to worry."

"I'm probably being overprotective." Abby sighed, grateful to Flann for taking the time to reassure her and feeling just the tiniest bit foolish for worrying. "A few bumps and bruises aren't going to hurt him. I just don't want any missing parts."

"Listen, you have nothing to be embarrassed about," Flann said with surprising insight. "I know what can happen and how quickly. I can't afford to get hurt, neither can Harper or Glenn, and we sure wouldn't let Blake do anything dangerous."

"I trust your judgment, but he's my son."

"Totally understood. But I hope you trust us, because we've got quite a lot of work to do around here and he's already volunteered to help out again."

"I see." She pursed her lips, pretending to consider. Secretly she was thrilled that Blake was making connections. "Free labor."

Flann grinned. "Everybody starts at the bottom, right?"

"Oh, I know." She'd been trained in the same hierarchical structure as Flann, where the lowest understood their position and counted on one day reaching the top. Then those who followed would take care of the scut work. "If he's having fun, I'm more than happy for him to spend some time working with you. Thanks for teaching him the right way to do things."

"Nothing to thank me for. Or any of us. He's a good worker and a nice kid. And we can use the help."

"He needs something to do, and needs to interact with people other than me." She exhaled softly, ambushed momentarily by Flann's sweat-soaked T-shirt clinging to her surprisingly broad shoulders and sculpted chest. "There's more to life than what I can teach him, and so many things here that I don't know anything about. I can't help him with those things."

"It seems to me you're doing a fine job. He's friendly, smart, polite, with a good sense of humor. That's a lot to say for a teenager."

"I know. But he's also spent a lot of time alone." Abby studied Flann, unveiled some of her secrets. "And he's vulnerable. I appreciate you looking out for him."

"My pleasure." Flann rubbed a trickle of sweat from her forehead with the back of her arm.

Abby followed the sweep of her bare forearm, caught by the way her sun-burnished skin gleamed over taut muscles. She resisted the sudden urge to thumb away a smudge of dirt on Flann's cheek. Flann had a way of capturing her attention when she wasn't being careful. Even worse, the way Flann said *pleasure* sounded as if she meant something far more intimate than simply befriending Abby's son on a sunny afternoon in the summer, and the idea stirred her. She needed to escape, away from Flannery Rivers and her unexpected sensitivity and sexy…everything.

"I've got to help Presley," Abby said, backing away.

Flann sensed the fast retreat and wondered what she'd said to cause Abby to run. They'd been having an easy conversation, a real conversation, about something that mattered, and the connection had felt good. Warm and solid and…good. Hell, if either of them should have reason to run, it was her. She'd been so busy reassuring Abby Blake would be in good hands, she'd forgotten all about charming her. A conversation without flirting was just not her style.

"I'll see you at supper," she called to Abby's retreating form. Abby didn't answer and Flann was left without a follow-up line. That never happened either. She hadn't even thought to comment on how great Abby looked. Abby's body did amazing things for simple shorts and cotton shirts, and the way her hair caught on the wind and tangled around her face made Flann think of how she'd look in bed, leaning over, face flushed… "Oh, for fuck's sake. Rein in your hormones."

Ignoring the sudden burn low in her belly, she stomped back to join the others. Harp gave her a questioning look and a raised eyebrow. She shook her head. "All good."

Flann welcomed the physical labor to keep her mind off Abby, who she didn't want to be thinking about, and Carrie, who had neatly avoided the topic of a date the night before at the game. She'd be better off not thinking about women at all, although she doubted that was possible. She grabbed the nail gun and focused on pounding in nails.

They worked another hour, racking together the external enclosure, stapling up chicken wire, and making sure nothing could get in by digging under. Before they put up the final side, they dragged one of the old coops around from the far side of the barn, hoisted it up on a couple of cement blocks, replaced some broken boards, and covered the old shingled roof with a new square of tin. When they were done, it was waterproof and could house half a dozen chickens plus the damn rooster. They could close the doors up if they needed to or leave them open and let the chickens roam within their enclosure until they were freed in the morning.

"How come you don't just close them in the coop at night?" Blake stuffed his work gloves in the back pocket of his jeans and drained a bottle of water. "Then you wouldn't need the outside fence."

"We could do that," Flann said. "But then the rooster would start making a fuss at dawn wanting to get out and wake up the hens and everybody else within a mile. This way they've got a yard they can peck around in until we're ready to let them free range. It's safer for them and easier on us."

"How come they don't run away when you let them out?"

"Wait'll you see how they get used to their routine." Flann piled wood scraps on the ATV. "Get the hammer and nail gun for me, will you."

Blake grabbed them and carried them over.

"They know where their roost is," Flann said as she packed the rest of the tools. "When the sun goes down, they'll start coming home. And once they get used to being fed in the morning, every time they see you they'll come running."

"When are we gonna go get the chicks?" Blake asked.

Flann looked at Harp. "What's your timetable for the big surprise, boss?"

"I think Margie wants to be along when we pick them out." Harp glanced at the sky and checked her watch. "Looks like the storm is going to hold off. We could go now and still make it back in time for dinner."

"Sounds like a plan." Flann noticed Blake perk up when Margie's name was mentioned. The kid would probably like someone his own age to hang around with after spending the day with them. "You want to go along, Blake?"

Blake looked from Harp to Flann, uncertainty and eagerness chasing each other across his face. "Could I?"

"Sure, unless you want to stay here and hang out."

Blake stared at Flann. "Is that a test?"

"Actually, no. Your mom and Presley and Carrie are pretty cool."

"Yeah, they are," Blake said. "But I'd rather help pick out chickens."

Flann laughed. "Go tell your mom you're coming with us, but wait—don't tell her why."

Glenn said, "I'll hang up at the house. There's not going to be enough room in the truck anyhow."

"Oh," Blake said, disappointment darkening his gaze. "I can stay here then."

"Not a problem," Glenn said. "Really, I've seen plenty of chickens."

Blake glanced at Flann eagerly. "Two minutes. I'll meet you at the truck."

He took off running.

Flann laughed.

Harper said, "Nice kid."

"Abby is pretty outstanding too." Glenn shouldered the roll of chicken wire.

"Nothing not to like," Flann grumbled.

"Nothing at all." Glenn smiled faintly as if she were thinking about some secret memory. "Don't be late. I can smell dinner from here."

"Yeah. We'll be back." Flann's shoulders tightened as she watched Glenn round the side of the barn. She was about as close to Glenn as she was to Harper. They didn't have history as long or as deep, but she worked with Glenn almost every single day, depended on her to look after her patients, relied on her to cover for her when she couldn't be available. She trusted her judgment, respected her professional skill, and knew without a doubt she could be trusted in every other way. But Glenn was a cipher too.

In the three years she'd been at the Rivers and the hundreds of hours she and Flann had spent together, Glenn never talked about her past, gave almost nothing away about her present life. If she dated, she didn't talk about it. She'd never commented on a woman. Ever. Her casual remark about Abby wouldn't have meant anything coming from anyone else, but from Glenn, it meant she'd noticed. Flann didn't like that for some reason. The surge of possessiveness made no sense and irritated her even more. So what if Glenn noticed Abby was a fascinating woman in a very attractive package? Okay, not just very attractive, absolutely smoking hot. Glenn wouldn't be the only one to notice. Not that Flann should care. And who was to say Abby cared either? She seemed to be all business all the time, except where Blake was concerned. Then she was a mama bear—a lot like her own mother. Abby hadn't given off any available vibes, at least not in Flann's direction. Quite the opposite.

"Hell, she might not even have an interest."

"Come again?" Harper said. "I missed something."

Flann muttered, "Nothing. Forget it."

"What's bugging you?"

"Abby's got a kid. Maybe she's straight."

"I'm still not following," Harper said, eyeing Flann curiously. "Maybe she is, or maybe she's bi. Does it matter?"

"Nope. It doesn't." Flann didn't make a habit of lying to her sister, or to herself. She really couldn't explain why she just had.

CHAPTER NINE

H ey," Margie said with a big grin as she climbed into the extended cab of Harper's pickup. "I didn't know you were going to be here."

Blake squeezed over as far as he could on the rear seat to give her room. Almost half of it was piled with medical equipment and supplies in plastic crates along with a big locked metal box that looked like it was bolted to the floor. He kind of felt like he was in a traveling ER van and couldn't imagine doing anything like this back home. In his *old* home, he reminded himself. He smiled, hoping Margie's smile meant she was glad to see him. "My mom and I were at Presley's, and I ended up helping build the coop."

"How's it look?"

"Awesome. It's really big. Flann says there'll be plenty of room for them all."

"I don't know how Rooster's gonna feel sleeping in a coop. Usually he sleeps in a tree," Margie said. "But it's not safe."

Blake pictured the limping rooster alone in the dark and got a tight feeling in his middle. "I guess it's good he's got the coop, then."

Flann said from the front seat, "He's going to be a lot happier about the chickens than he is about not liking the coop."

"Yeah, he'll be busy soon enough." Margie laughed. "How many are we getting?"

"I figured six would be enough," Harper said, turning in to Tractor Supply. "Depends on what they've got left in straight runs."

"That means all females," Margie said at Blake's questioning look. "Mostly you take your chances on the sex because it's really, really hard to tell the sex of baby chicks. They all look alike at hatch."

"Uh-huh," Blake said, trying to sound knowledgeable when he had no idea what everyone was talking about. Until last year, he'd had a circle of friends whose experiences were pretty much the same as his, even though he'd never quite related to some of their interests and never known why. They'd shared books and music and movies and school stuff, and that was enough. Flann and Harper were older, though, and he hadn't spent a lot of time with his mom's friends before this. She didn't have a lot of time to do much of anything except work. He couldn't actually remember her socializing with people at work. He didn't blame her. He knew what time she got up in the morning and when she got home from work. And when she wasn't at the hospital, she spent as much time as she could with him. He saw her a lot more than some kids saw their parents, even with her crazy schedule.

This was all different, though. Flann and Harper and Margie included him as if they'd known him for a long time. They acted regular around him, not studying him with questioning eyes. At least not very much.

He'd expected the stares and the questions and the comments. He'd watched dozens, probably hundreds of videos on YouTube of trans kids talking about their experiences of coming out, or not. Some were good and others bad, and he knew, or thought he'd known, what he'd be facing. Knowing didn't make it any less scary, but at least he could practice being prepared. He'd practiced a lot before he'd talked to his mom. That was the hardest, but the most important, even more important than telling Andy and April and Jill.

As long as he could remember, his mom and his grandmom were there for him. His grandmom practically all the time, and his mom whenever she could be. He couldn't not tell his mom, but he hadn't quite worked out what he would do if she totally freaked out. She hadn't. She'd sat quietly, studying him the way she did when she was trying to look inside him. He thought she probably could, because when he'd finished stumbling through his decision, she'd asked the right questions. Most of all she'd said the right thing. "I love you. You are my child, and you are who you feel you are.

You'll have to be patient with me as I've got a lot to learn, just like you. We'll do it together, agreed?"

Whenever he faced a new situation, he thought about what she'd said. He wasn't alone, even though he was lonely sometimes. He was lonely right now even though Flann and Harper and Margie treated him like a friend. They didn't really know him yet, and maybe they'd change their minds when they did. But he was excited too. He was part of this little group, at least for the next few minutes, and he was having fun.

"So tell me about raising chicks," Blake said, following Margie into the big warehouse-type store.

For the next twenty minutes while they watched the little round balls of fluff clamor around in big metal tubs, Margie filled him in on keeping them warm and making sure they had the right food and water and seeing that the rooster didn't bother them too much until they got bigger, and checking the weather forecasts because it could still get cold at night and they were vulnerable. The sign over the tub with the most chicks said *UNSEXED*.

"They all look alike," Blake murmured.

"Told you it was impossible to tell," Margie said.

"It's sort of neat not being able to tell males from females just by looking," Blake said. "Does it really matter so much?"

Margie looked him in the eye. "Not with people, I don't think. With the chickens it does, though. You can't have roosters in the town limits, for one thing, so anyone with a backyard flock doesn't want one."

A thrill of possibility rippled down Blake's spine. Margie as much as said she was okay with him being different. She hadn't asked for an explanation or a label. For the first time in a long time, he felt free to just be. Maybe it wouldn't last, but it was pretty awesome right now. "You can have chickens in your yard?"

"Sure—you have plenty of room at the old school—"

Harper cut in. "Maybe Abby isn't ready for chickens just yet, Margie."

"Besides," Flann said, joining them, "Blake has to work on the dog angle first."

"Okay," Margie said. "Next year, though…"

Flann put Margie in a headlock. "Enough helpful advice."

Margie laughed and tried to squirm free.

Blake grinned. "That's okay. I'm going to wage a long, careful campaign about a puppy."

"Oho," Flann said, letting Margie go. "Something tells me your mom won't be easily taken in."

"Nope," Blake said. "But she loves animals, so it won't be too hard."

"You two pick out half a dozen," Harper said.

Ten minutes later they were headed back to Presley's with a cardboard box of six peeping chicks balanced on the seat between Blake and Margie.

From the front seat, Harper said, "Presley's going to be pretty busy at work for the next few weeks. Maybe you two could drop over during the day and check on the chicks. Do you drive yet, Blake?"

"Not yet. I'll be able to get my permit in a couple weeks, but I haven't really thought about it all that much."

"Bike?" Flann said. "It's not that far a ride."

"I'm getting one soon." Blake shifted uncomfortably. "But I don't know much—like nothing—about chickens."

Margie said, "The White place is about the same distance for you as it is for me from home—about five miles. That's an easy ride. We could meet up and do it together."

Blake's heart jumped. He didn't care if he had to get up at dawn, as long as he had something to do and someone to do it with. And Margie was really easy to be with. She was smart and funny and she accepted him for him, at least she did right now. If he came out, put words to who he was, maybe she wouldn't. His chest hurt but he had to try. "Yeah, sure. We could do that. What time?"

"I'll talk to Presley, Harp," Margie said. "We can work out a schedule."

Harper glanced back and grinned. "You're in charge, Margie."

"Of course," she said and settled back in the seat.

Blake said, "I have to get a bike right away."

"We've got plenty at the house. You can borrow one of ours for a while."

"Yeah?"

"Sure," Flann said. "There's one of mine there I'm not using. Feel free. We're about the same height, so the fit should be good for you."

"Are you sure?" Blake asked.

"Absolutely. I'll bring it by your place tomorrow," Flann said.

"That would be so terrific. Thanks."

As Harper gave her a sharp look, Flann said, "Don't mention it."

Abby set out a stack of multicolored plastic plates, glasses, and disposable utensils on the red-and-white checked oilcloth that Carrie had spread over one of the two picnic tables. As she turned to go back in the house, Harper pulled up and Margie and Blake piled out of the backseat of the pickup, talking animatedly about something. Flannery jumped down from the passenger side, and for an instant, Abby had no thought in her head except how good Flann looked in tight blue jeans and her faded gray T-shirt. Better than any woman had a right to look. She caught her wandering mind and dragged her thoughts back into safer lines. Harper reached in to the backseat and came up with a cardboard box that she carried toward the house.

"Hey, Presley," Harper called. "You got a minute?"

Presley came to the screen door and looked out. "I'm just about to pull the roast out. What's up?"

"Got you a little something."

Presley hipped the door, wiping her hands on a pale yellow dish towel. "I hope it's dessert."

Harper, Flann, and the kids laughed.

"Not exactly."

Harper set the cardboard box on the porch and gestured for Presley to open it. "See what you think."

Presley knelt, folded back the cardboard flaps, and squealed, "Oh my God."

Abby didn't think she'd ever heard Presley squeal before in her life.

"Can I touch them?" Presley asked, wonder in her voice.

"Sure." Harper crouched beside her, a hand on her back.

The small possessive gesture struck Abby with an arrow of

longing she hadn't expected. Her life had slowed down enough for her to actually realize there might be things she was missing, things she might even need, and she wasn't at all sure she was happy with that. She still had so much to do—a new department to set up, a residency to establish, politics to maneuver. She'd be working twelve-hour days, if she was lucky. And then there was Blake. Moving a teenager to a new town and a new school was daunting enough. Dealing with his transition, and the challenges that came along with that, was a full-time job in and of itself. She had no time for anything else, and even entertaining the idea of dating was foolhardy.

She glanced away from Harper and Presley and discovered Flannery studying her, her deep brown eyes laser sharp and so focused Abby felt the heat. She also felt the flush climb to her cheeks and cursed her autonomic nervous system and the hormones that seemed to have suddenly awakened. Flann grinned, just a tilt of the corner of her mouth that seemed to say *I know what you're thinking right now*, and Abby schooled her expression, hiding the sudden rapid kick of her heart. Flann didn't need to know the way she looked at her made her feel intensely present, powerfully alive, and unfortunately, unwillingly aroused. Hormones and reflex. At least she was smart enough to recognize reactions she couldn't control and ignore them.

Carrie came through the door exclaiming, "What is it? What happened?"

Presley rose, a chick cradled in her hands. "Look."

"Oh my God," Carrie squealed in an exact replica of Presley.

Abby expected Flann to break their connection when Carrie arrived, but she didn't. Instead, she reached into the box, lifted out a chick, and carried it to Abby. "Here you go."

She'd cradled Blake against her breast moments after his first breath, held newborns hundreds of times, even delivered a couple in the emergency room. She cherished the innocence of new life, and the fragility of the tiny chick in her hands struck at what was most fundamental to her—the urge to protect and nurture.

"I'm not going to squeal," she murmured.

"Somehow, I didn't think you would," Flannery said just as quietly. "But I wouldn't mind just a little one."

Abby laughed but refused to look at her, would not give in to the urge to see that heavy-lidded stare concentrated on her. "Wrong woman."

"Oh, I don't know," Flann said, her voice low and soft and warm, too deep and thick for honey, more like molasses. The promise of a bite beneath the sweetness.

The other voices, the sensation of the other bodies nearby, faded away. Flann filled Abby's senses, the lure of her voice, the hint of spice that was her unique scent, the caress of her gaze. Abby took a quick step back and hit the porch post. She had nowhere to go, and Flann was so close. Too close. So close she couldn't draw a breath without tasting her, and the hunger surged so hot and hard she gasped. No. No, no, no. She eased aside and carried the chick back to the box to safety. Safety for both of them.

Frowning, Flann watched her retreat again. She'd heard the slight catch in Abby's breath, seen the faint flicker of her pupils when their gazes had caught and held. She *knew* Abby felt what she felt—the tug of recognition, a chain of connection as natural as breathing. She didn't understand it and she wasn't sure she wanted it, but denying it was as impossible as denying the pulse of desire in her belly.

Abby seemed bent on denying Flann even existed, let alone stirred anything inside her. Maybe she had the right idea. Flann folded her arms as Abby put a maternal hand on Blake's shoulder. Blake glanced at his mother with a quick smile. There was the bond Abby cherished, and rightly so. Flann had no business even thinking about a relationship— hell, she *wasn't* thinking about a relationship, more like a sizzling, incendiary night or two—with a woman like Abby. A woman who had a life and responsibility far greater than Flann ever wanted to have.

Flann looked away and caught Carrie's gaze. Carrie smiled. Flann relaxed a little. Safer, much safer. They were already friends with no dangerous undercurrents, nothing to pull her down and drag her into places she didn't want to go. No gut-deep tug of craving she was better off without. She smiled back.

CHAPTER TEN

"Why don't you two take the chicks into the barn," Harper said. "We'll get them set up with a heat lamp and a pen after we eat." "We'll put them in that back stall," Margie said. "That way the kittens can see them, and they'll get used to each other." "Good idea," Flann said.

Blake picked up the box of chicks and said to Margie, "Maybe we should put them up high on something for now, so the mother cat doesn't bother them."

"Good idea," Margie said. "Come on, I'll show you a spot."

The two of them ambled off toward the barn. From the bits of conversation Flann had heard on the ride back from Tractor Supply, Margie and Blake seemed to have bonded around the animals, books, and movies. Margie was the perfect person to introduce Blake into the local teen circles—she was popular, smart, and sure of herself. Any new kid needed a sponsor, and Blake almost certainly more than most.

"They're getting along well," Abby said from beside Flann.

"I was just thinking the same thing."

"Margie is special."

"Yeah. She's the baby and we might have spoiled her a bit, but it doesn't show. She's smarter than the rest of us already, and she's got a big heart."

"Blake is lucky to have made a friend like her so soon. I was worried he might not. He's not usually shy and never had any trouble making friends before…" Abby hesitated.

Flann glanced behind them. The others had disappeared into the kitchen. "Coming out can be hard enough. Coming out as trans must be tougher on a lot of levels."

Abby sighed. "Being different in any way is a hurdle for a teenager—this, well, I feel like I'm in uncharted waters most of the time. Did Margie say something about it?"

Flann shook her head. "I hope you don't mind. Harper told me in private that Presley mentioned it. We figured the kids would work that out for themselves."

"I'm trying to let Blake decide who he tells, and how much, and when—but sometimes it's so damn hard. I want to jump in and fix things for him."

"Sure you do," Flann said. "He's your son. I'd feel the same if it was Margie or a kid of mine. Looks to me like you're doing just fine."

"Thanks. I'm so close to the situation, I can't really tell sometimes."

Flann grinned. "Anytime you need a curbside consult, just ask."

"I'll remember that." Abby rested her hand on Flann's forearm. "I guess I could use a few understanding friends too."

Where Abby's soft fingers rested, Flann tingled. Heat bloomed in her belly. A rush of want surged through her. Any other place, any other time, any other woman, she would have reached for her, pulled her close, whispered an invitation. Flann stilled, at a loss.

"Sorry," Abby murmured, pulling away.

"No." Flann grabbed her hand. "I mean, you do. I...all of us... you're not alone."

"I'm glad," Abby whispered.

Presley appeared in the kitchen doorway. "Time to bring the food out. All hands on deck."

Abby dropped her hand and Flann stopped herself from reaching for it. A rumble of thunder rolled over the ridge on the far side of the back field, and she checked overhead. Mountains of blue-black clouds filled the western sky.

Flann frowned. "Be right there."

The air suddenly turned hot and heavy. Pent-up electricity raised the hairs on the backs of her arms. The leaves on the trees shading the yard turned underside-up with the shift in barometric pressure, sure signs of a storm bearing down.

"Hey, Harp," Flann called.

Harper walked out onto the porch. "What's up?"

"We might have to change our minds about eating outside," Flann said.

Harper craned her neck. "You're right. It's a big one."

"Yeah, and it's coming fast." Unease roiled in Flann's chest. The wind had picked up another notch in just the last few seconds. Summer storms were nothing new, and thunderstorms often tore through the valley in a matter of minutes, seemingly having risen out of nowhere and disappearing almost as fast, leaving behind brilliant sunshine and clear, clean skies. This one was barreling down even faster than most.

Abby stepped up beside her. "I can't believe how it's gotten so quickly." She glanced toward the barn. "The kids are going to get wet."

"They should be back before it hits."

Presley, Carrie, and Glenn crowded behind them. Jagged blades of lightning dueled above the horizon.

"Wow," Presley said, "are we getting rained out?"

"Looks like it." Flann kept watching the clouds. A blast of wind rattled the shutters against the wood clapboards on the old house and the maple trees bent with the force of it. Dirt devils spawned in the drive.

"Flann?" Abby's voice rose in alarm.

"I know. It's…"

The clouds coalesced into a solid wall of black from earth to sky.

"Fuck," Flann said. "Harp, I think—"

The funnel dropped from the sky between one heartbeat and the next, a whirling, churning mass twisting toward them.

"Oh my God," Abby breathed. "Is that—?"

"Tornado," Flann shouted. "Get in the house!"

Harper pushed Presley toward the house. "Everybody down in the cellar. I'll get the windows."

A roar of rushing air lifted the slates above their heads, the clatter like a thousand bones jerking to life. Carrie shrieked as a gust nearly toppled her over, and Glenn grabbed her around the waist. Together the two of them staggered inside.

"The kids!" Abby plunged into the yard, bending into the wind, her hair flying behind her in a wild tangle.

"I'll get them," Flann yelled. "Abby!"

Abby never slowed.

Flann cursed and jumped down. The wind plastered her shirt to her chest, the bottom lifting up like a sail. Leaves and sticks and loose stones cannoned across the yard. She caught Abby, twisted them both away from the force of the gale, and pushed her back toward the porch. "I'll go! Get inside. Harper!"

Harper wrapped an arm around the porch post, grabbed for Abby's hand, and pulled her protesting across the porch and inside.

Flann pivoted into the wind. Dirt stung her eyes. Loose branches ripped from trees and arrowed wildly. She blocked her face with her forearm and lowered her shoulders, struggling against a wall of air shoving back at her like a hundred linebackers. The eighty yards to the barn might as well have been eight hundred. She raised her head at the roar of a freight train closing in.

The twister crested the ridge behind the house and trees snapped off, sucked up into the funnel like matchsticks. Adrenaline dried her mouth and shot her pulse into overdrive. She kept pumping her aching thighs and staggered up to the open barn door. "Margie! Blake!"

The roof rattled and clacked, the walls shuddered, and the 200-year-old beams groaned, drowning out all sound. Flann staggered inside and stumbled down the aisle on numb legs. Sharp pain pierced her eardrums and she swallowed, trying unsuccessfully to clear them. Blake and Margie crouched in the last stall, the box of chicks shielded between them.

"You okay?" Flann dropped down beside them, searching for the best cover. Above their heads, foot-square beams supported the roof. If those held, they'd be safe; if they came down, they'd be crushed. She grabbed the kids by the arms. "Get over in the corner. Hurry!"

"Why?" Margie shouted.

Blake hugged the box of chicks to his chest.

"Twister's coming." Flann dragged them along.

"Can I see?" Margie cried, trying to pull free.

Flann yanked her back down. "Not this time, short stuff."

Blake yelled, "It feels like the building's going to blow away."

"We'll be okay. Just keep your head down." She herded them tightly into the corner next to the supporting post. If the walls came down, the corner might stand. And with any luck they'd be sheltered beneath the upright. It was the best she could do.

"What about my mom?" Blake looked ready to bolt.

"Harper has her. She's—"

A howl filled the air like the arrival of a marauding demon. Spears of light shot down around them, and the roof lifted away with a wrenching scream. Flann pushed the kids down and covered them as a torrent of wood rained down.

❖

A banshee wail filled the basement. Abby pressed her back against the stone foundation where Harper had directed her to crouch. The others huddled around her on either side. The power had gone out as they'd stumbled down the stairs, and a murky haze enveloped her. Her eardrums throbbed, threatening to burst. Terror clawed at her throat. Blake and Margie were out there somewhere, and she was helpless to protect them. Flann had disappeared too. Had she even made it to the barn?

Bile climbed into her throat. *She* huddled in the basement while Blake and Margie and Flann could be hurt, needing her, and she wasn't there. Every instinct screamed for her to force her way up those stairs and outside. She railed inwardly at the monster threatening her child. Of all the things she had imagined that might harm him, this was a foe she could not fight. A wave of frustration, of rage and fear, welled in her chest, and she choked on a cry.

Presley gripped her hand and leaned close. "Flann...be...right."

No reason would console her. No promise would convince her. She trusted no one to do what she must do, and she was impotent. Helplessness burned her throat, nausea curdling her stomach. The screaming wind grew louder and the floor above them creaked and heaved.

She shut her eyes and felt like a coward.

Minutes, hours passed and at last the screaming subsided. The terrible pressure in her ears relented and she could hear again.

"Is it over?" She jumped up and swayed, legs rubbery. "The kids. Flann."

"Wait." Harper grasped her arm. "We don't know what's up there. The house might be unsound. We have to go slowly."

Abby jerked her arm free. "I have to get outside."

"There may be secondary twisters." Harper blocked her path to the stairs. "It won't do anyone any good if you get hurt too."

"My son—Margie—"

"Flann is with them," Harper said grimly. "Come on, just stay with me."

At the top of the stairs, Harper shoved on the door leading into the kitchen. It didn't move. "Blocked."

Panic tore at Abby's throat. She couldn't be trapped. She had to get out. "Let me help."

Abby crowded onto the top stair beside Harper.

"On three," Harper said. "One, two...three."

Abby pushed against the solid wood door as hard as she could. It moved a fraction.

"Again."

On the third try, wood scraped on wood and the door opened enough for them to squeeze through. The kitchen table had upended and come to rest against the door. The light was out, but the walls and ceiling still stood. Someone had managed to get the windows open, and the only damage seemed to be broken furniture tossed around as if by an angry child.

Harper righted a chair and cleared a path to the porch. The screen door was gone. A tree on the far side of the yard had uprooted and lay in the yard in a mound of broken boards and pieces of slate. A wheelbarrow sat atop the pile. Abby jumped down the stairs and stared at the barn. The back half of the roof was gone, only a skeleton of rafters bare to the sky. Dread twisted through her. "Oh God."

Abby ran, skirting debris, sliding in mud and rivulets of water. Rain pelted down, sharp needles she barely felt. Broken branches clawed at her legs. The barn door hung down, half-unhinged. She pulled aside a tree limb and tugged at the end of a splintered board blocking her way.

"Here," Harper said, catching up to her. "Let me help. Don't try to go inside yet. The whole thing might come down."

"I'm getting my son." Abby peered into the dark interior. A jumble of debris filled the aisle. She pulled out another loose board and edged into the doorway.

"We're going to get them." Harper held her back. "But if we move something and bring all of it down, we're not helping them."

Glenn, Presley, and Carrie appeared out of the storm.

"Did you find them?" Presley asked.

"Not yet," Harper said. "But we will."

Glenn said, "I ought to try to get to the hospital. The ER is going to need us."

"Yes," Harper said. "Go."

Carrie said, "I'll go with you. We can take my car."

"I'll be there as soon as we get the kids and Flann." Harper gripped Presley's arm. "Can you try the phones? See if you can reach my parents, make sure everyone there is all right?"

"Yes," Presley said. "Be careful, okay?"

"We will." Harper kissed her. "You too."

Abby sucked in a breath. The control she brought to bear in the midst of an emergency rose to the surface, and she pushed the panic back into its dark corner. "Tell me what to do."

"We need some light—I'm going to get a flashlight from my truck. Call to them and see if we can get a fix on where they are. I'll be right back."

Harper hurried off and Abby peered into the dark depths of the barn. "Blake? Flann? Margie—are you there?"

Abby's heart stopped beating as silence crowded out the air in her lungs. "Blake?"

"Mom? Back here!"

Abby's heart started up again. "Are you hurt?"

"We're good," Flann called.

"Can you get out?"

"We're blocked in," Flann called. "What I can see of the roof looks iffy."

Harper returned and shone a light into the barn. Splintered wood and a jumble of beams filled the center aisle. "Flann? Can you see daylight?"

"No!"

"What about fire rescue?" Abby asked.

"They're all volunteers. Everybody in the area's probably dealing with the same thing," Harper said. "It could be hours."

"Then we have to get them out ourselves," Abby said calmly. "You're in charge."

Harper studied Abby and nodded. "Follow me."

CHAPTER ELEVEN

Flann couldn't move her left leg. Something heavy pinned her in the pile of rubble. Thank God, she could feel her toes, wiggle them, but she couldn't pull free, and every time she tried, the debris above her groaned and creaked. She'd rather not have the whole thing come down on their heads. Pain lanced down the back of her thigh and a warm wet sensation followed. Didn't feel like bone pain—probably just a laceration. The blood loss didn't seem extreme but she didn't want to make it any worse. They might be there for a long time.

"Are you two sure you're not hurt?"

"My shoulder's banged up a little," Margie said, her voice steady and quiet. "But it's not dislocated, and my arm is fine."

"Blake?"

"I'm okay." His voice was breathy and tight.

He was doing pretty good for a city kid. Hell, any kid.

"Harper's out there and she's going to get us out of here," Flann said. "Just don't move around too much, and do everything she says. No questions, just do it."

"What about the chicks?" Margie asked.

Flann would have shaken her head if she'd been able to. Had to love her. "That's a question."

"Yeah, but for information purposes only," Margie said.

"I've got them," Blake said. "The box is still in my arms, and it's not crushed. I can hear them cheeping."

"Good job," Margie said. "We can set them up in the kitchen when we get out."

Flann grinned. Margie was a rock. Someday, she'd be the matriarch of the coming Rivers generations.

"What about the kittens?" Blake said.

"My bet is they burrowed down in the hay," Flann said. "We'll look for them once we get this place secure."

A rumbling roar grew closer, and Blake gasped. "Is that another one coming?"

"That," Flann said with a wave of relief, "is an ATV. The cavalry has arrived."

❖

Abby clutched the roll bar on the ATV as Harper maneuvered over and around fallen branches, boards, and uprooted fence posts behind the barn. Abby recoiled at the scope of the wreckage. The back half of the barn had caved in. Only two uprights and one beam about halfway to where the roof had been remained standing intact. Piles of slate, tin, and other rubble from the collapsed portions of the roof filled the interior. Miraculously, the new chicken coop remained unscathed.

Blake, Margie, and Flann were somewhere beneath that horrible devastation. How were they ever going to get to them? If they'd been in Manhattan, dozens of emergency responders with all sorts of equipment would already be on scene. Here there were no flashing lights, no sirens, no one else at all.

"It looks like a giant heap of pick-up sticks," Abby said.

"And if we pull on the wrong one," Harper said darkly, "we'll bring the rest of the pile down."

"I guess a crane is out of the question."

"Even if we could get a backhoe in here, I don't think we want to leave them in there for days, and that's how long it would be. Besides, the debris is going to shift. Right now they're not injured, and we want to keep it that way."

"You're right." Abby couldn't imagine standing around doing nothing while Blake and the others were trapped inside. She had to trust that Flann had somehow kept them all safe. And she had to trust Harper to get to them. "Where do we start?"

"We find the shortest way in to them and then we can clear a tunnel so they can crawl out without shifting everything above them. If I know Flann, she's got them close to that upright."

Harper backed the Rhino over a mound of torn-up pasture and torn tree limbs to within a few yards of the barn. The foot-square hand-hewn post formed the center of a teepee of fallen beams, shattered slate, and splintered clapboards reaching twenty feet high. Flann and the kids were somewhere at the bottom of the rubble. Abby jumped down and vaulted over piles of debris, skidding to a stop at the edge of the wreckage. "Blake? Can you hear me?"

"Mom," Blake called back. "We're here!"

The sound of his voice stilled the last remnants of panic. She knew what to do in a crisis—she'd spent her life training for them. She also knew how to work in a team when she didn't know as much as her colleagues. She looked over at Harper. "They don't seem very far away."

"Good." Harper tossed her a pair of leather work gloves, crouched down, and switched on a big utility light. "Flann? What's the situation?"

"I'm pinned down. Feels like a big beam. The kids are closer to the upright. Get them first."

"Can you see light anywhere?" Harper called, shining the beam over the jumble of wood and stone.

"No," Flann called.

"Wait," Blake said. "I think—"

Harper played her light again over the same area, more slowly. "Now?"

"Yes," Blake shouted. "I can see it."

Harper retraced the same course even more slowly. "Call out as soon as you—"

"Now," Blake and Margie yelled simultaneously.

Abby's heart lifted. They were there, so close. "We're coming to get you."

"Be careful," Flann yelled. "We don't need the two of you getting buried too."

Harper muttered, "Always has to be giving the orders."

"Thank God she was with them." Abby kept seeing Flann forcing her way through the wind and flying debris toward the barn while she scurried toward the safety of the cellar. Flann had been right to force her inside—she wouldn't have known how to keep the kids safe. "Let's get them out."

Harper pointed to the base of the pile. "We start at the periphery and work our way in. Slowly and carefully, we'll make a pathway toward the spot where Blake saw the light. One board at a time, move it aside, don't pull out anything that's stuck underneath. Only things that look free. This is not the time to hurry."

"I understand." Abby tugged on the gloves, just as she did when preparing for the arrival of a trauma patient in the ER. No matter what was coming, no matter what she needed to do, she'd do it. She didn't think about time, or how much was passing. She didn't let the cold or the pain from bruised shins, sore shoulders, or aching muscles distract her. She forced herself to go slow, lifting broken tree limbs, splintered boards, and sheets of crumpled tin, one piece at a time. Harper worked silently beside her, bracing the sides of the emerging tunnel with chunks of wood as they slowly made their way toward the upright.

"How are you doing?" Harper called when they'd cleared an area three feet wide and five feet long.

"Your light is brighter," Margie called back.

"Good. Don't try to move anything from your side until we tell you to."

A sharp creaking sound emanated from somewhere inside the building and a shower of slate cascaded off the collapsed roof. Harper grabbed Abby and pulled her back. Stone splintered around them, and the building shuddered. Rock chips flew, several scoring Abby's bare legs. She gasped, waiting for the pile in front of them to rain down on the kids and Flann. The upright shuddered but nothing shifted.

"Everybody all right?" Harper called.

"It's getting a little tight in here," Flann called back. "It sounds like you're only a few feet away. I'd make haste."

Harper smiled grimly and yelled back, "You always were impatient. Just relax, and everybody stay still." She glanced at Abby and murmured, "Go as quickly as you can."

Abby crushed the urge to yank half-buried boards out of the way. Look, evaluate, assess. Just like in the ER. When you rushed, you missed things. Lift, carry, throw. She kept at it, shoulder to shoulder with Harper.

Presley climbed down to join them, carrying sweatshirts. "You two should put these on—you're both soaking wet. I put blankets in the ATV for the others."

Abby welcomed the warmth, not realizing she'd been cold until she wasn't any longer.

"Any news?" Harper asked, going back to work.

"Cell reception is spotty. I couldn't reach your parents or the hospital, but I got a couple of others on the emergency communications tree who will start calling everyone to report to the hospital. I need to go too, as soon as we get them out."

"We're close now," Abby said.

"I can see shadows moving," Margie yelled.

Relief poured through Abby's chest so fast she felt light-headed. "Soon!"

"Almost there," Harper said. "Are we coming right for you?"

"A little to your left."

"Okay. Don't move yet."

Abby lifted aside a two-by-four and cried out. A hand appeared in the space she'd made. Small and pale and beautiful. She knelt, grasped the fingers. "Margie?"

"Hi, Abby," Margie called back.

"Almost there, sweetie. Just another minute."

Abby hated to let go of those fingers, but she had to. Harper crouched beside her and they passed rubble back to Presley, cleared a path until Margie's face appeared at the end of the tunnel. Her face was streaked with dirt and a purple bruise blossomed on her left cheek. Her eyes were dry, and her smile wide.

"Can I come out now?"

"Nice and easy," Harper said.

Margie shimmied toward them, arms outstretched. When her shoulders appeared, Abby and Harper grabbed on and pulled her all the way out.

"Presley, take her to the ATV and get her warm," Harper said.

"I can help—"

"Go. Don't get any wetter than you already are."

Reluctantly, Margie let Presley lead her up the slope to the vehicle.

Abby inched deeper into the tunnel. "Blake, can you see the way?"

Blake's head appeared in the tunnel. His hair was caked with dirt and blood smeared the side of his neck. Not much blood, but the sight of it made Abby bite her lip. She forced a smile.

"Hi, baby."

"Jeez, Mom, come on," Blake said, his eyes shining.

"Sorry, I forgot. Come on out of there."

"Here…" Blake pushed the partially crumpled cardboard box out first. "Be careful they don't get wet."

Abby's throat closed and she nodded, passing the chicks back to Presley. "Now you."

Abby held her breath as he inched toward them. His shoulder dislodged a board and several more sluiced down from the heap. Abby twisted aside as one barely missed her head. Blake's eyes widened.

"Mom?"

"It's okay," Harper said. "Keep coming."

Abby reached for his hand and, when she clasped his fingers, fought the urge to pull him all the way out. She let him come to her, but it was the longest wait she'd ever experienced. At last he was free, and she hugged him close, checking him with quick strokes for damage.

"I'm good, Mom," Blake finally said, pulling away.

"Go get in the ATV with Margie. You kids try to keep warm."

Blake didn't move. "What about Flann—"

"We'll get her," Abby said. "Go on now."

Blake looked back one last time, then stumbled over the littered ground to the ATV. Margie held out a hand and he climbed in next to her, sliding his arm around her shoulders. They cradled the box between them, their heads close.

"Flann, your turn," Harper called.

"I can't," Flann said. "I can't move."

Abby's throat closed. Oh God. Harper's face blanked, her body freezing in place. *Evaluate, assess, act.*

Abby crouched and peered into the tunnel. "Can you feel both legs?"

"Yes, it's—"

"Any numbness or tingling?"

"It's not my spine. I'm pinned by something."

Abby heard Harper start breathing again.

"Any other injuries?" Abby said.

"I don't think so. Something's bleeding, but not a lot."

"Jesus," Harper said. Her face paled, and for the first time, Abby saw panic in her eyes.

"Harper," she said sharply, "it's not serious. But we need to get her out of there."

Harper shuddered, and her gaze cleared. She let out a long breath. "We need to make sure the tunnel doesn't collapse. I'm going to get her."

"It's not big enough for you," Abby said.

"Then we'll make it bigger."

They went back to work, widening the path into the depths of debris, shoving blocks of wood under canted uprights to keep the structure from shifting. Abby followed Harper, holding the light. An endless time later, Flann's face appeared, ghostly and pale.

"Hey." Flann grinned and the cold, hard fist in Abby's chest eased.

"Hey, yourself," Harper said. "Abby, I need a two-by-four about five feet long."

"Right." Abby braced the light between two boards in the rubble, called out to Presley what they needed, and backed out.

"Here," Presley said a moment later, passing her a wet length of wood. "Is she all right?"

"I think so." Abby crawled back in with the board. "Harper— here."

"There's a big beam across your left leg, Flann. I'll lever it up and you need to crawl toward me."

"If you move things," Flann said, "this whole thing might come down."

"We'll go slow."

"Leave me. When you get more people, you can take this thing apart from the top down."

"It'll be a day. I'm not leaving you in there."

"It's not gonna help for both of us—"

Abby's frayed nerves snapped. "The two of you, *hush*. Harper, how long before you can get more help?"

"Twelve hours minimum, maybe a day."

"What's the chance this whole thing might come down before then?"

"Fifty-fifty, maybe worse."

"Get her out."

Flann cursed. "Look—"

"Risk assessment, Dr. Rivers," Abby pronounced. "This is the safest course."

"Then at least you should get out of the way so you can pull Harper out if it goes bad."

"I'll take that under advisement." Abby murmured, "Be careful, Harper."

"Yeah." Harper jammed the two-by-four under the beam pinning Flann's leg and pushed another hunk of wood under it.

"Get ready to move."

"I'm not sure my leg will work right away," Flann said.

"Just get close—we'll take it from there." Harper pushed down on the lever and the pile of wood groaned. Abby watched from the mouth of the tunnel, ready to grab Harper and pull her out if the pile started to shift. Endless moments later, Harper eased aside and an arm appeared next to her.

Abby crowded forward and grabbed Flann's hand. "I've got you."

"I'm not at my fighting best," Flann said weakly. "So don't let go."

Abby tightened her grip. "I'm not going to."

CHAPTER TWELVE

Flann pushed herself to her knees but didn't have the strength to stand. Her leg might as well have been a dead log attached to her hip for all she could control it. "Leg's useless for a bit."

Abby slipped an arm around her waist, saying gently, "Take your time. You can make it."

A second later Harper was on her other side, and Flann managed to get both legs under her and wobble to her feet. Her injured leg burned like someone had rammed a hot poker down the middle of her quad. Congealing blood soaked her jeans to the knee.

"Jesus, Flann," Harper said, "you're a mess."

"Thanks, sis."

"Are you dizzy?" Abby asked.

"No," Flann croaked. "A little weak in general, but I don't think I lost that much blood.

"We'll see when we get you to the ER."

Flann grunted and put a little more weight on the leg. It held. "By the time we get to the ER, it'll be filled with patients and I'll be too busy to worry about it."

"You're not going to be doing anything tonight," Abby said.

"You don't know what you're dealing with here, Abby." Flann didn't have the patience to argue. "Look at the damage here. If that twister went through town or even stayed on the ground on the outskirts, there's gonna be a lot more than property damage. People are going to be hurt. I've got work to do."

Abby gritted her teeth and stared at Flann's set jaw. The woman was so stubborn that reasoning with her was about as effective as trying to hold back the tornado with a bedsheet. "Harper, maybe you can talk some sense into her."

Harper cleared her throat. "Uh…how about we get everybody inside and we'll do a quick check on the three of them. I'll take the kids, you look at Flann. If her leg's not too bad, then for the short term, at least, it makes the most sense to let her try to work. I've got everything you'll need to treat a straightforward injury."

"Oh for God's sake," Abby muttered. Two against one was hopeless odds, but she was counting on Harper's concern for Flann's welfare to win out if she found anything serious. "Let's get inside. If the wound is manageable as an outpatient, okay. But if I say she needs the OR, then what I say goes."

"No," Flann said.

"Okay," Harper said.

"God damn it, Harp," Flann said.

Harper held firm. "If it's not bad like you say, then you've got nothing to complain about."

Flann didn't argue. She'd just work on Abby when she got her alone.

"Everybody okay?" Presley called.

"We're good," Harper said. "Take Flann and the kids back to the house. Abby and I will catch up."

Flann didn't argue about riding—she couldn't maneuver through the rubble. Once she got situated next to Margie, Presley navigated a circuitous path back to the house. Miraculously, the house was undamaged other than a few slates lying scattered around on the grass. Margie and Blake carried the chickens inside, and Presley gave her a hand climbing down from the ATV.

"How are you doing?" Presley asked.

"Better," Flann said. "I'm starting to feel my leg again."

Inside, Margie and Blake immediately settled into one corner of the kitchen, discussing how best to create a temporary pen for the chicks. Harper appeared a minute later with a medical bag in one hand and a plastic crate filled with instrument packs and surgical bandages. Presley put flashlights on the counter and table.

Abby immediately joined Blake and Margie. "You two need to get into dry clothes."

"We just need to get the chicks settled," Blake said, barely giving her a glance as Margie set a big cardboard box on the floor.

"Five minutes," Abby ordered.

"I'll see what I can find for them," Presley said, pausing by Abby. "They look like they're doing better than the rest of us."

Abby glanced over at Flann. "Right. Harper, can you take a look at these two while I get a look at Flann's leg."

"Sure." Harper pulled out a kitchen chair. "Margie, sit."

Flann desperately wanted to sit down too, but she didn't. Any sign of weakness now would get her benched for the rest of the night. She'd be fine as soon as she had something to drink and a little bit to eat. Time to get on top of the situation.

"Let's go in the sitting room, Abby. You can check me over in there."

Surprised that Flann acquiesced so easily, Abby grabbed the container of surgical supplies and one of the big lantern flashlights, and followed Flann down the hall. Flann moved slowly and Abby suspected she was trying hard to hide a limp. The sitting room was a large cozy space with a fireplace, an overstuffed sofa and matching easy chair with a floral pattern, and a big hooked rug on the wood floor. An oversized coffee table that looked as old as the house sat in the middle of the room with a few business magazines and general medical journals scattered on top. Harper and Presley obviously used this room to relax, and the companionable image gave her a pang of envy.

"Stretch out on the sofa." Abby put the supplies and light on the coffee table. "Can you get your jeans off?"

"I don't want to get blood on their rug." Flann stopped just inside the door, unbuttoned her jeans, and started to push them down. She winced and stopped. "I might need a little help."

Abby pulled on a pair of disposable gloves. "Hold on to the door frame for balance. I'm going to have to tug."

Flann braced one arm against the doorway. "All set."

Abby crouched, gripped the waistband of Flann's jeans, and rocked them down over her hips to midthigh. Flann could think of a lot of scenarios where she wouldn't mind Abby on her knees in front of her, but this definitely wasn't one of them. She hated appearing helpless in front of Abby and hated being tended to as if she were incapable of looking after herself—or anyone—even more. Abby tugged on her jeans, and Flann swore.

"Sorry." Abby rocked back on her heels and looked up at Flann. "It's stuck to the laceration and I can't tell how bad it is. I'll have to soak the material with some saline and try again."

"Go ahead."

Wordlessly, Abby opened the liter bottle of sterile saline and poured it onto the front of Flann's jeans. Maroon-colored water dripped from the bottom of her jeans as the material soaked through. When she was done, she grasped the material and tried again. Flann's breathing was short and raspy.

"I'm sorry," Abby murmured. "I can check the supplies for analgesics, but they probably won't kick in soon enough to do any good."

"It's okay," Flann said through tight teeth. "Just get it done."

With one final pull, the jeans slid down over her knees to the tops of her work boots.

"Almost there." Abby unlaced Flann's boots and steadied her with a hand on her good hip. Flann's T-shirt came to the middle of her dark briefs. Her legs were lean and muscular. Abby focused on the ten-inch laceration angled across the anterior portion of her thigh, deep enough to have separated the tissue down to muscle. The saline had cleared most of the clot, but she couldn't tell yet how serious it was. "Can you step out of your boots and jeans?"

Carefully, Flann eased one foot free and then the other.

Abby rose and slid an arm around Flann's waist. Flann was pale, her pupils wide and dark with pain. Abby steeled herself against the surge of sympathy. She couldn't stroke away her hurt the way she wanted to. She'd have to hurt her a little more before she could help her. "Come on, sit down so I can get a good look at it. I need to clean it up a little bit more."

Flann looped an arm around Abby's shoulders and leaned into her, a sure sign she was in more pain than she wanted to admit. "How's your suturing?"

"Very good, as a matter of fact." Abby recognized Flann's attempt to deflect her attention with humor. Flann was very good at hiding her feelings behind a cavalier attitude, but that wouldn't work here.

"However, I don't plan on sewing you up here. It'll be easier in the OR."

"It *would* be, if there were a surgeon around to do it, but there won't be. I'm telling you, you and I and Harper, probably my father and a couple other local GPs who can get in to the hospital, are going to be it tonight. We'll be swamped. We've got two choices—either suture it now or pack it open and suture it later."

"If we don't close it right away," Abby said, propping a cushion against the arm of the sofa for Flann's head as Flann slowly stretched out, "the scarring will be much worse and there's a greater chance it will get infected."

"I agree. So like I said, let's get suturing."

Abby didn't intend to commit herself until she had a better look at the wound. Flann's reasoning wasn't bad, but she didn't altogether trust her motives. Flann was the macho type, and she'd likely risk her own well-being and certainly risk being in pain for the entire night if it meant she'd be able to work. Abby had handled plenty of patients like her, and part of her job was protecting them from themselves. Although she doubted anyone had much success with Flannery, she intended to win this contest.

She found an impermeable drape in the med kit and slid it under Flann's thigh to protect the sofa. After donning another pair of gloves, she soaked gauze with more sterile saline, carefully cleaned around the wound, and pulsed saline into it from a sterile syringe. Flann tensed as she worked but said nothing, and Abby ignored the fist of anxiety in her middle. She stirred up a little bit of bleeding, but it wasn't excessive, and as she got a better look at the wound, her unease lessened. "Is there any sensory loss in your calf or foot?"

"No numbness that I've noticed. The leg feels weak, but I think that's just me in general." Flann laughed. "I missed dinner."

Abby smiled faintly. "The wound is down to muscle but nothing major seems involved. It's deep and long and will hurt like hell if you try to stand on it tonight. You know that as well as I do."

"I know." Flann sighed. "Look, I'll get off my feet as much as I can, if I can."

"If you agree to that, I'll suture this here. But I'll want you to check in with me every few hours."

"If I—"

Abby rose and folded her arms. "No ifs, Flann. You come by the ER every two hours and let me check you over, or I tell Harper you're not fit for duty."

Flann's eyebrows rose. "That's blackmail."

Abby shrugged. "Take it or leave it."

"Harper always has lidocaine in her emergency supplies. You'll find a suture pack in there too."

Abby turned away to hide her smile. She drew up local anesthetic, changed gloves, and after wiping down the periphery of the wound with Betadine, anesthetized the laceration. It took her half an hour to close the wound with several layers of suture. While she worked, Flann lay back with her eyes closed. "I thought you'd be supervising."

Flann kept her eyes closed, but her lips curved into a smile. "I trust you."

"Why?" Abby asked absently as she tied and snipped a suture. She loaded the needle holder with nylon for the skin and started a running suture to close the long laceration. "You've only seen me work that one time."

"That's all I needed to see."

"I could have terrible hands, though."

Flann laughed. "Do you?"

"No," Abby said, suturing steadily. "I actually have good hands."

"Then why aren't you a surgeon?"

Abby smiled. "I like the variety in the ER. There's more patient education involved too. And I like working with doctors whose egos don't come through the door before they do."

"Yours seems pretty healthy."

Abby laughed. "You noticed."

Flann opened her eyes at the same moment as Abby looked up at her. Flann's eyes had lost their sheen of pain. They were dark and intense again, the intensity Abby was coming to like when turned on her. She stilled.

"I noticed a lot of things," Flann said softly, each word a subtle caress. "I noticed you're smart and strong and compassionate."

"You forgot stubborn and controlling," Abby said, her throat tight.

Flann grinned that damnably charming grin. "No, I didn't. I just didn't want to make you mad."

Laughter threatening to bubble out, Abby pulled her gaze away and went back to work. Flann was too good at distracting her. "That's probably smart considering your position right now."

Flann pushed up on her elbows and surveyed her leg. She nodded. "Not bad. I'd put you at about a third-year resident level."

"Oh, please," Abby said, snipping the last suture. "That's as good as half the attendings you work with, I bet."

"Three-quarters, maybe."

Secretly pleased, Abby found gauze and wrapped Flann's leg with the circular bandage. "I still would not recommend standing on that."

"If I don't, I'll have a tough time keeping my balance in the OR."

Abby stripped off her gloves, sat on the edge of the sofa, and rested her hand on Flann's uninjured calf. "Be serious for a minute."

"I'm always serious."

"I doubt that you ever are," Abby said with a snort, "but you need to be now. You've been through a lot. Your body has been bruised, battered, and exposed to the elements. That's a nasty laceration on your leg and I know it hurts, even though you're too macho to admit it. You won't do anyone any good if you get halfway through a case and collapse."

"What if I promise I won't start a case if I don't feel a hundred percent?"

"Do you mean it?"

"If I promise, I mean it."

"All right then. Your word."

Flann leaned over, grasped Abby's hand. "My word."

Harper came through the doorway. "What's the verdict?"

Abby realized she was sitting with a half-naked Flann on the sofa, and Flann was holding her hand. She jumped up and started collecting supplies. "A deep laceration, but fortunately the muscle's spared. We've closed it."

Harper strode to the side of the sofa, jammed her hands on her hips, and stared down at Flann. "Are you bullshitting or can you really work?"

Flann pushed herself all the way up and eased her legs off the sofa. Her back ached, her shoulders ached, and her leg really hurt. "I feel like you kicked my ass like you used to do when we were kids playing football, but I'm okay. Do you hear anything from Dad?"

Harper shook her head. "I've been trying him and Mama and Carson, but I'm not getting anybody."

"One of us should go by the house—probably you. Any of the urgent traumas will need me."

"You're right. I'll go there, and then straight over to the Rivers. Presley needs to get to the hospital too."

"What about the kids," Abby said. "Are they both okay?"

"Fine." Harper smiled wryly. "I had to make them promise not to go out kitten hunting."

"They can stay here, and Presley, Flann, and I can go in my car to the hospital," Abby said.

"That's a plan," Harper said.

"I need some pants," Flann said.

"Might be a good idea," Harper said dryly. "I've got some scrubs that I keep here to hang around in. They'll fit you."

"If you get them for me, I'll get dressed and we can go."

Abby packed up the rest of the supplies. "I want to talk to Blake for a minute. I'll meet you in the kitchen."

As Abby left, Harper said, "How're you doing, really?"

"I'll make it for a few hours. Abby did a good job."

"I don't doubt it. She's solid."

"Yeah," Flann said slowly. "She's something."

"What are you doing there, Flann?" Harper asked.

"Not a thing." Flann gave her a long, flat look until Harper shrugged and shook her head. Satisfied, Flann said, "How about you get me those scrubs so we can get to work."

CHAPTER THIRTEEN

Y ou should take the truck, Harp," Flann said.

"Presley's car will do me," Harper said. "The three of you have farther to go."

"Yeah, but the road's likely to be washed out along the river. Presley's car won't handle that." Flann got a stubborn set to her jaw, a look Abby was coming to recognize.

Flann was used to being in charge, of making decisions that no one—except Harper, apparently—ever questioned. Abby wondered if Flann had always been that way, or if her training or some other experience conditioned her to be most comfortable when she shouldered the responsibility for the welfare of others. She wondered too what happened if Flann was wrong—imagining those inevitable mistakes must eat at her. A wave of sympathy washed through her.

"No one should take any unnecessary chances," Abby said. "We're all going to be needed at the hospital."

Presley slipped an arm around Harper's waist. "I'd feel better if you took the truck."

Harper caressed her arm. "Okay. But if the three of you run into any problems on the way in, you turn back, okay?"

"I'll look after them," Flann said.

Since Abby didn't know what she faced, she could hardly object to Flann being Flann and assuming she was in charge, but she wasn't going to be a bystander either. "How about Presley drives, and I'll watch the roads for obstacles. Flann, you can stretch out in the backseat and keep your leg elevated."

"Wait a minute," Flann grumbled. "I should drive. I know the roads—"

"So does Presley." Abby plucked Presley's keys from the table, slipped them into her pocket, and gave Flann a no-discussion glare. "If you expect to work later tonight, you need to rest now."

Flann scowled. "I can see how you got to be chief so fast."

Abby grinned. "By being right, you mean?"

"I was thinking more like hard-as—" Flann glanced over at Blake and Margie, who didn't seem to be paying them any attention. All the same, she muttered, "Not quite what I was thinking."

Presley set the roast that was to have been their picnic dinner in the center of the big oak table. "Everybody should grab a sandwich. If the power is out at the Rivers, the cafeteria won't have food for long. Grab water from the fridge too."

"Double-check you have flashlights," Harper said, slicing thick slabs off the roast as Presley set out bread and sandwich bags.

"Good idea." Abby put together sandwiches. "Blake, Margie—come and eat."

When they'd grabbed sandwiches, she made two more and handed one to Flann. "Eat this now. I'll pack some more for later."

Flann took the sandwich, her fingers grazing Abby's. "Thanks."

"Sure," Abby said, not entirely sure why she'd made Flann's without even thinking about it. And that was not anything she wanted to keep thinking about right then.

Inside of ten minutes, they were ready to go. Presley walked Harper to the back door and kissed her. "Be careful. I wish you weren't going alone."

"I'll be fine," Harper said. "I'll meet you at the Rivers just as soon as I've checked the homestead. Don't worry if you don't hear from me. Phone reception is likely to be iffy."

Presley nodded, her lips tight.

Harper hugged her, murmuring something too quietly for Abby to hear. Presley's expression softened and she leaned into Harper for an instant, her arms locked around Harper's waist. Abby looked away, directly into Flann's eyes. Flann's pensive gaze skimmed her face and settled on hers, capturing Abby again in the dark, seductive undertow Flann exuded with effortless force. Abby broke away reluctantly and physically turned aside, not trusting herself to resist the strange pull of Flann's attention. "Blake, Margie—remember, no searching outside."

"We should check for Rooster," Margie said.

Blake nodded.

"Rooster is a survivor," Presley said. "If he hasn't made an appearance by morning, we'll all look for him. Abby's right, though, it's not safe out there until we're sure the storms have passed."

"You're all going out," Margie pointed out with her usual certainty.

"Yeah, Mom," Blake added in solidarity.

Great, Abby thought. *Now there's a pair of them to bargain with.*

"Besides," Margie said, "if we keep an eye on the sky and promise to—"

"No deals," Flann said, joining Abby. "You stay inside until one of us comes back. Let's have your word on it."

Blake and Margie glanced at each other in some kind of silent communication, then at Abby and Flann. Whatever they saw must have convinced them, and together, they said, "Word."

"Good enough," Flann said. "Margie, you've got all our numbers. We'll call when we hit the Rivers."

"Thanks," Abby whispered to Flann.

"No problem." Flann grinned. "Never try to negotiate with my sister. She always wins."

"Runs in the family?"

"Usually." Flann dropped her voice and leaned close. "You've been doing pretty well on that score with me, though."

"I'm not counting." Abby savored the heat of Flann's bare arm against hers for an instant, an unexpected guilty pleasure, before snatching up the bag of sandwiches. "All right then, we're ready."

Harper drove out first with Presley close behind. They had to stop twice before the end of the long driveway so Presley and Abby could climb out and help Harper clear downed tree limbs from the road. Flann grumbled about not helping but stayed in the car.

When they reached the two-lane, Harper turned in the opposite direction and was gone. Abby shivered at the sudden sense of being very alone in an alien landscape. Despite it being only early evening, the sky was unnaturally dark, layered with angry black storm clouds. Their headlights were the only illumination as they traveled slowly toward the village. The farmhouses they passed had no power and stood as blackened silhouettes against the ominous horizon. Presley, both hands gripping the wheel, managed to circumvent all of the downed limbs in the road for the first few miles. When they rounded a bend, she let out a sigh. A distant glow heralded the village up ahead.

"At least some of the village has power," Abby said.

Presley said, "Hopefully the hospital does too."

"They've got the generators," Flann said, "but they'll only do for twenty-four hours or so."

"I'll get on the line with the power company as soon as we arrive and get an idea of what the local grid looks like," Presley said.

Abby leaned forward and narrowed her eyes, trying to make out the shape in the road ahead. Her breath caught. "Pres, there's a truck off the road."

Presley stopped quickly, ten yards from a pickup truck leaning precariously on its side, its rear wheels barely on the shoulder and its front pointed down a long slope that ended in a ravine filled with pine trees. Abby lifted her door handle. "I'll have to go check and see about the driver."

Flann gripped her shoulder from behind. "Wait a minute. You're not equipped for field intervention, and it's dangerous trying to work around a vehicle like that. It could shift, slide down that incline, and take you with it."

"I can't take the chance someone might be trapped."

"Dammit, Abby—" Flann sounded more worried than angry. "At least try 9-1-1 first. If they can be here soon, they're the best hope for anyone trapped in the car."

"I know that." Abby ought to be annoyed by Flann's objections and offended by the restraining hand on her shoulder, but she wasn't. Flann made sense, but that wasn't the reason she accepted Flann's protests either. Flann didn't want her to get hurt, and being cared for rather than caring for someone else was so unusual she'd forgotten what it felt like. Oh, her mother and Blake cared about her, but they didn't *take care* of her. She hadn't thought she needed or wanted it, but it was nice. "I'll call them just as soon as I see about the driver. I've got to at least see if he's in there and alive."

Flann opened her back door. "I'll come with you."

"You won't. There's no way you can manage that slope on your leg." Before Flann could argue more, Abby jumped out.

"Abby!" Flann called.

A car door slammed and Presley yelled, "Wait for me. I'm coming too."

"Don't try to get inside," Flann called again as Abby and Presley slogged away through the puddles and tangled branches.

When they reached the spot where the pickup had gone over, Abby started down the steep, slick slope first, testing each step carefully as her foot sank into wet soil and loose gravel. The humid air smelled of ozone and the thick, cloying odor of drenched earth.

"Oh!" Abby's foot slipped, her legs flew out from under her, and she barely caught herself on an outstretched hand. Sharp stones gouged her palm, and she bit back another gasp of pain.

"Are you all right?" Presley asked.

"Yes. The footing's treacherous. Be careful." Turning, Abby held out a hand and they helped each other down the last few yards to the truck cab. The truck canted toward them on its running board, the passenger-side wheels elevated into the air. Abby felt the hood of the red pickup truck. It was cold. The engine had either shut off or run out of gas. She pulled aside branches of a shrub caught in the wheel well and peered through the driver's window. A dark form leaned against the door, a seat belt strap angled across the window.

"He's belted in place." Abby rapped on the window. "Hello! Hello, can you hear me?"

No response.

"Is there anyone else in there?" Presley asked.

"I don't know. I can't see past him. I need to open the door if I can."

"Be careful," Presley said. "If the truck slides while you're trying to open the door, you can get caught underneath."

"You should stand back out of the way."

"You just be ready to jump too." Presley scrambled back up the slope. "Clear."

Abby grasped the handle, hoping the door wasn't locked. She squeezed and the door gave a little. Holding her breath, she carefully pried it open. The lower edge hit the ground and stuck, but she had enough space to wedge herself into the opening. If the truck shifted now, she'd be carried down the rest of the way with it. Flann would never let her hear the end of it. Grinning at the absurdity of the thought, she shouldered into the narrow crevice.

A man in his sixties sagged against the steering wheel, the seat belt holding him upright. The windshield was shattered and his forehead was bloodied in a starburst pattern from the impact.

"Sir? Sir, can you hear me? I'm a doctor." He didn't move as she pressed her fingertips over his carotid artery. Strong and steady.

A light shone in over her shoulder. Presley with a flashlight. "How is he?"

"Alive." The light helped and Abby quickly ran a hand over his chest and abdomen. She couldn't find any signs of external bleeding. "He's not shocky yet, but he could have internal injuries. Definitely has a closed head injury. He's alone."

"What do we do?" Presley asked.

"We can't get him out of the cab without proper equipment. We could make a spine or back injury worse. Shine the light into the backseat."

"Good right there?"

"Yes. Just give me a minute." Abby stretched an arm behind the seat and snagged an old wool blanket from the floor. "Okay—you start back up. I'll be right behind you."

She covered him, carefully backed out of the cramped opening, and edged her way up the slope to Presley. Going up was a lot harder than going down and she slipped a few more times. She'd need a shower before she'd be able to see patients. She concentrated on getting back to the top, trying to keep as much dirt and contamination out of her lacerated palm as she could.

Flann leaned against the hood of Presley's car, shining a light to guide them back. The night had gone black. Her face was mostly in shadow, but Abby could feel the tension radiating from her from ten feet away. Her solid presence chased some of the cold from Abby's middle, and she realized she was shaking.

"There's a man down there with a head injury," Abby said.

"We're not going to get him out without more help," Flann said. "You look like you took a fall. You okay?"

"Just muddy." Abby resisted the ridiculous urge to straighten her clothes and tame her tangled hair. Like it mattered what she looked like just then.

"Get in the car and get warm," Flann said, her tone gruff. "Pres, you okay?"

"Just wet. If we can't reach emergency services," Presley said, "we'll have to drive the rest of the way into town and find the sheriff or someone else."

"I hate leaving him here," Abby said.

"Getting the proper help is the best thing we can do," Flann repeated. "Come on." She circled Abby's waist. "Inside."

Abby climbed into the car before she realized Flann had directed her into the rear seat. Flann slid in and shut the door, blocking her exit. When Flann's arm came around her shoulders, she didn't pull away. The warmth felt good. So did Flann's body.

"Presley, you good to drive?" Flann asked.

"Fine."

"Wait." Abby pressed 911 and prayed for a connection. After what seemed like an interminable period of time, a woman answered briskly.

"Fire rescue, what's your emergency?"

"This is Dr. Abby Remy. I'm on—" She looked at Flann.

"County Road 54."

"County Road 54 just east of 71. There's a red pickup truck off the road with an unconscious driver inside. We need a response team."

"Is there any evidence of gas leaking or fire?"

"No."

"Are there any other passengers?"

"No. The driver's pulse is strong and I didn't see any evidence of external hemorrhage. How long until a team can get here?"

"I have one on the way. They'll be there in under five minutes."

"Thank you."

Flann said, "Pres, you should go. We can't do anything here, and we can at the Rivers."

"Abby?" Presley asked.

"I agree. We need to get to the hospital."

"Let me see your hand," Flann said, taking Abby's wrist as Presley pulled away from the wreck.

"What?" Abby said.

"Your hand is bleeding."

"Oh," Abby said. "It's nothing, just a few scrapes."

"I'll check it when we get to the ER," Flann said.

Abby was too weary to argue. Presley drove slowly through town, detouring around intersections blocked by police and fire trucks. Sirens blared intermittently and emergency vehicles passed them, most headed toward the Rivers, a few out of town. When the hospital on the hill came into view, glowing like a beacon from lights in dozens of windows, Abby sighed with relief.

"It looks like the village was mostly spared," Flann said quietly. "Power's out here and there, and the water main on River Road looks like it sprang a leak, but hopefully there won't be too much more damage. The houses out of town are far enough apart that the twister probably missed most of them. We might've gotten lucky."

Presley turned into the winding drive up to the Rivers.

"I'm not too sure about that," Abby said, taking in the line of emergency vehicles pulled up in front of the ER. "It looks like we've got a full house."

CHAPTER FOURTEEN

When the kitchen lights came back on, Blake blinked and Margie whooped.

"All right!" Margie jumped up. "Come on."

Blake followed Margie down the hall into a room that looked like a library, although most of the bookcases were empty. "What are we doing?"

"Getting lamps."

"Why?" He whispered, although he wasn't sure why. The whole night resembled one of those movies where a bunch of kids go into the woods and some maniac shows up. Though now that he thought about it, those movies seemed really stupid compared to what had just happened.

"You'll see. Here." Margie handed him a desk lamp. "We'll use these to keep the chicks warm."

He followed her back to the kitchen, the lamp under his arm. "Do you think these will be enough?"

"As long as the kitchen doesn't cool off too much," Margie said.

Blake wiped the sweat from his neck with his arm. The storm hadn't helped the heat at all. It was worse, the air a heavy thick blanket he could almost feel sitting on his shoulders, even inside. "Not much chance of that."

"They need to be kept at ninety degrees at this age." Margie placed her lamp on the floor next to the box and passed Blake the cord. "Put yours on the other side."

Blake positioned his, plugged them in, and angled the round metal shade so the beam fell into the box. The chicks huddled in one corner in the straw. They were about the size and color of tennis balls. They looked awfully fragile. Blake's chest tightened. "I wish we had the right stuff for them."

"It's just for tonight. The regular lamps aren't as good as heat lamps," Margie said, "but it will help."

Margie filled a saucer with water and placed it in one corner of the box. The small noisy balls of fluff hopped in a scrum over to the dish and pecked at the water.

Blake grinned. Weird that watching chickens, something he'd never given a thought to before, could create a little spurt of happiness. He laughed and didn't even feel dumb about it. "They're really cute."

"Wait'll they start to molt in a few days. They look so totally alien, half down and half feathers."

"What about food?"

Margie sighed. "Yeah, I know. The chicken food is in the barn."

"Oh." Blake didn't need to say it. Off-limits.

"Do you think starving chicks constitutes an emergency?" Margie's blond brows were drawn down, like she was working out a difficult math problem. Or plotting how to avoid getting caught coming in after curfew.

"Well, we can't let them go hungry." Blake was okay being stuck inside overnight, especially since he'd given his word on it, and he could live forever and be happy never to get caught in another storm like the one that just tore through, but the chicks… "We didn't figure them into our decision."

"The tack room is up at the front of the barn. That part didn't look damaged."

Blake walked out onto the back porch. Other than the glow from the kitchen, there were no lights anywhere. The sky was completely black. No stars, no hazy cloud of reflected illumination hanging on the horizon. "Hey, Margie? Isn't there supposed to be a light over the barn?"

Margie joined him. "Yeah. The line down there must be out."

"We have the flashlight, right?"

"Yep. What do you think?"

"We promised Flann and my mom we wouldn't go out, but…" Blake wrestled with the dilemma. "That was about us being safe, right?"

"Right. We didn't discuss contingencies and emergencies. Flann wouldn't want us to stay in the house if it caught on fire."

"I think letting the chickens starve constitutes about the same level of emergency as the house burning down."

"Totally." Margie's eyes sparkled in the slanted light from behind them, and the gold in her hair almost looked like a halo, but her grin was anything but angelic. Her tilted smile said she'd take a risk and not mind facing the consequences. "Flann will kill us if we get hurt."

"So will my mom." Blake knew they both knew they'd most likely get grounded and lectured at, which they'd survive, but he hated disappointing his mom. And he didn't want to look bad in front of Flann. He pictured the little yellow fluff balls and how eagerly they went after the water. They must be hungry. "It's not raining anymore. What are the chances another one of those twisters will come through?"

"I don't know. This is the first one I've been around for." Margie looped an arm around the porch post and swung out and back. "It's only gonna take us five minutes, max, to get to the barn and back."

"I say we do it." Blake stepped down onto the ground.

"Yep. Me too. I'll get the light."

Margie led the way to the driveway with the flashlight, holding Blake's hand. "There's a tree down just there. We can skirt around it."

"What about power lines?" Blake hopped to avoid a huge puddle and almost managed it. On the landing, water soaked into his right tennis shoe. He tried not to think about what might be in the water.

"The lines are buried out here, so we should be okay."

"Great." Blake eased off his grip on Margie's fingers, but didn't let go. It was *really* dark.

The chicken food was just inside the tack room in a big aluminum can. Margie played the light around until they spotted an empty feed bucket. Blake filled it with a couple of inches of chicken feed. "You think we should look for the kittens?"

"I want to," Margie said, "but if we go toward the back and anything comes down, we might as well hope it buries us for good."

Blake sighed. "Yeah, you're right. I guess this is as much as we can do right now."

"Wait—listen."

Blake tensed. Shadows filled the barn, and not being able to see beyond the small cone of light made everything extra spooky. "What?"

A sound like an animal being eaten alive came from somewhere close by. Blake jumped and dropped the feed pail. "What is that?"

Margie laughed. "Rooster."

"Where?"

"He's probably hiding nearby."

"How do we catch him?"

Margie handed Blake the feed pail and looped her arm through his. "We don't. Come on."

They picked their way quickly but cautiously back to the porch, and Margie propped the door open with a chair and set the flashlight on top. "Can you find another dish for the food and feed those guys?"

Blake found one on the drain board, filled it from the pail, and placed it in the box with the chicks. They chirped and pecked at it, and he knew they'd made the right decision. "They're good."

"Okay." Margie turned out the rest of the lights in the kitchen and plopped down on the floor with her back against one of the cabinets.

Moving carefully in the near dark from the little bit of illumination from the flashlight, Blake straddled a wooden kitchen chair and folded his arms on the back. He rested his chin on his arms. "What are we doing?"

"Look," Margie said excitedly.

Rooster landed in the doorway, swiveled his head back and forth a few times, and hopped into the kitchen. He fluttered his wings and pooped.

Blake winced. "Oh boy. Something tells me he's probably not supposed to be in here."

"Crap." Margie laughed. "But there are extenuating circumstances, right?"

"Are you sure you don't want to be a lawyer?"

"Family of doctors, remember?" Margie said. "Besides, I'm not interested in verbal arguments. I like doing things."

Rooster one-legged it over to the box of chicks. Blake got ready to jump. Weren't male animals—birds, whatever—supposed to be dangerous around babies? "He won't hurt them, will he?"

"I wouldn't ordinarily put the babies in with the big ones, but Rooster's not your ordinary chicken. Let's see what he does."

Margie sounded calm, but Blake wasn't so sure. Rooster peered over the box, trumpeted a few more earsplitting screeches, and fluffed up his feathers. A few more screeches and he hunkered down beside the box and appeared to go to sleep.

"All good," Margie said. "Anyhow, I've been thinking I might be a vet."

"Yeah," Blake said, "I can see that. It's still medicine, but you'd be outside more, and animals are so cool."

"More cool than people sometimes." Margie moved the flashlight and set it upright between them, enclosing them in a circle of light beyond which the night ruled. "Wait till you've spent some more time with some of the bigger animals."

"I'd like that." Blake had never thought about learning about animals, but then why would he. He grew up in the city and did what city kids did. He didn't know anything about farms or animals, and the idea of finding out hadn't interested him. Until now. The only other time he'd ever felt quite so happy inside had been when he'd escaped into a fantasy world between the pages of a book. Spending more time with Margie would be cool. She was smart and logical, but adventurous too. She was just fun to be around. "You said the other day I could go to the 4-H thing with you. I could still do that, right?"

"Sure. You live here now. I'll take you with me when we go to the convent to look after the kids."

"Whoa, back up a minute. Convent kids?"

Margie smirked. "The nuns over at St. Mary's raise goats, and it's kidding season. At least the second round of kids for this year. 4-Hers volunteer looking after the babies—feeding them and holding them and stuff. Makes them friendly and calm. Some of us show them at the county fairs. They're way cute, and it's really fun."

"Okay, sure. If you think it will be all right."

"Trust me, everybody likes volunteers."

Blake worried he'd stand out. The new kid. The different kid. The weird one. "I'm not gonna know anything."

"You will before long." Margie nudged his foot. "I'll teach you."

"Thanks." He sat in silence for a few minutes, listening to the chicks scrabble about and then slowly quiet. The night grew heavy with silence, like the air was growing thicker. "Weird, without any noise— nice."

"You miss the city?"

"Not so much. I mean, I miss having everything I want being really convenient—restaurants and shops and movie theaters and things like that. But I don't miss how crowded and dirty it is. You don't really notice it when you live there, until you get out here and there's no garbage on the sidewalks."

"No sidewalks."

Blake laughed. "Yeah, that too."

"I guess it's hard leaving your friends and school and everything, though."

Blake's heart jumped. He really liked Margie, and he didn't want to screw up being friends, but he hadn't really had anyone to talk to except his mom for a while. The support group was okay, but it was different talking to the group. They understood where he was coming from, which was super, but they weren't there when he went to school every day. They weren't part of his everyday life like Margie might be, weren't maybe going to be friends like she was. He hoped. Margie was different, special. He wasn't sure how far he could go. What was safe to say. "I miss a couple of them, yeah."

Margie tilted her head, watching him like she was waiting for more.

"You know, some of the kids I went to school with, my friends, they had a hard time with the trans thing." There, he'd said it out loud. Trans. He'd owned it. Now he just had to wait to see what happened. Again. A sick feeling rolled through his stomach. Maybe he'd just screwed up.

"Why?" Margie asked.

The big hand squeezing Blake's chest let go. Hopeful, he said, "I keep trying to figure out why, exactly, so, you know, maybe I can explain better. My best friends were these three girls and a guy I'd gone to school with forever. When I told them, one of the girls weirded out even though she tried to pretend she was cool with it. Allie said she felt like she'd been sharing secrets with a guy all along, and she never would have said some things if she'd known. And how now she couldn't be herself with me."

"Wow," Margie said thoughtfully. "It seems kind of backward, don't you think? Because you were sharing secrets with them too, probably."

"Yeah. But you know, not the big one."

"True. I can see how it might be hard when your really close friends have to think of you differently—like if one of my sisters said she was really a guy. But they'd still be them, right? I mean, you're still the same person. It's on the other people to see the real you."

Blake sat down on the floor next to Margie and wrapped his arms around his bent knees. The sick feeling was gone, and a flame of excitement kindled in his middle. Maybe this would be all right. "I guess when you find out the person's different than you thought, you don't know quite how to act. Because we expect guys to be a certain way and girls a certain way."

"I think we ought to just take people as they are, girls or guys or whatever, as they put themselves out there, you know?" She laughed. "I guess you must. Since that's what you're doing. Being the way you know you are."

"I'm kind of glad we moved up here." Blake hadn't told his mom, but in a way, it was a relief to be in a new place and maybe have a new start. "I do miss my friends, but I feel like here, I can just be me and no one will be comparing me to the me they think I should be."

"Are you gonna tell the school…the teachers, I mean?"

"Yeah, I think so. When I'm eighteen, I can legally change my sex—you know, on forms and stuff like that, but I don't want to wait to be treated like…like me."

"Yeah, that makes sense." Margie pursed her lips "So, what about…the other. You know."

Blake let out a breath. He knew. "I haven't talked to my mom yet, but I'm ready. I just started the shots a couple of months ago, but I'm ready for the surgery. For the top, anyway."

"You should get my sister to do it," Margie said with conviction. "She's the best."

"You don't think it's too out there? A lot of trans guys don't ever have surgery."

"Do you think it is?"

"No. It feels…not right this way."

"Well then, you should do it. You know who you are, right? You know what feels right for you. I think you should do whatever feels right for you."

"Thanks."

Margie bumped his shoulder with hers. "I didn't do anything. You're the one who's brave."

Tears pricked Blake's eyes and he blinked to keep them from falling. He'd heard it before, from his mom, from his therapist, from the others in the trans group. Margie was the first friend he'd made since he'd determined to be out with everyone. She hadn't freaked out. She understood. She gave him hope.

"You think we can sleep down here with Rooster and the chicks?"

"I don't see why not." Margie jumped up. "Let's find some pillows and stuff."

"And popcorn?"

Margie grabbed his hand. "Most definitely."

CHAPTER FIFTEEN

A bby counted eight emergency vans in the line extending down the drive from the ER entrance. Who knew how many had arrived in the time it had taken them to free Flann and drive over. "Stop and let me out here."

"Wait." Flann grasped her arm. "You're in no shape to see patients just yet. You're wet, cold, and…ah, dirty. Plus your hand needs some cleaning up."

Abby couldn't argue. Flann was never more annoying than when she was right. Abby's legs below her shorts were scraped and mud caked, her shoes were a ruin, and her palm stung from the dried blood and grit stuck to the lacerations. "Fine. I need you to get me some scrubs. Where's the locker room?"

"Presley," Flann said, "pull around to the side entrance. I'll take Abby up to the OR for a shower and some scrubs."

"All right." Presley swung around the circle in front of the main entrance to the white colonnaded brick building and into the side lot. "I'm going to head to the ER to see what the situation is, but I want to try Harper first." She pulled out her phone and swiped the screen. "I've got a signal."

Abby dug out her cell. She had a weak signal but at least there was hope the service would be back to strength soon. "I'll try the kids."

After a minute, Presley sighed. "I'm not getting through."

"I'm not either." Abby powered off.

"The circuits are probably overloaded with everyone trying to check in with family and friends," Flann said. "We'll have to just keep trying."

"I should have gone with Harper," Presley said.

"Harp knows these roads. She'll be fine," Flann said. "You're the boss—you need to be here, especially if we have to call in reinforcements."

"And I'm going to need to decide that," Abby said. Blake and Margie were as safe as they could be. She would've felt better hearing Blake's voice, but that comfort would have to wait. From the looks of what was ahead in the ER, they were probably already at capacity. "I'll have a recommendation for you in twenty minutes, Pres. Let's go, Flann."

"Yes, ma'am." Flann held the door as Abby climbed out and led her up the walk to the side entrance.

The security desk was unmanned. Abby followed Flann into the stairwell to the second floor and into the OR lounge. A redhead with a curvaceous body undisguised by her faded green scrubs let out a cry of delight when she saw Flann.

"Thank God you showed up. Glenn called up from the ER to say she's got a couple of cases that will need to come up soon. You're the only surgeon who's shown up so far."

"How urgent?" Abby asked.

The nurse gave her an inquiring look.

"Jeannie," Flann said, "this is Abby Remy, the new ER chief."

"Great initiation," Jeannie said. "Both level threes but Glenn said they shouldn't wait too long in case we get backed up overnight. An open tib for a washout, and facial lacerations on a teenager that are too extensive to do in the ER."

Flann said, "We'll get cleaned up and head down there. How many OR nurses do you have in?"

"Three so far. And one nurse anesthetist."

"That's a start. See if you can get another team together so we can run two rooms."

"Already on it. I've been calling, but I can't reach a lot of the on-call staff. Hopefully everyone knows to show up."

"I'm sure they do, but they might not be able to get here."

"We'll make it, Flann. Just let me know what you need." Jeannie barely took her eyes off Flann's, her tone eager and just a little breathless.

Abby recognized the signs of infatuation. So far every woman she'd seen around Flann appeared a little bit smitten. She suspected Flann's effortless charm worked on just about everyone, gay or straight. Then again, maybe Flann and Jeannie had history—or something more current. Pushing the flare of annoyance aside, she said, "We should get going."

Her tone was more forceful than she intended, but Flann just nodded and pointed to the door marked *Surgeons*. The other read *Nurses*.

"Seriously?" Abby asked. "Not Men and Women?"

"The hospital is a hundred years old. It's tradition."

"It's archaic."

"Good thing you're friends with the CEO—you can take it up with her."

"Not my battle. The locker rooms in the ER are appropriately labeled."

"I kind of like making the guys jump for their pants." Flann grinned, pushed the door open, and yelled inside, "Rivers on deck."

No one answered, and they trooped in.

"We've got two showers in the back." Flann pulled scrubs from a metal rack and looked over her shoulder. "Mediums?"

"That should do it."

"You can go ahead. I'll rustle up some OR towels. Won't be fancy, but it will do the job."

"Thanks." Abby took the scrubs and, expecting the bathroom to be a grungy example of male dominion like the ones she'd had to use from time to time in training, was surprised to find the long marble counter with inset sinks, the white octagonal floor tiles, and the brass fixtures all sparkling. Like everywhere else in the hospital, the elegance of an earlier age remained. She stacked her dirty clothes and clean scrubs outside the last shower stall. The water was hot, plentiful, and blissful. Her palm stung as she carefully scrubbed it free of dirt and debris, but she took her time. She couldn't afford to get sidelined with cellulitis. She used soap from the dispenser to wash her hair and quickly rinsed off.

She would've stayed under for a half an hour if she'd had the choice, but she didn't. She'd have to ignore her aching muscles and stiff joints for now. Less than five minutes later, she pulled back the plastic curtain and checked outside. A stack of green OR towels sat next to her scrubs. They were just large enough to cover her as she wrapped one around her torso and stepped out to dry off.

Flann rounded the corner, a pair of OR clogs in her hand, and stopped abruptly. "Hey. Feel better?"

Abby tried to pretend she wasn't standing there nearly naked, but she felt the flush rise up her chest to her throat. The towel came to just the tops of her thighs. If she breathed too deeply, she'd give Flann a show. She resisted the urge to grab another one and hold it up in front of her. Flann had undoubtedly seen naked women before, and she had changed her clothes around dozens of other women over the years. This was different, though. This was a woman whose briefest gaze made her heart race. She grabbed another towel and briskly rubbed her hair with one hand and surreptitiously held the other down against her middle. "About a million times better."

"I brought you some OR clogs—they might be a bit big, but they're clean."

"Thanks. I'll see you down there."

"I need to look at your hand."

"Go shower," Abby said. "You're just as cold and dirty as I was. My hand is fine."

"Let me see it. Thirty seconds."

Since she'd waste more time arguing, Abby stepped forward with her hand out, palm up. "Your verdict, Dr. Rivers?"

Flann cupped Abby's hand, her fingers a gentle cradle. "Not too deep, but your whole palm is scraped up. You ought to put some antibiotic ointment on it when you get downstairs."

"I will." Abby pulled her hand away when Flann showed no signs of letting go. They'd probably only been touching for ten seconds, but her whole arm flashed with heat. Why attention from a woman she barely knew could rock her so completely left her as shaken as the trembling in her depths. The need that pulled at her when Flann focused on her was foreign and terrifying and bittersweet. Everything she'd forgotten how to want. "You need to keep your leg dry."

Flann held up a big sheet of adherent plastic. "Jeannie got me this. I'll wrap it around the dressing."

"You'll need help with that."

"I'll get Jeannie to do it."

"I'm right here."

"If you don't mind."

She minded the idea of Jeannie doing it a lot more, for some reason. "Just give me a minute to get dressed."

"Sure." Flann leaned against the tile wall.

Really. As if she couldn't tell when she was being teased. Abby pointed. "Flann. Out."

"Oh," Flann said, her smile widening. "Just checking."

"Well, you can stop. I'll call you."

Flann laughed and backed out. Abby wanted to be outraged at Flann's outrageous presumptions and her interminable flirting, but she wasn't really. Flann's exuberant confidence and relentless charisma made her feel young in a way she couldn't remember ever feeling. She must've, once, before she'd made a colossal mistake that had left her pregnant and also given her the greatest gift of her life. She'd lost her youth, but she'd gained so much more and had not one iota of regret. Still, Flann's playful seductiveness woke something in her, and allowing herself a few moments' secret pleasure couldn't do anyone any harm. But the moment was over. She pulled on the scrubs over her bare skin and stepped into the clogs. "Ready."

Flann came back and dropped scrubs and more towels on the floor. She untied the pair of scrub pants she'd gotten from Harper and let them slide to the floor.

The shower enclosure was steamy and very quiet. They were very much alone and Flann was not her patient now. Flann's legs were tanned and toned, and a little bit of bare, lean midriff showed above the black briefs. Flann was a very sexy woman, and Abby was not immune.

"Okay, how do we do this?" Abby kept her gaze firmly on Flann's face.

Flann held out the eighteen-inch square of adherent plastic. "You hold both corners on your end, and I'll peel off the backing. Keep it tight so it doesn't wrinkle, lay it down over the bandage, and wrap it all the way around. Make sure you get skin on both sides of it so it sticks."

Abby had to crouch in front of Flann again, and she ordered herself back into physician mode. She grasped the plastic as directed, Flann peeled off the thin paper backing, and Abby pressed the adherent film to Flann's thigh. Flann's muscles jumped.

"I'm sorry. You're tender, aren't you?"

"I'm okay. You're doing great."

Abby carefully wrapped the plastic around Flann's thigh, completely enclosing the gauze bandage she'd placed earlier. When she was done, she looked up. "All right?"

Flann's teasing grin was gone. In its place was an expression Abby had never seen directed at her before—a dark flash of hunger that flared in the shadows of Flann's gaze.

"Really good." Flann brushed a strand of hair from Abby's cheek. "You do have good hands."

Flann's fingertips were soft and warm, and heat flowed down Abby's body. She leaned into Flann's palm and Flann's fingers slid over the edge of her jaw onto her neck. Her nipples tightened.

Abby swallowed. "I should get downstairs."

"I'll be right down." Flann didn't move.

Abby rose. They were inches apart. Flann's lips parted, full and moist.

"Abby—"

"Don't forget," Abby said, slipping around Flann. "I expect you to check in every two hours." She didn't wait for Flann to answer.

CHAPTER SIXTEEN

Flann finished her sixth case of the night at five in the morning. They'd commandeered a couple of floor nurses to work in the recovery room until the regular staff could get in, hopefully sometime in the next few hours. Presley had sent word into the OR that she'd been in contact with local police and county sheriffs' offices, and reports were that many roads were closed due to downed trees and mudslides. With so few roads connecting the outlying communities, many of the staff members would not be able to get into work for at least another twenty-four hours. Those who lived close enough to the hospital to make it in or who were on duty when the storm hit would be eating and sleeping at the hospital until relief arrived. Sometime during the night one of the old-timers Presley had once referred to as a dinosaur had shown up in the OR in scrubs. Franklin Thomas had spent his life as a general practitioner, but when he'd started practicing, around the time Flann had been born, he'd delivered babies, set bones, and on occasion removed an appendix or two. He'd pitched in and put on casts, washed out wounds, and performed other minor surgical procedures to give Flann a chance to concentrate on the most serious repairs.

"Jeannie," Flann said as she stretched some of the kinks out of her back, "if there's no one on deck, I'll head to the ER and see what else might be down there."

"Hopefully, not much." Jeannie's shoulders sagged with weariness. She and the few OR nurses they'd been able to assemble had been working flat-out for over twelve hours.

"I think Glenn would've called up if she'd had anything, but I want to be sure before we let people start taking breaks."

"Right. We'll be waiting."

Flann changed out of her sweat-soaked scrubs into clean ones, grabbed a white coat from a peg by the door, and took the stairs down to the first floor. The almost empty ER waiting room was a relief. The big board across from the nurses' station indicated eight of the dozen rooms were occupied, but the emergency receiving bay was unoccupied. No pending traumas. The exhaustion she'd been keeping at bay seeped in, and she rubbed her forearm across her eyes.

"Hey."

Abby's voice cut through Flann's fatigue like a sharp scalpel, energizing her. Flann straightened, and there she was. A few feet away, a chart tucked under her arm, her hair held back with a tie at the base of her neck. Faint circles smudged the pale flesh beneath her eyes, but that was the only sign she'd been up all night working. Her gaze was bright and focused and her smile—Flann hadn't realized until just that moment how precisely like sunrise Abby's smile was.

"What are you doing down here?" Abby asked.

"I escaped."

Abby laughed. "You've also missed several check-ins."

"I know, I'm sorry. They were stacked up like firewood there for a while. I couldn't get away."

"I know. We were sending them up to you. How's everybody doing?"

Flann leaned against the wall, moving out of the way of a nurse pushing a stretcher toward the elevator at the end of the hall. The aches in her muscles disappeared as pleasure lightened the heaviness in her chest. Abby stirred a surge of energy, like a breeze chasing away the clouds after a summer squall. "Fortunately, most of the fractures were straightforward and they'll be able to go home in a day or two. The guy from the car accident is in the ICU being monitored. His CAT scan shows contusions, but nothing that looks surgical. Last I heard, the nurses were waiting for neurosurg to evaluate."

"We really need our own neurosurgeons on call."

"We need a lot of things," Flann said with an edge. "But we're not a level one, Abs."

Abby's eyebrows rose. "Abs?"

"Okay then. What do people call you for short?"

"Abby."

"Right." Flann grinned. "Have you heard from the kids?"

"Not yet. But they have to be okay, right?"

"They'll be fine. Margie has a good head on her shoulders—she won't do anything too crazy."

"Now, that's reassuring," Abby said dryly. "How are you feeling?"

"Fine."

"Uh-huh. And now for the real answer."

Flann shrugged. "I wouldn't mind sitting down for a while."

"I'll bet. Are you hungry?"

Flann gave that some thought. She'd wolfed down the sandwich Abby had made between cases a few hours ago. When she was operating, she forgot about everything except what she needed to do to get through the case. "I think I will be before too long. What about down here? Need a hand?"

"Between Glenn and Andy Bucknell, who got here a few hours ago, we've been able to clear the board more or less. We're waiting to transfer an acute asthmatic up to a telemetry floor, and a couple more are waiting for X-rays and test results, but I think everyone is pretty much squared away."

"Are you going to be able to get out of here for a while?"

"Maybe. At least long enough to check in on Blake. What about Harper?"

"I got a short message from Harper in the OR about three. She and my dad are fielding local calls."

Abby gestured for Flann to follow. "I'll stand you a cup of coffee and we'll try calling again."

"You're on."

Instead of going to the cafeteria, Abby led her to the ER break room where a fresh round of coffee was just dripping into the pot. Flann sank into a chair at one of the chipped Formica tables, the beige top discolored in places from too many spilled cups of coffee. Abby pulled two Styrofoam cups from a stack and looked over her shoulder. "Cream? Sugar?"

"Black is fine."

Abby poured two cups and leaned down to pull cream from the under-counter fridge.

Flann took the opportunity to study Abby unawares. She looked great even in scrubs—full in all the right places and sleek in others. Added to that, she moved with confidence and grace. She was pretty spectacular on all fronts. Flann would have sworn she was too tired to even entertain sex, but her belly heated and she couldn't help imagining Abby naked and lying beside her on cool white sheets while a late-night breeze blew in an open window. Yeah, right. The scenario worked, but Abby Remy was not a good candidate for the rest of the picture. Flann sighed. She and Abby kept getting thrown together in the middle of a crisis, and every time Abby came out looking more and more desirable. Just the circumstances. Adrenaline and hormones. Nothing more.

Abby handed Flann a coffee and sat across from her. "Considering that we don't have any protocols in place for a disaster of this magnitude, I think everything went really well tonight."

Flann sipped her coffee. Abby's eyes glowed and her voice lilted with excitement. "You've been having a good time."

Abby looked as if she might protest, then with a small smile, nodded. "You don't really think I'm an ER doc because I like to take care of colds and UTIs, do you?"

"While there's nothing wrong with doing that," Flann said judiciously, "no, I see you preferring a lot more high-powered situation. I'm surprised you're not an intensivist or some kind of critical-care doc or something."

"I thought about it, but like I said, I enjoy the variety in the ER. And I like the tough cases. I like the pace."

"Then why are you here? Tonight's an anomaly, you must know that. Ordinarily, you're going to get the occasional car accident, some farming injuries, kids with broken bones from playing sports, and a whole hell of a lot of MIs, pulmonary problems, and…female-type issues."

Abby laughed. "I know that."

"Then I repeat, why are you here?"

Abby stared at her coffee, contemplating how much she really wanted to say. She hadn't even talked to Presley about everything that had happened in the last year, not really. And Flann, Flann was hardly the confidant type. And yet, the intensity of her gaze and the thoughtful timber of her voice were genuine. She actually wanted to know, and

Abby wanted to say the words out loud, rather than whisper them in her mind when lying alone late at night. "Most of it has to do with Blake."

"You mentioned that, at least a little bit. That's a big sacrifice to make—leaving a major trauma center for a quiet place like this."

Abby's head snapped up. "I don't think so."

Flann held up a hand. "Whoa. I'm not saying I don't agree with it. But there's no point in pretending you didn't have to give up something."

Abby's first instinct was to argue, or at least tell Flann she had no idea what she was talking about until she was in the same situation. Until she had a child for whom she was completely responsible. A child who needed love and protection. Flann gazed back steadily, no touch of arrogance or superiority in her expression. Just calmly waiting. Abby took a deep breath. "It's hard to think of it that way. He's my child. I'd do anything for him."

"I believe you." Flann smiled. "My parents are like that too. Especially my mother. I respect you, more than I can say."

Abby had heard that before, in one form or another, from her own mother, from the parents of some of the teens in Blake's trans support group, from Presley. Hearing those words from Flann touched her in a way she hadn't expected—Flann knew what it had taken to get where she was. Flann understood the thrill and the tremendous sense of accomplishment that came with treating critically ill patients in a crisis situation. Abby's throat tightened, and to her horror, her eyes stung with unshed tears. She brushed a hand across her face. "Well, I must be more tired than I thought."

Flann took her other hand and squeezed gently. "Long fucking night."

Abby laughed shakily. "You can say that again. I don't think I ever thanked you for saving Blake during that storm."

"No thanks necessary. And I didn't, really. But I'm glad I was there."

"God, so am I." Abby tightened her grip on Flann's fingers, barely able to picture the horror of what might have happened. "He's been through so much already. I never dreamed of a natural disaster as our next challenge."

"Was it bad for him, before you moved?"

"I wish I knew the answer to that. He doesn't always tell me everything, I don't think. Partly that's just being a teenager, and partly probably trying to protect me."

"He's his mother's son," Flann said softly.

"I know his friends, of course. I've known them most of their lives. He went to preschool with them, and then with a couple of them all the way through into high school."

"Private school?"

Abby nodded.

"It must not have been easy raising him, with you being a resident."

"My mother lived with us. That made a difference. I had some insurance money from my father's death, so that helped pay for Blake's school."

Flann knew she was pushing, but she wanted to know. Needed to know in some deep way she couldn't even name. "What about Blake's father?"

Abby laughed. "David? He's a nice enough guy, but…I would call him something of a flake. He's into tech and always looking for the next big wave. He hasn't caught one yet. He never had enough financial resources to really help out."

"He's not in the picture?" Flann's chest tightened, waiting for the answer.

"He's never really been in the picture," Abby said slowly, not taking time to ask herself why she was answering. Why she wanted to answer. "He was my best friend in high school—the two gay kids against the world. We came out together, had our hearts broken at the same time. Presley was my best friend in college, maybe my only real friend. The sorority gave me a kind of community, but I was lonely, I guess. David showed up in the city one night, chasing a job. I wasn't quite twenty yet, away from home for the first time. It was wonderful to see him and we went out to dinner, had a lot to drink, and ended up back in his hotel room reminiscing. Turns out he was a little lost and lonely too. Somehow…" She shook her head. "God, I don't even know to this day how it happened. But it happened."

"Wow. And you never considered—"

"Never. Not from the second I found out. I wanted the baby. David, on the other hand, was running before the sentence was out of my mouth." Abby shrugged. "That was fine with me. I didn't expect anything from him, and I'm just as glad things turned out the way they did."

"Does Blake see him?" For some reason, Flann hated the idea of Blake feeling rejected or hurt because his father wasn't in his life.

"Oh, sure. David's always been in and out of his life. I left it up to Blake as he was growing up to decide how much he wanted to see him. It's been a couple of years since his last visit. David lives out west with his lover now."

"Blake's okay about it?"

Abby smiled, hearing the protectiveness and the concern in Flann's tone. They were still holding hands, and she didn't want to let go. "He's good."

"Does David know about Blake?"

"Blake told him on the phone. David seemed to take it well, but you just never know until you're really confronted with it. Besides, the next time David sees him, Blake is likely to be a lot different from the child he remembers."

"Is he taking hormones?"

"Yes, for about six months." Abby realized Flann was the first person other than her mother and parents in the support group with whom she'd discussed any of the details of Blake's transition. Talking about it with someone she trusted helped make all the changes feel less foreign. "I keep looking for changes. There are some, but he still looks baby-faced to me."

"A lot of boys do at that age." Flann smiled. "Is it hard, watching him change?"

Abby wanted to say no. Part of her thought she should. Slowly, she nodded. "Sometimes. I think back and remember Blake as a child, trying to see what I missed, trying to pick out the moment when he knew and I should have. I can't. I feel guilty."

"You're amazing," Flann said softly. "Blake is so fucking lucky."

Abby grimaced. "I don't feel amazing. Sometimes I feel completely inadequate. A couple of the friends I told you about shut him out, hurt him. I can't tell you how much I want to shake every single person who hurts him or *might* hurt him. And I can't and I don't know how to keep it from happening again."

"Blake seems like a pretty strong, together kid. He'll be okay.

He'll get some bumps, and it's got to be damn scary. But he's got you. That's probably the single most important thing he needs."

"I hope so. I hope he and Margie get to be good friends. She's the kind of friend he needs."

Flann grinned. "Margie? She's a freaking Amazon."

"From what I can tell, all the Rivers siblings are Amazons."

"You should meet my mother."

Abby laughed. "Oh, now there's a line I didn't expect to hear from you." As soon as she said it, she flushed. Flann might think she was flirting.

Flann didn't laugh. "You know what? I think that's a great idea." She pulled out her phone, punched in a number, and waited. "Mama? Where are you?...Have you heard from Dad and Harper?...Uh-huh. If everything stays quiet, maybe an hour or two...Uh-huh. Hold on." Flann held up the phone. "Here's Blake."

"What?" Abby took the phone. "Blake? Are you okay? Where—?"

"I'm great. Everything's cool. Margie's mom is here. Are you coming home soon?"

Abby hesitated. "I don't know, honey. I can't leave until some other doctors show up. Maybe."

"Hold on."

Abby frowned. Now what?

"Dr. Remy, this is Ida Rivers."

Abby sat up straight and released Flann's hand. Ida Rivers's voice was kissed with a hint of the South that did nothing to make it any less commanding.

"Hello, Mrs. Rivers. This is Abby Remy."

"Nobody can work around the clock without food. You're ten minutes from the house. I can have breakfast ready for you and the rest of the family by the time you get here."

"Um." Abby glanced at Flann, who was grinning slightly maniacally. She shot her a glare. "Well, I…"

"I'm tracking down my husband and the rest of my children now. Seven o'clock. You can go back to work after that if needed."

"If at all possible, of course."

"That will be just fine. See you at seven."

Abby held the phone out to Flann. "I can't believe you did that."

"Makes sense. Cafeteria is probably not going to open for a while.

And it doesn't take much longer to get to Presley's than it does to chase down food in town."

"I suppose we could all use a break and some food. If it's quiet."

"I'll check on the postop patients, and you can get the ER sorted."

Abby knew when she'd been beaten. "You should let me change the dressing before we leave."

"Good enough. I'll meet you down here as soon as I'm finished upstairs."

Abby stood. "I'll round up Presley and Carrie." She paused. "What about Glenn? She's been up all night."

Glenn was practically part of the family. Flann would have mentioned inviting her herself in another minute. "Sure."

"Great." Abby jumped up and hurried for the door. "I'll find her."

"Great," Flann muttered, ignoring the quick spurt of jealousy. "Terrific."

CHAPTER SEVENTEEN

"Call me if you need me, Angie," Flann said, clipping the postop order sheet to the front of the patient's chart. The computer network was iffy with the power outages, and she didn't want to chance the orders being lost. She'd never really given up the habit of writing notes by hand anyhow. She'd watched her father do it when she'd followed him around as a kid, and the mystique of pulling charts from their racks and delving into the mysteries within still lingered. "I'll be back in a few hours."

The recovery room nurse, who usually covered the ICU, nodded. "I don't know what we would have done if you hadn't gotten in last night, Flann."

Flann grinned. "Where else would I be?"

Angie laughed. "I can't imagine."

"Besides, Franklin got in and really made a difference."

"Like old times." Angie, a fifty-year-old who'd trained at the Rivers's nursing school before it had shut down, shook her head sadly. "Sometimes I wish we could turn back the clock. I miss the old days."

"Maybe with the new administration, we can bring back a little of the old too."

Angie snorted. "You think? Now there's a new head in the ER. More change."

"Abby's great. She's not going to hurt us." Flann had seen Abby in action enough to believe what she was saying. And she'd gotten to know her now, believed in her commitment to the Rivers.

"I hope you're right."

A patient's IV machine beeped, and Angie went off to check it.

Flann took the stairs down to the ER, eager to see Abby again. She was nowhere in sight but Glenn was at the nurses' station, filling out a chart. She looked as alert and unfazed as she did at six in the morning at the start of a routine day. Her sandy hair was unruffled, her shoulders straight, her blue eyes crystal clear. Now that Flann thought of it, Glenn was damned good-looking. Just the kind of steady, solid woman who'd appeal to someone looking for a relationship.

"Have you seen Abby?" Flann asked abruptly.

Glenn looked up. "Hey, Flann. She's in ten, giving discharge instructions to a woman with a fractured wrist."

"How's it going down here?"

"Everything's pretty much cleared out. Abby just checked with fire rescue, and they've only got one in the bus. Mrs. Wilcox—shortness of breath again. Andy is set to handle that."

"Can we sneak out for a little while?"

Glenn nodded. "Sorry I didn't get up to the OR, but Abby was swamped. I figured it would be more efficient for me to get the pre-ops ready down here so you could just keep them rolling through."

"It was a good call. Better to get them triaged down here as fast as possible."

"That's what Abby thought too. She had things working like clockwork. She's got a way of getting everybody to put out a hundred and ten percent without even trying." Glenn grinned. "Abby's like a general directing troops, but she leads from the front. I've never seen the ER click so well."

Abby, Abby, Abby. Flann bristled a little. "I don't know, I thought we always did pretty well."

"Hey, it wasn't a comment about you. I didn't mean to suggest—"

"I know. Forget it." Flann waved her off. Her ego wasn't so sensitive she couldn't hear something good about someone else. No doubt Abby was great at her job. She wouldn't have risen to the top at a competitive program as she'd done without being excellent. Besides, she'd seen for herself how good Abby was. Glenn was obviously taken with her, and that bothered her more than the commentary on how well Flann ran the ER, and *that* was just plain ridiculous.

"Abby said if you got down here before she was free, to take a look at your leg," Glenn said. "Three is open."

"It's fine. It can wait."

"That's not what I heard." Glenn closed the chart and regarded her with a steady, unwavering gaze.

Flann recalled Glenn had been a ranking officer in the military. She never talked about it, but it showed in her demeanor. She wasn't going to budge, and Flann had to admit a dressing change was probably a good idea. She blew out a breath. She was being an ass on just about every level. "You're right. Thanks."

Glenn was halfway through the dressing change when Abby poked her head in through the curtain. "How's it looking?"

"Fine," Flann said from her perch on the treatment table. Glenn sat on a stool in front of her, cleaning the incision with sterile saline.

Abby stepped up behind Glenn, rested a hand lightly on her back for balance, and leaned forward to study Flann's leg. "It looks pretty good. Some swelling. If you can manage to keep off it for the rest of the day, it would help."

"I will if I can," Flann said.

Abby squeezed Glenn's shoulder. "Thanks for taking care of that, Glenn."

Glenn glanced up, giving Abby a smile. "No problem."

"When you're done, I think we're clear to sneak out of here for a while. Glenn, can you give me a ride?"

"Sure."

"We should probably take two cars," Flann said quickly. "In case we have to come back at separate times. Why don't you take Presley and Carrie back in Carrie's car, Glenn? I'll ride with Abby."

Abby's brows rose. "Glenn?"

"Sure." Glenn rose, wrapped a fresh gauze quickly and efficiently around Flann's thigh, stripped off her gloves, and washed her hands. "I'll tell them to meet us in the parking lot."

"Great." Flann carefully climbed down from the treatment table and pulled on her scrub pants. She was aware of Abby watching her, and the tingle in her belly that started every time Abby was near ratcheted up a notch. She took her time tying her scrubs, and when she looked up, Abby's gaze was still on her. Flann couldn't read what was behind her pensive look, but she knew she liked it. "Ready?"

Abby nodded, still thinking about Flann's long, agile fingers sliding the green ties through her hands. Clever, sensuous fingers. She turned away. "We should go. We might not have much time."

Presley met them in the parking lot and gave Abby her keys. "See you there!"

Abby pulled out first, hoping the drive back to Presley's would be less adventurous than the trip in to the hospital had been. In daylight, everything looked both less forbidding and more devastated than the night before. The road crews must've been working around the clock too. Downed trees had been cut and dragged to the side to clear the roads. Uprooted trees and fields smashed flat by the high winds punctuated the countryside. They passed a white farmhouse and red barn looking bucolic in the bright sunlight, tall stalks of corn waving in the fields. A quarter mile farther on, bent and broken cornstalks lay strewn across pastures surrounding a tumbled-down barn and a house with portions of the roof missing.

"This is terrible," Abby said. "It's not just property damage. These fields are people's livelihoods."

"I know," Flann said. "It's still early enough in the season that some of these fields can be replanted, though. Everyone who lives out here is a survivor. Nature has been trying to drive us out for a couple hundred years, but it hasn't won yet."

"Have you ever thought about leaving?"

"Oh," Flann said lightly, "for a while. When I first got to the city for medical school, I was pretty seduced by the…life."

Abby grinned and shot her a look. "Don't you mean *night*life?"

Flann grinned back. "Well, it's not as if there's an abundance of available females in this area. So, yeah, I was a little taken with the increase in the dating pool."

Abby laughed. "I don't doubt it. Where did you go to school?"

"My father's alma mater. Vanderbilt."

"Southern girls at that. That must have been a change."

"It worked out pretty well for my father."

"But neither you nor Harper came back with a bride."

"I wasn't looking for one, and Harper…well, I guess Harper was waiting for Presley."

Abby smiled, taken aback by the seriousness in Flann's voice. "That's a terribly romantic thing to say, Dr. Rivers."

"What, you don't think I have any romantic tendencies?"

"I think I'd better not comment on that."

"Is that what you're looking for? A romantic?" Flann asked. For some strange reason, Abby's assumption she wasn't capable of romance bothered her. Not that she'd ever considered herself romantic or had been looking for romance. Far from it. But Abby's quick dismissal rankled.

Abby frowned. "How did we get from your love of the city life to my love life?"

"Natural progression."

"This is my turn, isn't it?" Abby frowned, feeling oddly displaced. The countryside looked practically foreign despite the bright sunshine and clear skies. She'd traveled the road barely twenty-four hours before, but subtle changes in the landscape, as if someone had rearranged familiar pieces on a chessboard while she hadn't been looking, left her uneasy and wary. Even the discussion with Flann had started out innocently and veered into areas she'd rather not discuss, areas she'd rather not even think about.

"Yes—turn right."

Abby signaled and turned in to the drive leading to Presley's, hoping to derail the strange turn in the conversation. Her personal life was barely existent, and romance had never been on the horizon. She'd been a mother before she'd barely had a chance to date other women. Oh, she'd been tempted now and then during medical school and after to do more than casually date, but there'd just never been time. She'd hardly had the energy to maintain the grueling training schedule while helping to raise Blake. Personal relationships weren't even a consideration. "I'm not in the market for romance."

"Is there someone back in the city, then?" Flann asked, a tightness in her voice that sounded almost like anger. "A trail of broken hearts?"

"No," Abby said, "nothing dramatic at all. I've been a little busy the past few years, so…nothing serious." She wasn't about to admit to nothing at all. Really, how pathetic would that seem?

"Blake is fifteen, isn't he?"

"Almost sixteen," Abby said.

"So in sixteen years, nothing serious?"

Abby looked away from the road long enough to meet Flann's questioning gaze. "That's a little personal."

"I know." Flann didn't sound the least bit apologetic.

Clearly, Flannery Rivers would not be put off when she wanted something. Abby had never run into anyone who probed beneath the surface of her personal shields with such unabashed arrogance and persistence. She ought to be irritated. She *was* irritated, but more with herself than Flann. Irritated because she didn't want to keep her shields up. Protecting herself, protecting her privacy, protecting Blake's privacy, was exhausting. She couldn't remember the last time she'd let anyone see the needs and hopes and desires she harbored beneath the surface. She couldn't even remember the last time she'd thought of them herself. Maybe the last time she and Presley had talked, really talked, before Abby had gone off to medical school and Presley had left to pursue the life her family had raised her to live.

"You first," Abby said, thinking a reversal might dissuade Flann from probing any further. "What are you looking for?"

"That's easy. Someone smart, adventurous, with her life together, and no serious aspirations."

Abby nodded wryly. Why was she disappointed? "A good-time girl."

"More or less. I'd prefer she'd only be having a good time with me."

Abby raised a brow as she pulled up in front of Presley's house. "Fun for how long?"

Flann grinned. "Until we aren't having fun anymore."

"For how long?" Abby shut off the engine and turned to face her. "For how long will it be just fun?"

Flann's grin disappeared and a muscle jumped along her jaw. "I don't know. I don't think I'm cut out for anything else."

"I'm not sure I believe that," Abby said quietly.

"You should. Your turn," Flann said just as quietly.

Abby shrugged. "I used to think, a long time ago, I'd have a traditional family—spouse, couple of kids, a comfortable house, a few animals. And my career, of course."

"2.5 kids, station wagon, and a house in the suburbs?"

"Not exactly. I grew up in the suburbs, but my grandparents had a place in the Adirondacks. Ten acres on a lake. I'm not looking for a lake, but I'd like to have a place where the neighbors aren't too close, where my children...where Blake can have a dog and we wouldn't have to worry about traffic." Abby laughed. "Maybe even a few chickens."

Flann laughed too. "You said you used to think that. You don't anymore?"

"Tell me about your mother," Abby said. She didn't want to talk about herself anymore. She didn't want to think about a relationship, and even if she did, Flann wasn't the person she wanted to share her dreams with.

"My mother?" Flann's voice held a note of surprise and affection. "She's…she's amazing. If it weren't for her, I don't know how any of us would've turned out, really."

"What about your dad? From what I understand, everyone at the hospital thinks he's close to God."

"My father is a remarkable physician, and a good father. I love him, but like most doctors in his situation, he wasn't around a lot when we were growing up. When we were hurt, when we were scared, when Kate…" Flann blew out a breath. "Well, anyhow, my mother is the rock our family rests on."

"Kate?" Abby couldn't remember anyone mentioning Kate.

"Our sister between Carson and Margie. She died of leukemia when she was eleven."

"Oh God, I'm really sorry. I didn't know."

"No reason you should have. My father was there, as much as he could be, but it was my mother who was always there, for everyone, all the time. More than anyone." Flann grimaced. "More than me, for sure. I…I didn't handle Kate being sick very well."

"You couldn't have been very old yourself."

"Old enough to be a hell of a lot stronger than I was." Flann's voice was tinged with bitterness and self-reproach. "Harper was the strong one. No surprise there. I decided to rebel instead. I was pretty much a jerk, really."

Abby grasped Flann's hand and squeezed. "That must have been a terrible time for everyone. And not everyone handles that kind of loss the same, especially not at first."

"Yeah, well, my mother and Harper did just fine," Flann said softly. "You'll like my mother. You're like her."

"I am?" Abby caught her breath. "Why?"

Flann drew their clasped hands onto her thigh, gripping her fingers tightly. Her dark eyes held no levity, only solemn sincerity. "She's strong, fierce, protective of us. She's never let any of us down, ever."

"Thank you," Abby said softly. "I'm not at all sure I'm that strong, but I'm honored that you think so."

"I know so."

The front door opened and a woman looking like a regal version of Harper walked out. She called down to them, "Are you planning to bring her in for breakfast, Flannery, or let her starve out here?"

Flann grinned and pushed open the car door just as Carrie pulled in behind them. "We're coming, Mama."

Abby followed her out, for once as happy as Flann to pretend all that mattered was medicine and an occasional good time. She already liked the serious side of Flann a little too much for comfort, or safety.

CHAPTER EIGHTEEN

Abby climbed the steps to meet Flannery's mother, more nervous than she had any reason to be. She rarely worried about the impression she made, but this meeting had an air of importance others didn't. She remembered the way Flann spoke of her mother, with deep affection and a little awe. This woman was Flann's hero. Abby held out her hand. "It's good to meet you."

"I'm sorry it took a night like last night to get us in the same house." Ida squeezed Abby's hand in both of hers. "My apologies, Dr. Remy, for not having you out to dinner when you arrived."

"Oh no, please. Call me Abby, and apologies are not—"

"Nonsense. My daughter knows better. Now go into the kitchen, you two." Ida slid an arm around Abby's waist and gently but firmly led her forward.

Helplessly, Abby glanced over her shoulder at Flann, who merely grinned, shrugged, and fell into line.

The kitchen looked completely different than the last time Abby'd seen it. The table had been righted and put back into its original position, the rain-streaked floor scrubbed, the counters wiped down, and the windows cleaned. The one over the sink was cracked, she noted, and the back door stood open to the morning without benefit of the screen door, which was propped against the railing. "You've done a lot of work in here. What else can I help you with?"

"Not a thing," Ida said. "Blake and Margie pitched in. You can help me best by sitting right there at the table and drinking the coffee I just made."

"Where is my son? Not in the barn, I hope." The box of chicks still sat in the corner with the new addition of two lamps shining into it. "I know they were worried about the kittens."

"I told them the barn was off-limits until Flannery and Harper got a good look at it in daylight. I sent the two of them off to shower. They both looked as if they'd crawled out of a mud pit."

"Uh…" Abby said.

"Separate bathrooms," Ida said without turning around. She set a flame under a cast-iron pan and laid strips of bacon into it. "What's wrong with your leg, Flannery O'Connor?"

"Just a scratch, Mama."

"Then why are you limping?"

Ida hadn't raised her voice or even glanced at Flann, but Flann actually squirmed in her chair. Abby watched, fascinated, and shook her head when Flann sent her an imploring look.

"A little stiff, that's all. It's fine."

"Mm-hmm." Ida cracked brown-shelled eggs into a big ceramic bowl. "How are things at the hospital?"

"Under control, Mama." Obviously relieved at the change in subject, Flann poured coffee for Abby, set a small pitcher of cream next to her cup, and sat next to her. "Abby's got the ER humming like a watch."

"Nothing too serious last night, I hope."

Flannery grabbed a roll from a basket on the table, broke off a piece, and munched it. She passed the basket to Abby, who took one, suddenly ravenous. "Mostly broken bones, although Fred Endee gave us a little bit of a challenge with a punctured lung."

Flannery's mother shot her a look. "He's going to be all right, isn't he? You know his wife hasn't been doing well for the last couple of years. If the both of them are laid up, it will be a problem taking care of Patty at home."

"I hope to have him out of bed tomorrow and home in a couple of days. I'll ask Carson to get visiting nurses to stop by the house to check on Patty until then."

Ida nodded. "That sounds fine."

Presley, Carrie, and Glenn trooped into the kitchen from the back porch.

"Oh my God, Ida, you're a saint!" Carrie beelined for the coffeepot.

Glenn pulled out a chair next to Abby. "I just called the ER. Dewers made it in, it's quiet, and unless something changes, Dewers says for you to take half a shift off."

Six hours free. Abby sighed. "Glenn. Thank you for calling. My brain must not be firing on all cylinders, or I would have done that myself as soon as I got here."

"You would have as soon as you had something to eat," Flann interjected abruptly. "Give yourself a break, Abby. You're running on fumes."

Abby stared, surprised at the edge in Flann's tone. "I didn't do anything the rest of you—"

"Flann's right," Glenn said, resting a hand on Abby's forearm. "You saw twice as many patients as everyone else last night. You deserve to coast a few minutes, Abs."

Flann abruptly pushed back her chair and stalked out onto the back porch. Abby squelched the urge to follow. She'd seen Flann irritated, exhilarated, cool and calm, and forceful and commanding. She'd never seen the dark, brooding expression in her eyes before, and she wanted to soothe it away. Bad idea. Not her problem, and definitely not her woman to soothe. Still, the urge to go after her gnawed at her like an unfinished refrain.

Presley paced, coffee cup in hand. "Ida, have you heard from Harper? I haven't been able to reach her for the last few hours."

"The last I heard from her and her father was about midnight. They were heading out to start answering calls. I imagine—"

"Hey, baby." The back door opened wide and Harper strode in, her dark eyes alight and fixed on Presley.

Presley set down her cup and launched herself at Harper all in one motion. "How are you? I was really worried."

Harper gathered her up, kissed her soundly, and after a long moment, let her go. "Everything's good. Just tired."

Edward Rivers entered, glanced around the room, nodded to Abby and Glenn as if their presence was completely expected, and kissed his wife on the cheek. "Good morning, my dear. How was your night?"

"I checked on the neighbors up and down River Road. Everyone was doing fine." She wiped her hands on a towel and pressed her palm to her husband's cheek. "Carson, Bill, and the baby are fine. They had some flooding and they'll be busy with cleanup for a while, but nothing too bad."

"Good, thank you."

He covered her hand with his, turned her palm up, and kissed it. Ida smiled and turned back to the stove. Edward took off his suit jacket, shook out the wrinkles, and hung it carefully on a coat tree in the corner. Tall, fit, and clear-eyed, he exuded quiet confidence. His white shirt had lost the creases in the sleeves, but he nevertheless looked as crisp and fresh as when Abby had been introduced to him in Presley's office the first time. Abby could see Harper in his quiet surety, just as she could see Flann in Ida's brisk authority and effortless command. Edward accepted a cup of coffee from Harper and sat at the head of the table. Everyone else filled in on either side. Flannery, Abby noticed with an odd twist of disappointment, sat at the opposite end of the table and did not glance her way.

Keeping half an ear out for some sign of Blake and Margie, Abby joined in as Edward, Harper, and Flannery brought each other up to date on patients and follow-up situations. Presley and Carrie, both looking tired but content, sipped their coffee and quietly made plans to draw up emergency protocols for similar situations.

Just as Ida began placing breakfast on the table, Blake and Margie tumbled into the kitchen like a pair of playful puppies. Blake's hair was damp and stood on end as if he'd toweled it dry and not bothered to comb it. He wasn't usually so casual about his appearance, especially not recently. He wore a blue-denim button-down shirt and faded jeans, both at least a size too big for him, and a wide grin. "Hi, Mom."

"Hi, hon—Blake. Hi, Margie."

"Hi, Dr. Remy." Margie had scooped her long blond hair into a green John Deere cap and pulled the damp strands through the back tab. She wore shorts and a scrub top with flip-flops. "Hi, Daddy."

"Good morning, darlin'," Edward said, pausing in his conversation with Harper.

Ida said, "Presley, I hope you don't mind, I raided your laundry room and grabbed some clothes from the clean pile for these two. I recognized Harper's and figured they'd do better for Blake."

"No, of course I don't mind." Presley smiled at Harper and took her hand.

Blake dropped into a free chair and Margie took one beside him. Abby couldn't remember the last time she'd seen him so unselfconscious and confident. She caught her lip between her teeth and swallowed hard. She just had to make everything here work out.

Ida took her seat and everyone attacked the food. The breakfast was delicious, although Abby was almost too tired to eat it. Now that she was sitting, she realized how long it'd been since she'd had to work straight through the night with no relief. Everyone at the table was tired, but an undercurrent of exhilaration filled the room all the same. They'd faced down a crisis and everyone had spent the night doing what they did best. Despite the fatigue, the satisfaction won out.

Abby joined Ida at the sink when everyone had finished and started piling their plates on the counter by the sink. "Really, I'd like to help."

"Ordinarily, Flannery and Harper would have dish duty," Ida said, rinsing dishes and stacking them. "Under the circumstances, they'll get a pass this morning. You too."

"Oh, really, I'd like to—"

"I'm just going to fill the dishwasher and run it, and the rest of these can wait until later. Everyone should take a nap."

"That should include you too, then," Abby said. "You've been up all night."

Ida smiled. "When you raise a house full of medical people, you get used to that. I'll get my rest this afternoon when you all head back to the Rivers."

"You've raised a wonderful bunch, every one of them," Abby said.

"I'd be bragging if I agreed, but I can't argue." A glow of pride passed over Ida's strong, bold features. "Your son seems to have handled the excitement of the evening very well himself."

Abby smiled at Blake. He and Margie were discussing something while staring earnestly into the chicks' box. "He seems to have fallen in love with all things farm related. I have no idea why. I would have sworn he would always be a city boy."

"Some just take to it, like it's in the blood. He might be one of those."

"Margie's a wonderful teacher." Abby met Ida's steady gaze. "She's just the kind of friend I was hoping he'd find."

"It looks like the two of them have taken to each other."

Abby tensed. Blake hadn't talked to her about how he identified sexually, but his affection for Margie was obvious. Maybe Ida wouldn't find Blake ideal friend material if she thought their friendship might become more than that.

"It's nice to see two kindred spirits connect," Ida said.

A weight lifted from Abby's heart. "It is."

"Although I'll wager the two of them are capable of raising a bit of Cain, if I know my daughter."

Abby laughed. "The two of us ought to be able to handle them."

"Most assuredly." Ida glanced over to where Flannery and Harper were discussing patients who needed follow-up. "Exactly how serious is Flannery's leg?"

Abby hesitated.

"She was limping when she came in, and she's favoring it even when she's sitting down," Ida said.

"I guess the kids didn't tell you they were in the barn when it came down during the storm."

"They were too busy trying to explain why there was a rooster perched on top of one of the kitchen chairs when I came in this morning."

Abby folded her arms, just the memory of the night before giving her a chill. "Flann went after them when we saw the tornado touch down. I think she probably saved them from serious injury. She sustained a fairly deep laceration on her leg. It should be fine. I sutured it this morning."

"Did you now."

"I am an ER physician. It wasn't—"

"Oh, I have no doubt you're more than qualified. Flannery, however, isn't an easy patient. There were times when she was younger I practically had to tie her down so her father could to tend to some injury or other."

Abby smiled, watching Flann run a hand through her hair, a habit that only left her tousled locks more ruffled and her looking even more attractive. She was dangerously good-looking, and Abby had to work at not staring whenever they were in the same space. "I found threats to be effective."

Ida chuckled. "You seem to be fitting in very nicely."

Abby met Ida's gaze. "I hope so. I want things to work out with… here."

"I can't think of any reason why they shouldn't."

At that moment, Flannery caught Abby's gaze, and the dark brooding stare slowly turned to a simmering perusal that bordered on indecent. Deliciously indecent. Abby's heart sped up, and heat flooded her cheeks. She hoped Flannery's mother didn't notice it, but of course not very much escaped Ida Rivers's notice.

"Now," Ida said, "a few hours' sleep will do you good. This place has a slew of bedrooms on the second floor. Presley and Harper have the room on the left at the top of the stairs and Carrie's is on the right all the way at the back. Any of the other ones are fine."

Abby needed to wrangle her emotions back in line more than she needed sleep. Escape was her best option. At least then she wouldn't be anywhere near Flann in a weakened state, since she couldn't seem to resist her outrageous appeal. "I should just drive Blake home and—"

"Nonsense. That will take extra time, and you're already tired. You could get a call at any time." Ida crooked a finger at Flannery. "Flannery, take Abby upstairs and find a bedroom for her. You too. Get some sleep."

Flannery rose, her grin widening as Abby blushed furiously. "Sure thing, Mama."

Abby surrendered. "Blake, I'll be upstairs. If you need—"

"All's good, Mom. See you."

"Right." Abby sighed and followed Flann into the hall and up the wide curving staircase. "Outnumbered and outvoted."

CHAPTER NINETEEN

Flannery pushed open a big oak door in the center of the hall. "Sorry if my mother made you uncomfortable."

"No, she didn't," Abby said. "To be perfectly honest, it's nice to be so well taken care of, I'm just not used to it."

"That's too bad." Flann motioned Abby inside. "You don't need it, maybe, but you deserve to be tended to now and then."

Abby laughed, embarrassed by the attention and a little breathless from the yearning Flann's words stirred. Flann kept blindsiding her with these tender statements out of nowhere that struck a deep chord inside her. What had she revealed that let Flann see her secret needs so clearly, when no one else ever had? She turned to the room to hide her confusion. "This is a fabulous place. I could hide out here forever!"

The big, bright, high-ceilinged room faced a sweeping panorama of green pastures and distant mountains beneath a robin's-egg-blue sky. Swaying branches of an oak tree framed the bay window with its wide, deep rose-patterned cushions, and the early morning sunlight fanned across wide plank floors in a golden tide. A big four-poster bed stood against one wall, the covers turned down, and a pile of white ruffled pillows beckoned. It looked so inviting she almost wept. "I didn't realize how tired I was. I'm not so sure it's a good idea to go to sleep."

Flann let the door ease closed behind her. Abby's face glowed in the slivers of sunlight showering her form. She'd pulled out the tie holding back her hair and thick waves tumbled onto her shoulders. Flann's fingers itched to dive into them. Her throat suddenly dry, she rasped, "A little sleep is better than none, especially if it gets busy later. A couple hours, and we'll head back."

Abby was suddenly aware they were alone and the bed suddenly looked less inviting and a lot more threatening. Flann stood absolutely still only inches away, but she seemed to fill the space with pent-up energy and heat. Abby pulsed inside, a warning and a plea. She couldn't look at her, didn't dare see her own desire reflected in Flann's dark gaze, couldn't bear the disappointment if she didn't. "Yes, well, you should get some sleep too."

Somewhere else, anywhere but here. Go. Go away before I beg you not to.

"I will, in a little while. I never really thanked you for looking after me earlier," Flann said.

Abby took a breath, chanced a glance into her eyes. God, she had beautiful eyes. Bittersweet chocolate this morning, flecked with gold. They spoke, her eyes, of passion and pleasure. "You don't need to thank me. You might have saved my son's life, and you got hurt in the process. And even if that hadn't been the case, I wanted to look after you."

"Did you?" Flann brushed a strand of hair from Abby's throat. Her fingers lingered.

"Yes."

"You think I need looking after, do you?"

"Oh no, not you. I forgot, you don't need anything except a little fun and companionship." Abby meant to say it lightly, but it came out more seriously than she intended. "I'm sorry, that was inappropriate and—"

"You're right, most of the time. You're not right now, though." Flann clasped her upper arms gently and drew her forward. "Right now I need something else. Something very, very specific."

"Flann," Abby protested.

"You, Abby. Right now I want you so much I can't think." Flann slid her palms from Abby's shoulders and down onto her forearms, tugging her until they were a whisper apart. "You looked really good sitting at the table this morning. Like you belonged there. You fit this place, Abby, this world."

"Flann, I don't—"

"Don't think." Flann leaned close. "Just take, Abby. Take."

Impossibly, Abby couldn't think. Somewhere a voice, *her* voice, cried *Yes, for once, yes, take.*

Flann kissed her, the first silky caress of her mouth barely more than a whisper, gently at first, building with each teasing pass to possessive and sure.

Abby stiffened, swamped by a hunger she'd never experienced. A little afraid, and terribly greedy for more. Flann held her firmly, unapologetically, as if Abby belonged to her. She'd never been held with so much authority, never been kissed with so much assuredness. Their bodies weren't quite touching, but heat enveloped her. She tilted her head to get more of Flann's mouth, slid her arms around her neck, breathed her in. Her nipples tensed and her thighs trembled. Another kiss stole through her, lightning fast, heat lightning, setting her ablaze. She pressed closer, heard herself moan softly.

Flann groaned and swept her hand down Abby's back, tugging her scrub shirt up and spreading her fingers over Abby's lower back. Her touch was a claim. Mine. *Mine.* Abby arched into her, pressing close, closer, her heart beating against Flann's.

"God, you feel so good." Abby laced her fingers through Flann's hair, cupping the back of her neck, sealing the kiss as Flann's lips parted and they delved deeper.

"Abby," Flann groaned again, leaning back on the door and dragging Abby hard against her. A dizzying swell of desire rocketed through her. Flames raced across her skin, burning her with pleasure. Abby tasted so sweet, like hot honey on fresh biscuits, rich and full. Her kisses were wild, and so, so ready. Flann swept her palms down Abby's sides and up again, thumbs stroking the undersurfaces of her breasts. "I want my hands all over you."

"Your leg," Abby gasped.

"It's fine," Flann growled, kissing her again. Abby's breasts were firm against her own, the pressure a tease that shot to the pit of her stomach. Abby's skin was soft and Flann let her hand drift beneath the top of her scrub pants until her fingers feathered the swell of her ass. Abby fit, every curve and sensuous plane of her. Their bodies were perfectly aligned. Every tilt of her head, every sweep of her tongue and Abby was there, answering. Passion for passion, need for need.

"Come to bed," Flann gasped against Abby's ear.

Abby pressed her palms flat against Flann's upper chest and pushed away an inch. "Flannery, we can't. Your family's right downstairs."

"They're downstairs, we're up here." Flann's eyes were dangerously dark, ravenous.

"I'm not going to bed with you."

"Why not?"

Abby shook her head. She'd lost her mind. She couldn't be kissing Flannery Rivers. "Because I'm not. I'm not—I'm not a good-time girl, Flann. And this is a really, really bad idea."

Flann grinned, a ferocious smile that reminded Abby of a lethal predator about to pounce, and tightened her hold on Abby's waist. "It's a fucking great idea. Just kiss me again."

"Absolutely not. I'm sorry, I don't have any excuse. I—"

Flann's eyes sparked, flame in obsidian. "What excuse, Abby? We're both adults. You want me, I want you. What's so complicated about that?"

Abby jerked back. "Really? That's all it takes? A little bit of lust and you just follow your hormones wherever they lead? Well, I don't. I've got a lot more to think about than taking care of an itch."

"Maybe you should try scratching that itch sometime. You might find out you like it." Flann's voice was low but nearly a snarl.

"When and if I decide to *scratch*, it's not going to be with you." Abby managed to extract herself from Flann's grip. "Now, if you don't mind, I'm going to try to get a little sleep before I have to go back to work. I'd like you to leave."

Flann's jaw clenched, and she battled down the haze of lust. What the fuck was she doing, with Abby of all people? She reached behind her, found the doorknob. "I'm sorry. You're right. I apologize for taking advantage where I wasn't invited."

Abby's head spun. "Advantage? Hardly, I—"

"I can assure you, it won't happen again." Flann yanked the door open. "I'll let Glenn know she'll need to ride back to the hospital with you."

"What? I…"

Flann disappeared, and Abby stared at the closed door. Dammit. How had she let that happen? Flann thought she'd taken advantage? Please. She'd practically climbed up Flannery like a tree. Where had all that need come from, and how did she get rid of it? Her lips still tingled. Her belly throbbed with the demand for release. She hadn't let it happen, she'd wanted it, almost from the first moment she'd seen

Flannery Rivers in the ER. Flannery was the forbidden fruit she'd secretly been longing to taste. Well, now she'd tasted her, and she'd just have to figure out a way to stop wanting more.

❖

Flann stared at the closed door and cursed viciously under her breath. Of all the stupid, asinine moves she'd ever made in her life, jumping on Abby Remy had to be at the top of the list. She never made a move on a woman that she hadn't planned in advance. She always judged the field, made sure she had a good read on the signals, analyzed the defense—and the offense, for that matter—and mapped her play down to the last detail. She didn't like complications and had learned early on to recognize when she and her date weren't working the same game plan. When she'd first discovered girls, she thought everyone was as eager and crazy to explore sex as she was. It didn't take too many hysterical breakups and broken hearts—fortunately short-term at that age—for her to realize otherwise. By the time Harper had hauled her down to the tree house and lectured her on the right way to go about treating a girl, especially one she wanted to have sex with, she'd pretty much figured it out for herself. She'd gotten herself into a few other snags in college and medical school, mostly from dating more than one girl at a time, and she'd finally given that up too. Now she was strictly a serial dater—usually short-term—and she made sure the game plan was clear from the beginning.

Until tonight. She'd thrown away the playbook where Abby was concerned. She'd just walked up to the plate and started swinging away. Christ. She turned on her heel and stomped down the stairs, nearly bumping into Harper and Presley at the bottom.

"I thought you were headed to be—" Presley began.

"Changed my mind." Flann swerved around them, avoided the kitchen and her mother, and escaped through the side door at the far end of the hall. Once outside she took a deep breath of morning air. A layer of ozone lingered, biting at her eyes, and her skin instantly misted with sweat. All the same, the sky was clear and promised a brilliant day. She tilted her head back and closed her eyes, waiting for her heart rate to come down and her body to lose the razor edge of arousal that had stripped her control *and* her reason. When she had half a brain back, she strode toward the barn. She'd never be able to sleep, and even if she could, she wasn't about to go back upstairs and stretch out on a bed with Abby a room away. The state she was in, she'd probably end up scratching at Abby's door like some pitiful stray, begging to be let in for crumbs.

"Fuck."

"What's the matter, Flann?" Margie said, coming around the corner of the barn.

Flann growled. "What the hell are you doing out here?"

Blake appeared behind Margie, his arms full of kittens. Belatedly, Flann noticed Margie had one tucked under her arm.

"I thought I told you not to go in that barn until—"

Glenn stepped into view. "Harper and I checked it out a few minutes ago. That one corner is pretty bad. You all are lucky no one got hurt any worse." She scratched a tiny kitten head cradled in Blake's arms. "These guys were raising hell in the hayloft. We put a ladder up against the side to get them out through the hatch. The kids didn't go inside."

Flann raked a hand through her hair. "Right. Sorry. How's it look?"

"It's salvageable. The roof needs shoring up in the back, about a quarter of the slates are gone or broken and need to be replaced, and we'll need to put on new siding." Glenn dropped a hand on Blake's shoulder. "Luckily, we've got a pretty good crew. As soon as Harper says the word, we'll get going."

"I'll talk to her. Maybe next weekend we can get started."

"Good enough."

"Glenn," Flann added with calm she didn't feel, "I'm going to head over to my place. Can you grab a ride with Abby when she wakes up?"

Glenn shot Flann an appraising look and nodded. "Sure. No problem."

Flann turned away as the trio continued to the house. Glenn and Abby—perfect match. Perfect. Duty done. Now she could forget all about Abby and the hot, hard press of Abby's body cleaving to hers or the way Abby tilted her head to deepen the kiss, guiding Flann right where she wanted her. God, the woman was all flame and sweet temptation. And off-limits.

The barn had taken a beating. The chicken coop they'd built just before the storm hit was miraculously still standing. Sections of roof had blown away but most of the structure remained. Glenn was right. The damage was primarily to the exterior. The barn was worth saving, and they could do it.

"What's the problem?" Harper said from behind her.

Flann didn't turn around. "No problem."

"Didn't look that way when you were storming down the stairs."

"Leave it alone, Harp."

"Something happen with Abby?"

"Nothing happened." Flann gritted her teeth. "Why don't you go find your perfect woman and curl up in your perfect house and have perfect sex and leave me the fuck alone?"

Harper debated tackling her, dragging her to the ground, and pummeling her until she talked. It would be faster and probably easier for both of them. However, their mother was in the kitchen, and they'd catch hell if she found out, and she was too damn tired to wrestle anyhow. She stepped up beside Flann and stared at the mess of the barn. "What did you do?"

"Don't you ever get tired of being the family hero?"

"It's a burden, I'll admit," Harper said quietly, "but I've learned to bear it."

Flann barked a laugh. "You ass."

Harper grinned. "Since we both know I've made plenty of mistakes, I'll take that comment as self-directed. What'd you do?"

Flann gripped a handful of hair and twisted. The pain cleared her head a little but didn't make her feel any better. "I kissed her."

"Can't say I'm surprised," Harper said. "You've been wanting to do that for a while."

"Now you're a mind reader as well as a saint?"

"You've been practically drooling every time you look at her."

"Bullshit."

"Have it your own way. You kissed her. And?"

"Let's just say it wasn't welcome, and I should've known that from the beginning."

"Did you barge in with your usual lack of finesse? Maybe you just caught her off guard."

"Fuck you," Flann said for form, but she couldn't muster up much heat. "It was a mistake, all right?"

"Why was it a mistake?"

"That should be obvious."

"Not to me," Harper said. "You're single, she's single, you've got the hots for her, and if I'm not mistaken, she's been sending you a few appreciative looks too."

"Oh, for chrissakes, Harper. It's not about hormones."

Harper stared. "Excuse me?"

"It's not about wanting to get laid, okay? Abby's—she's just not somebody I want to fool around with, okay? She's got a kid, she's got a new job, a whole new life to get settled into. Christ, she's actually *got* a life. The last thing I want, or she wants—which she made abundantly clear—is for us to get mixed up in anything."

"I thought you said you just kissed her. Was there a lot more you left out?"

"No."

"Sounds like a lot of overreacting to me."

"Look," Flann said. "It was a bad idea. I know it. She knows it. Won't happen again."

"Flann," Harper said, "if you care—"

"I don't, okay?" Flann turned and stalked away. "I don't."

CHAPTER TWENTY

Abby opened her eyes in an unfamiliar room, sunlight washing over her face. The ornate tin ceiling was painted a soothing taupe. A breeze fluttered through the open window, scented sweetly with hay and clover. Had she really slept? She must have. A collage of memories bombarded her. Presley's farm. The beautiful bedroom. The storm. The long night in the ER and the morning...Flann. Oh God, Flann. Heat stroked through her, settling unerringly in the pit of her stomach. Flann's kisses—arrogant and unapologetic, simmering and demanding. Her kissing Flann back, just as greedy. Where had the greed, the need, come from? She'd kissed women before, felt desire before, but never such all-consuming hunger. The mindless, endless want haunted her still. Her breasts tingled with the memory of Flann's hands just barely grazing her flesh. Her clitoris swelled and pulsed. The ache between her thighs grew heavier, an unfamiliar and ecstatic beat. How easy it would've been to say yes. Her body was still saying it. Her heart and mind, though, were retreating from emotions and sensations she'd never expected and wasn't entirely sure she wanted to embrace.

Abby pushed the covers aside and swung her legs over the bed. Sometime in her sleep coma she'd shed her clothes. They lay in a heap by the bed. She brushed her hand over her breasts and down her belly, experiencing the swell and planes of flesh as if for the first time. This body, alive with sensation, felt nearly as unfamiliar as the longing that even now rose through her. She hadn't just opened her eyes in a strange room, she'd awakened in a body transformed to a world that looked and smelled and felt different than the day before. She laughed out loud. Sleeping Beauty indeed, roused from oblivion by a kiss. And in Flann's case, the handsome prince couldn't have been handsomer, but Abby's erstwhile prince had been anything but gentle and refined. More a marauder than a royal courtier, storming the castle to make her claim. Flann had urged her to take, and she had, but she'd wanted to be taken as well.

Come to bed, Flann's dark eyes commanded.

And Abby'd almost said yes.

"But I didn't," Abby whispered. She was no fairy-tale princess, there was no prince in the guise of a drop-dead-gorgeous surgeon coming to save her when she didn't need saving, and the only fairy-tale ending she needed was a nice stable life with no drama and a secure future for her and her son. And if her body thought otherwise, there were logical reasons for that. She was, after all, living breathing flesh, and she knew very well where desire came from: the pulse of blood, the rush of hormones, the burst of pheromones that ignited neural pathways. All perfectly rational and explainable. No reason to attach any extreme significance to that kiss. Okay, those kisses, plural. Now that she'd had time to slow down, take a metaphorical breath, she was simply aware of sensations she hadn't had time to acknowledge before. And other than that, life went on just as it had before. Still the same responsibilities, the same obligations, the same plan to fulfill. And right now, that plan included taking care of her son and getting her butt—her naked butt—to work.

Instantly, she saw herself naked in Flann's arms, and after seeing Flann's bare legs more than once, she had no trouble imagining the rest of her unclothed. The pounding between her thighs jumped into overdrive. For a millisecond she contemplated sliding back under the sheets and finishing the fantasy with her hand between her thighs.

Wonderful. Now she'd regressed to the age of fourteen. When exactly had she lost all control of her senses?

Resolutely, she gathered up the crumpled scrubs and prayed the bathroom was nearby. A shower would make all the difference. At this point, she'd even try a cold shower and see if the old adage was true. Spending the rest of the day in a state of unrequited arousal was not her idea of fun. She halted at the end of the bed and took in the small wicker basket someone had placed just inside the door with a neat stack of scrubs and an array of toiletries. She opened the folded note atop the pile.

Bathroom is across the hall on your right. I thought you could use these. Talk to you later, Pres.

"I'm going to kiss you for this." Abby quickly pulled on the old scrubs, picked up the basket, and dashed across the hall to the bathroom. The doors up and down the hall were closed and she couldn't help wondering if Flann slept behind one of them. As soon as the thought occurred to her, she saw Flann and Carrie wrapped up together. The image prompted a mental snarl, and she twisted the shower dial hard enough to send a blast of water splashing onto the tiles outside the enclosure. She yanked off the old scrubs, pushed them into a clothes hamper in the corner, and stepped under the spray.

After the first few minutes with her arms braced on the wall and hot water beating a tattoo on her back, she started to think rationally again. She'd sent Flann on her way, not that she'd really had any choice. They couldn't very well have sex in Presley's house with half the hospital plus Flann's parents and her son in attendance! That was beside the point anyhow—she didn't *want* to have sex with Flann. Okay, she did, but not in the real world. Just in the little slice of fantasy world that had bled over into hers when she wasn't looking. Flann and Carrie were a much better match—hell, Flann had practically described Carrie when she'd said what she was looking for in a woman. Bright, beautiful, sexy, and not ready to settle down. If Flann had pulled her Prince Charming routine on Carrie, all the better.

Yes. Better for everyone.

Abby resolved to put the whole issue of who had slept where out of her mind. After a long sumptuous shower, she dressed, toweled her hair dry, slipped into the clogs Flann had lent her what felt like a year ago, and headed downstairs.

Carrie sat alone at the kitchen table drinking a cup of coffee. Abby hesitated at the doorway, that morning's kiss suddenly looming large. If Carrie and Flann had something going on, the last thing she wanted to do was get in the middle. She not only liked Carrie, but Carrie was Presley's good friend. Now she was even happier she'd sent Flann away. "Morning."

"More or less." Carrie grinned. "Hot coffee, biscuits on the counter, and ham in that covered dish next to them."

"There is a fairy godmother," Abby muttered, her hunger making itself known with a vengeance. She poured coffee, grabbed a biscuit and several slices of ham, and sat down across from Carrie. "Mrs. Rivers?"

Carrie shook her head. "Lila. Presley's housekeeper. She was here a few hours ago, apparently."

"I forgot she cooks too."

Carrie grinned. "That's an understatement. I'm really gonna miss that when I move out."

"I can't believe the wedding is in just a few weeks."

"And we've still got a lot of planning to do." Carrie's eyes brightened.

"Whatever you need me to do, just let me know."

"Oh, don't worry, you'll be plenty busy."

Abby finished the biscuit and ham and got up for a coffee refill. "More coffee?"

Carrie handed her the cup. "Thanks."

"Where's everyone else?" Abby tried to sound casual. She didn't know how she'd feel seeing Flann again, but the sooner she did and they got back onto neutral ground, the better. She'd be working with Flann more closely than with anyone else at the hospital, and she wanted their relationship to be cordial. Hopefully, they could just treat the kiss as what it was—a spontaneous physical encounter born out of lowered inhibitions brought on by fatigue and the aftermath of the crisis. Flann undoubtedly was regretting it just as much as she was right now.

"Margie and Blake are asleep somewhere—I think in the sitting room. Harper's parents left right after breakfast. Glenn and Harper are around somewhere, and I think Presley might still be asleep."

"And Flann?" Abby tensed, waiting for Carrie to say Flann was still asleep somewhere too, possibly in her bed.

"Oh, I thought you probably knew," Carrie said. "Flann left hours ago. I was just getting ready to go to bed and she borrowed my car. I think Glenn is looking to ride with you."

"Right." Abby handed her the coffee and sat down again. "She didn't get any sleep, then."

"Glenn?" Carrie colored faintly. "I'm not sure."

"I meant Flann."

Carrie regarded her over the top of her coffee cup. "She said she was going home. If I know Flann, she's probably back at the hospital by now."

"Of course," Abby said cheerfully. Could she be any more obvious?

"In case you were wondering," Carrie said lightly, "we're not an item."

"That's really none of my business," Abby said, caught between embarrassment and relief, and uncomfortable with both reactions.

"Okay, but just being clear. She's sex on a stick, for sure."

Of course she was, and anyone with two eyes and a beating heart could see that. Abby pursed her lips and sat back down, assuming a nonchalant expression. "Attractive, yes. No denying."

"And smart and funny and...did I mention sexy?"

Abby had the strangest urge to growl. "I think you did."

"And she looks at you like she wants to drag you off to her cave and have her way with you." Carrie grinned.

Abby choked down the coffee she'd just sipped. "I'm sorry?"

Carrie laughed. "Don't tell me you haven't noticed. She was practically staring holes in you all morning at breakfast."

"I doubt that. She was all the way at the other end of the table and barely looked—" Abby realized she'd just admitted she'd been watching Flann too. "Well, hell."

"Uh-huh. It's the old avoidance reaction. She's interested and running scared."

"I can't believe anything scares Flann when it comes to women," Abby said dryly. She certainly hadn't acted scared that morning. If anything, Abby had been the one to run. The idea made Abby pause. Really? Run? That wasn't her. She didn't run—not when she'd discovered she was pregnant, not when Blake was born and she'd had to leave him with her mother so she could finish school, not when the demands of residency and parenthood had nearly killed her. Why on earth would *she* run from a simple kiss?

"I think there might be," Carrie said.

Abby blinked. "Sorry?"

"Flann. Scared. I've known her awhile now and seen her around a lot of women. She does casual really well, but something else would probably scare her."

"I don't know her well enough to say," Abby said, "but there's nothing going on between us that could possibly be frightening." *At least not to Flann.*

"Ah. Okay, then we're all squared away."

"Right, the field is clear."

"Good," Carrie said. "On to more important matters, then—once everything settles down at the hospital, I'll text you about the wedding meeting."

"Absolutely. I'll be here." Abby got up and carried her dishes to the sink. "I'm going to collect my offspring and head back to work."

"I'll probably see you there later."

The only thing she wanted was to collect Blake and put Flannery O'Connor Rivers out of her mind. She found Blake and Margie in the sitting room, asleep as only teenagers could sleep, so deeply the world could come to an end around them and they wouldn't notice. They were stretched out on the same sofa where she'd treated Flann the night before, foot to foot, their heads at opposite ends. She stood for a moment in the doorway, taking them in. They were beautiful. Blake had two kittens curled up in the crook of his arm. Margie's golden hair framed her oval face like a halo. Abby wished for a second they could always stay as peaceful and content as they were right at that moment, but then life wasn't always peaceful and happy, and some of the greatest pleasures grew out of turmoil and challenge. She couldn't stop Blake from growing up and wouldn't want to.

She knelt by his side and shook his shoulder gently. "Hey, time to go home."

His lashes were long and dark, the kind people always said were too beautiful for a boy, but she didn't think so. Boys had their own kind of beauty, and he was growing into his, day by day. His eyes opened and focused on hers. His smile was swift.

"Hi, Mom."

"I have to go back to the hospital, and I want to take you home first."

"Okay." He looked down at the kittens, a pair of black and whites with brilliant blue eyes, just stretching with their tiny paws flailing in the air. The pair of them would've fit in a soup bowl. "Can I keep them?"

"Are they old enough to be separated from their mother?"

"Margie says so."

Abby smiled. Margie was obviously the source of all farm knowledge. "Then I don't see why not. I guess we should check with Presley to be sure."

"Maybe I could take them home, and we could call her later."

"How about we leave a note on the table and let her know you've borrowed them for the day. I suspect she'll be happy that they've got a good home."

"Thanks, Mom."

"No problem. But"—she ruffled his hair—"no dog. Not until we have a house with a bigger yard."

"Deal." He grinned and glanced at Margie, who was awake and regarding them sleepily. "I can keep them."

"Awesome," Margie said with a yawn. "Is it lunch yet?"

Abby laughed. "Come on. We'll find Glenn and I'll treat you all to lunch before I go back to work."

She herded the kids and cats outside. Glenn sat on the front steps, reading her phone.

"Cell tower's back up," Glenn said.

"Great," Abby said. "Maybe that means things aren't so bad. Hopefully people will start getting in to work today."

"Most of the afternoon shift has called in they're coming or have already arrived," Glenn said. "I just checked the OR and ER."

"You're wasted as a first assist in the OR," Abby said. "Come down to the ER and be my assistant director."

Glenn laughed. "I don't know who Flann would shoot first—you or me."

Abby grimaced. "Probably me. But the offer stands. Think about it. You're qualified, and when we start growing, there'll be plenty of challenges."

"I'll think about it." Glenn stood and stretched, wincing as if something bothered her.

"You okay?"

Glenn's expression shuttered. "Fine."

"Can I treat you to lunch?" Abby said, recognizing a closed subject.

"Sure." Glenn smiled and Abby realized how good-looking she was in a quiet, contained way.

Abby smiled back. "Wonderful. I can't promise I won't keep trying to seduce you away from the OR."

Glenn laughed as she and Abby walked to the car. "Seduce away."

Abby laughed too, not the least bit inclined to run from the playful banter. Glenn was attractive, thoughtful, intelligent, and interesting, and so much easier to be with than Flann. Abby wasn't plagued by the unsettled, simmering emotions Flann incited. She should have been relieved, but for some strange reason, she wasn't.

CHAPTER TWENTY-ONE

A little after seven in the morning, Flann finished up a trauma case that had run all night. She'd been up almost two days and two nights with only a few scattered hours of sleep. The world had condensed to the surgical field in front of her for so long that when she lifted her head to glance at the clock, it took her a few seconds to orient herself. She grinned at Glenn across the table, and Glenn grinned back. Glenn's face was hidden behind a surgical mask, but she could read Glenn's emotions from her eyes after years of doing it. Glenn was as exhausted and exhilarated as her. They'd won another one. "Good job."

"Same to you," Glenn said in her husky alto.

The twenty-year-old motorcyclist had gone off the road on a slippery curve in a rainstorm and arrived in the ER a little after midnight. With his broken leg, wrist, collarbone, and punctured lung, she would have ordinarily stabilized him and sent him to a tertiary care center for ortho treatment and rehab. Unfortunately, he'd had no blood pressure when he'd been wheeled in by the paramedics doing CPR. His belly had been as hard as a board. Her bet had been ruptured spleen. Glenn voted for liver laceration. They'd both been right and then some. His abdomen was a war zone. Along with a ruptured spleen and lacerated liver, he'd torn his small intestine.

They got the bleeding under control as soon as they got his spleen out, repaired the liver laceration, and put his small bowel back together. Somehow, he'd managed not to break his neck or fracture his spine, and he was young enough he'd likely survive the multiple trauma and insult to his major systems without too much in the way of long-term side effects. He'd still be looking at a week in the intensive care unit and six times that in rehab if he was lucky. But then, he was damn lucky.

Flann stepped back from the table as Glenn carefully applied the dressings and secured his chest tube and other lines for the transfer to the gurney. Flann pulled off her mask, shed her gown and gloves, and called thanks to the anesthesiologist and the nurses on her way out of the room. Her legs were rubbery and her head muzzy. She contemplated taking herself off emergency call, but chances were another one wouldn't come in anyhow. If it did, she could always punt or transfer if she couldn't handle it. Once in the locker room she stripped, stumbled like a zombie back to the shower stalls, and stepped under the spray.

"Cripes," she gasped, when the cold water doused her head. While she fought with the dial to regulate the temperature, her mind cleared and she got her second wind. She'd be good for another half a day at least. And the day stretched ahead of her like a long, empty hallway. Not knowing how long she'd be tied up with the trauma, she'd left a message with her answering service halfway through the case to reschedule her morning hours. Barring emergencies, her time was her own. She didn't really have anything to do with it—work was her recreation as well as her profession. Other than playing softball four nights a week in the spring and summer, she didn't do much else except work, take a woman out to dinner or a movie a few times a month, and find reasons not to leave the hospital. The hospital was the core of her social life. Like a lot of single doctors, or those who weren't single but weren't in any hurry to get home, she spent a fair amount of time hanging around, talking to other staff in the cafeteria or the OR lounge or the ER.

Unfortunately, the only person she really wanted to talk to was Abby, and she'd been avoiding her. She hadn't seen her since the morning she'd left Presley's while Abby was asleep. Abby hadn't been on call the night before when the trauma came in, and she'd managed not to see her the day before either. Avoiding her turned out to be a lot easier than not thinking about her. When she wasn't completely focused on an operation or patient evaluation, like now, memories of those few moments in Abby's room replayed in vivid detail. Who knew her body had perfect recall? She didn't usually dwell on a physical encounter, but she couldn't get those few moments with Abby out of her head. Every second seemed imprinted on her skin—when Abby had been pressed so close against her even air couldn't find room between them, when Abby's arms had wrapped around her neck and her fingers drove into her hair, pulling her head down for a deeper kiss, urging her to plunder and claim.

Flann's clitoris twitched. "God damn it."

She was too damn old to get riled up from just a kiss, and definitely not from only *thinking* about a kiss. She slid her palm down her belly and pressed the swelling between her thighs with her fingertips. She caught her breath. She wasn't too old for jerking off in the shower, but not in the locker room. And not while she was thinking about a woman she'd already moved past.

She twisted off the dial, stepped out, and grabbed one of the skimpy towels housekeeping provided for staff use. She'd taken the dressing off her leg the day before, and she carefully dried the area around the sutures before cursorily mopping up the rest of the water on her skin and hair. The leg looked fine. Abby had done a good job. As she patted the sutures, the image of Abby kneeling before her, wrapping a bandage around her thigh, jumped into her consciousness and the faint throb between her legs became a piercing ache.

She'd seen herself then, could see herself now, sliding her hand into the hair at the nape of Abby's neck and guiding her face upward until her mouth closed over her. Her thighs suddenly weakened and she shot out her arm to brace herself against the wall. Her belly tightened, the need a fist twisting in the pit of her stomach. She blew out a long breath and forced her mind to blank.

Glenn came in as she was pulling on jeans and a plain white T-shirt, and gave her the diversion she needed. "Everything quiet?"

"Looks like it." Glenn opened her locker and pulled out her street clothes and a motorcycle helmet. "I'll have my beeper if you need me."

"Aren't you off today?"

Glenn grinned as she changed and tossed her scrubs. "Yeah, but it's more fun being here."

Flann laughed, but the sound rang hollowly in her ears. "True."

"See you," Glenn said on her way out the door.

"Ride safe." Flann dialed the recovery room from the phone by the door. When the clerk answered, she said, "This is Rivers. Can I talk to George Baker's nurse?"

"Hold on."

"Hi, Flann," another woman said a moment later.

Flann recognized the voice. Becky McAllister. Twenty-five, blond, bright, great breasts, and dynamite in bed. They'd had a few breathless weeks half a year ago before Becky decided she'd rather settle down with her old high-school boyfriend. No hard feelings on Flann's part. She'd known Becky was experimenting, but that didn't bother her. In fact, it made things a lot easier. Becky was looking for a good time in bed, and Flann knew just how to deliver that.

Abby, now, she wasn't looking for a bedmate. She wasn't looking for anything at all, at least she didn't think she was. Flann wasn't sure she agreed. Abby was passionate, intelligent, sensitive, and giving. She wasn't the kind of woman to spend her life alone, if she'd look past all her responsibilities and see she deserved a life. What was it Abby had said? A couple of kids, a house with a yard, a dog or two. Yeah, she could see Abby there. Abby was born for family.

"Flann?"

"Hey, Becky," Flann said with a start. "How's Baker doing?"

"He's good. Vitals are stable. The last blood gas was normal," Becky said. "How are you?"

"Great. You?"

"Oh, sure, great." Becky paused. "You know, no law says we couldn't get together for a drink sometime. Talk about old times."

Flann laughed. "Talk about them?"

Becky's laughter pealed, and Flann flashed on Becky straddling her, her blond hair flying about her shoulders, her breasts rose-tipped and bouncing gently as she rocked on Flann's hand. A nice image that did nothing for her.

"Well, you know…I miss…some things," Becky said.

"Be surprised how much fun you could have giving lessons. You should try it," Flann said lightly. "Call me if there's any problems with my patient."

"Of course," Becky said, a distinct chill in her voice.

Smiling wryly, Flann hung up the phone. She didn't have any strict rules against dating married women in general, but she preferred they not be actually living with their husbands when she did. Besides, Becky was way too close to home. She didn't care to advertise her bedroom activities to the world. And all that aside, the idea of climbing into bed with her just didn't appeal. She might think differently after a good night's sleep, but she doubted it.

Halfway back to her apartment on the outskirts of town, Flann changed her mind and reversed course. No way could she sleep yet, and sitting around in her apartment was the last thing she wanted to do. Ten minutes later she turned down the drive to the homestead, but instead of pulling under the porte cochere where she usually parked, she followed a winding dirt road past acres of cornfield down to the main barn. The big doors were open and the clank of cows at the milking station rang like bells as she stepped from the Jeep. The Rivers family had leased their land for crops and dairy cows for as long as she could remember to a farming family who owned the adjoining land a mile or so downriver. Melanie Cochran, the oldest daughter, was supervising the morning's milking. She waved to Flann. "Come to help out?"

Flann laughed. "Those electronic robot milkers are way too high-tech for me. The cows are safer with you."

"Chicken."

"How's the summer going?"

"Great," Melanie said with obvious pride. Her older brother had opted for a teaching job in the city, and Melanie appeared to be the heir apparent to follow in her father's footsteps. "We got a good round of heifers this spring, rain's been good, temperature's been high." She grinned and shrugged a shoulder. "It's a good season if you don't mind a tornado now and then."

"Everything okay over at your place?"

"We lost half a field of soybeans, but we've got time to replant. All our stock are fine. We were lucky."

"You know it. The whole village was pretty lucky."

"I hear Harper's new place got torn up a little bit."

"The barn took a hit, but it's repairable."

Melanie adjusted one of the suction tubes on a cow's udder and dusted off her hand. "I heard there's going to be a barn raising. You gonna be there?"

"I didn't get an invitation," Flann said with a grin, "but I haven't talked to Harper since yesterday. When?"

"This weekend."

"Barring emergencies, I'll be there."

Melanie cocked a hip and sent Flann a slow grin. She was a good ten years younger than Flann, but more than a few above legal age. She was strong, sunburned, and pretty in a wholesome way. "Well then, I'll see you. There'll be dancing, I hear."

"Wouldn't miss it." Flann walked toward the tack room, shaking her head. Must be the day for invitations. Nothing to complain about, but the usual thrill of the hunt eluded her. She pulled down one of the bikes that looked about Blake's size from hooks along one wall. The tires were in good shape and she dug out a foot pump and filled them to make sure they held up before she gave it to him. She wheeled it back out of the barn and wrestled it into the back of her Jeep. As she made the turn into the drive, her mother came out onto the back porch, set her hands on her hips, and fixed Flann with a stare she could feel through the windshield. She pulled over, cut the engine, and climbed out. "Morning, Mama."

"You were thinking to leave without stopping by, I take it?"

"Ah—"

"Come on in the kitchen. I imagine you haven't had breakfast."

"I could do with some food."

Ida laughed. "When can't you?"

Flann stepped into the kitchen and was immediately enfolded in the scent of warm bread, fresh ham, and sweet strawberries. The smell of home stirred an ache in her depths, and she settled at the table with a sigh.

Her mother set a cup of coffee in front of her. "Long night?"

Flann rubbed her face with both hands. "Long couple of nights. How are things with Dad?"

"He finally got a break last night and didn't get a call out until after breakfast this morning. He's fine."

Flann nodded and swallowed some coffee. "Good."

"What were you looking for down at the barn?"

"Oh, I was getting one of my old bikes out for Blake."

"That's nice of you."

"Well, he and Margie are planning on looking after the chicks over at Presley's, so he needs some transportation since neither of them drives."

"I imagine the two of them will be getting their licenses at about the same time."

Flann winced. "Don't remind me."

Ida sat with her own coffee and studied Flann unhurriedly. "You and your sisters survived, they will too. We'll all keep an eye on them."

"I'm not worried about them—it's the rest of the idiots out there."

"We'll see that they know what they're about."

"I know."

"Blake seems like a nice boy."

"He is."

"He and Margie hit it off."

Flann searched for any sign that her mother had concerns and didn't find any. The idea that Blake wouldn't immediately be accepted for the great kid he was bothered her and she could only imagine how Abby must feel. "Margie is teaching him the wonders of farming."

Ida smiled. "Abby is quite remarkable too."

Flann flushed and stared at her coffee. "Uh-huh."

"I admire her, being a single mother. It doesn't much matter if it's one child or five, it's always easier when there's two people sharing the raising."

"You managed."

"That's not fair, Flannery," her mother said gently.

"I know, I'm sorry."

"It's not me deserving the apology." Ida stroked her arm to signal she was forgiven. "And if anybody ought to be complaining, it would be me."

"You're right again, I'm just—I don't know, probably just tired." She didn't know why the hell she was mad, or even who she was really mad at. "I should go."

Ida took her hand. "No, you should stay and tell me what's bothering you."

"I don't know," Flann said, when she meant to say *nothing.* "I love Dad, you know that, right?"

"Course I do, and so does he."

"Harper always wanted to be just like him."

Her mother said nothing.

"And I was always afraid I was."

"What do you mean?"

"I love what I do, just like he does. Maybe too much. Sometimes I thought he'd rather be taking care of other people than taking care of us."

"It must've seemed that way when you were younger."

"But I'm not young anymore, and I do know better." Flann shook her head. "It's hard to let go of feelings you've had for a long, long time."

"That's because you're still angry at him about Kate. You think he should have known, and he should have fixed her."

"No, of course I don't. I know no one could have—"

"You know it now, but you didn't know it then. And like you said, those feelings take a long time to change."

"I don't even know why I'm thinking about all of this right now." She avoided serious relationships so she'd never have a chance to let anyone down, so she'd never fail to take care of the people who needed her. The decision had never bothered her, until now.

Ida smiled. "Don't you?"

Flann frowned. "I think you better let me in on it, if you do."

"Oh no. There're some things a mother ought to stay clear of."

"I'm gonna remind you you said that someday."

"I'll remind you not to sass, Flannery."

Flannery grinned. "I love you."

Ida got up, kissed Flann's cheek, and gave her shoulder a squeeze. "I love you too."

Flann carried her dishes to the sink. "I guess I'll be seeing you at the barn raising this weekend."

"We haven't had a good old-fashioned barn raising in a long time," Ida said.

"Just another excuse for a party."

"Mm-hmm. Everybody loves one."

"I'll see you." Flann headed for the door. "Save me a dance."

"I suspect you'll have a full card. And Flannery," Ida called after her.

Flann turned.

Her mother's eyes twinkled and Flann couldn't quite decipher her smile. "Remember, women enjoy being courted."

Flann's mouth dropped open. "What?"

"Just a little motherly advice."

CHAPTER TWENTY-TWO

A bby sat on the back steps with an honest-to-God newspaper spread open on her knees. Granted, it was the *Argyle Post*, a ten-page weekly filled with some of the most fascinating stories she'd ever read. The headliner described the daring rescue of an escaped parrot by the local sheriff's deputy (with photo of officer and parrot). Another stated the fine received by a local resident whose backyard pig had apparently destroyed a neighbor's vegetable garden. Another listed the names of five residents cited for speeding on the county road connecting the township to parts beyond. The rest of the paper was filled with births, deaths, and marriage announcements, and a surprisingly full calendar of upcoming events including the Fourth of July Fireworks on the Green celebration, a two-day local artists' exhibition, a play put on by the theater group in a neighboring village, and the annual pig roast.

"Blake," Abby called, "there's going to be an art exhibit in a couple of weeks I think you might like—local artists."

Blake came to the door, munching a piece of toast slathered with peanut butter. "Okay, sure."

"Good." She pulled out her phone and made note of the date so she could adjust the on-call schedule to be sure she was free. One of the great benefits of no longer being an underling was she could actually make a few plans that might come to fruition without needing to sell her soul to other residents to arrange coverage.

"What are you doing today?" Blake asked, in an odd reversal of their usual conversation.

Abby had the entire day free, another oddity. She actually had a day off. She had thought to go in to the hospital a little later in the day to take care of some paperwork, but now that she considered it, the idea seemed like a pathetic way to fill the unexpected hours. "I don't know. Is there anything you want to do?" She glanced over her shoulder. Blake looked faintly chagrined. "What? Not interested in spending your free time with your mother?"

Blake grinned. "I kind of told Margie I'd meet her at Presley's. We were going to look at the chicks. After that, you know, we were probably just gonna meet up with some of Margie's gang and hang out."

"I interpret that to mean you're *not* interested in spending the day with your mother."

"Well, I guess—"

Abby laughed. "It's fine. You need a ride?"

"Yeah, about that. Maybe I could drive—with you in the car, you know."

"Maybe we'll be waiting until you get your permit."

He made a face. "Margie says all the kids around here know how to drive a long time before they ever get their permits, and I've never even been behind the wheel."

"I don't think tractors quite count as knowing how to drive."

"How about an ATV?"

"We don't have one of those."

"Margie does."

Abby sighed. "Why do I feel like I'm being expertly maneuvered?"

He grinned again, that incredibly infectious grin that had always claimed her heart and, she suspected, would break a few in the future. She shook her head. "No deal."

"Aw—"

"So," Abby asked, conscious of not wanting to push her way into Blake's personal space, "have you met these other kids yet?"

"No."

His lack of embellishment told her he was nervous. She was too. Would this new crowd accept him, view him as just a new guy, or see him as someone who wouldn't fit? "They're Margie's friends?"

"Yeah."

"Good." What else could she say?

"Mom," Blake blurted, "I want to have surgery."

Abby's stomach twisted. She'd been waiting, wondering when, if. God, he wasn't even sixteen. Everything she'd been able to learn had said the most important criterion for moving ahead was the certainty of the teens themselves. Blake was sure, she believed with her heart and her mind. "What kind?"

"The top." Blake met her gaze squarely. "Before school starts and I meet a lot of new people."

"Okay, wait, let me catch up." Abby stood and leaned against the porch rail, working through a million questions to find the right one. "How much is this about the way you feel physically versus wanting to be accepted in your new school?"

"Does it matter?"

"I'm not sure, maybe. What do you think?"

He frowned. "Remember when I said I wanted to start the hormones, because I wanted to look and feel male?"

"Yes."

"This is like that—I want my body to match the way I feel about myself, and I'll feel better if I look like I feel."

Abby blew out a breath. "It sounds circular, but then it is, isn't it. Mind and body are fluid."

Blake grinned, looking relieved and amused. "Mom, you're thinking too hard."

"I love you."

"I know. So—can I talk to Flann?"

"Flann?" Abby's mind blanked for a second. "You want Flann to do the surgery?"

"Margie said she's the best."

"Undoubtedly, but…" Abby pictured Flann during a trauma alert, saw her quick deft hands and certain actions. The surgery itself wasn't all that dangerous or complicated, and Blake was lucky. He hadn't had much breast development before the hormones suppressed it. Blake obviously trusted Flann, and so did she. "All right. We'll start there. Information first, deal?"

"Deal." Blake looked over his shoulder. The house was small enough to see from the back porch all the way through to the front if the doors were open, which they were to capitalize on any kind of breeze. "Hey! Flann's here. She brought a bike!"

Blake disappeared and Abby panicked. Flann. She looked down at herself. Oh God. Cut-off sweatpants that seconded as pajama bottoms, a T-shirt that had to be older than Blake—faded and literally see-through in places—and of course, no underwear. She had at least brushed her hair and taken care of other necessary hygienics. Maybe she could just stay out of the way. But then if she hid, she wouldn't see Flann, and she very much wanted to. If she was honest, she'd been wanting to see her since she'd sent her out of the bedroom.

She folded up the paper, tossed it onto one of the two rocking chairs she and Blake had found in a hardware store down the street, and hurried through the house. Flann and Blake hovered over a bicycle in the front yard. She walked to the edge of the porch and observed their animated expressions. Blake was transformed—his face alight with pleasure. Flann looked Abby's way, and her smile was as potent as a harpoon striking her in the center of the chest, slowly drawing her toward Flann.

"Good morning," Abby said, hoping her voice sounded nonchalant despite the piercing pleasure filling up her chest.

"Thought I'd take a chance on finding someone home," Flann said.

"Mom," Blake said excitedly, "look at the great bike Flann brought me."

"It's super," Abby said. The bike did indeed fit the description—a newish road bike built for speed. "Flann, that's an awfully nice bike—I appreciate you lending it—"

"No problem. I'm not using it. Besides"—Flann grinned at Blake—"you gotta have wheels. These will do until you get your license."

Abby resisted the urge to grind her teeth. She really didn't need anyone else encouraging Blake in the pleasures of automotion. "Fortunately everything around here is in walking distance."

"Mostly," Flann said agreeably. She grinned at Abby. "But then again, a car isn't just for transportation."

She folded her arms and gave Flann a pointed frown. "It better be in this family."

Flann laughed and Blake blushed, although he tried to pretend he hadn't heard the exchange.

"Keep it as long as you need it," Flann said. "Really, I don't use it."

"Maybe I could buy it," Blake said.

"Why don't we discuss a work trade? There's going to be plenty to do out at Harper's place."

"Yeah, I could do that." Blake looked back at Abby. "Can I go, Mom?"

"Sure. Be back by dinner or call me or—" But he was already on the bike and headed out to the road, waving one arm without looking back. Abby sighed. "I wish it was another year before he gets his license."

Flann climbed the porch steps. "I know what you mean. I just had the same conversation with my mother about Margie."

"At least your mother's had some practice with it. I bet you and Harper were devils behind the wheel."

Flann brushed a hank of hair out of her eyes, and Abby followed the motion of her hand before skimming her gaze down Flann's body. Abby's attention heated her skin, and the memory of Abby's fingers on her neck when they'd kissed chased away the last of her fatigue. She was instantly very much awake. "Not Harper, she was never wild. She always followed the rules."

"Not you though, I'll bet," Abby said softly. Flann looked tired, shadows under her eyes, her face paler than she'd ever seen her. She even looked thinner, if that was possible after two days.

"No, not me. I've never cared for rules."

"You look like you haven't caught up on your sleep yet," Abby said. "You should go home, get some rest." Abby wanted her to stay, but that was absurd. The woman was probably almost out on her feet, even if she was too macho to admit it.

"I was thinking," Flann said, although she hadn't been until just a minute ago. She had a day free and Abby was standing right in front of her and she didn't want to say good-bye. What she wanted was another kiss, and she wasn't going to think too hard about why. "There's a farmers' market in Saratoga. Maybe you'd like to go, walk around, see what it's like."

"If you've been up all night—"

Flann took her hand. "I'm fine. Besides, the fresh air will do me a lot more good than rolling around in a hot apartment trying to sleep during the day."

"No air-conditioning?" Abby said lightly, though all of her attention was focused on Flann's fingers wrapped around her hand. Flann was probably used to casual contact with women, but she wasn't. Why couldn't she seem to do casual around Flann?

"Don't have any," Flann said, her eyes drifting from Abby's face down her body. "I figure I'm never really home much, so why bother. Usually I can sack out in the hospital if I want to."

"But today you decided to bring Blake a bicycle. That was really kind of you."

"Nothing kind about it. I like him, and besides, I need him to be able to get around for work."

Abby laughed and she couldn't think of a reason to say no. She didn't even want to think, she just wanted to enjoy a day in the sun with a woman who looked at her like she was delectable. Oh God, her clothes. "I'd love to go to the farmers' market with you. Give me a minute to change."

"Why? You look terrific."

"Sure, if we're going to a pajama party." Abby extracted her hand and backed toward the door. Flann followed. "There's lemonade in the refrigerator. The kitchen's in the back."

Flann was very close and her eyes had turned dark and hungry, the way they had right before she'd kissed her. The house was empty and Blake wouldn't be back for hours. Abby took a breath. "I'll be right down."

"All right." Flann slowly leaned forward, giving Abby time to turn away. She didn't. Flann kissed her softly, a brush of her lips over Abby's, repeating the easy caress until Abby's hand came to her neck again, tugging her a little closer. Flann teased her tongue over Abby's lips until her control wavered and she was in danger of sliding her hands under Abby's T-shirt. With another woman, she already would have. She pulled back, her vision a little blurry, the rush of blood in her ears a drumbeat of desire more potent than anything she'd ever known. "Take your time. I'll be waiting."

Abby's lips parted, her pupils wide and black and a wee bit hazy. Her hand dropped from Flann's neck. "Good."

Flann leaned against the door and watched her disappear. Today Abby didn't look as if she wanted to run. She looked as if she wanted to be kissed again. Flann liked that idea herself, although the usual self-satisfaction when a woman signaled she was ready for the game to begin was missing. Maybe because she wasn't playing a game, or if she was, it was the most important one she'd ever played. Instead of feeling triumphant, she was…nervous. Hell.

She waited on the front porch in one of a pair of wicker chairs set on either side of a small round table, her feet propped on the rail, her body pleasantly simmering, the scent of Abby—some intoxicating blend of honey and sunlight—still clinging to her skin, and watched the world go by. She rarely sat, rarely even slowed down. She liked action. Harper was the one who went in for quiet contemplation. But right this moment, she was as content as she could ever remember being. The sensation was novel, and she was anything but bored. Every cell simmered with excitement.

Women like to be courted.

She didn't have any experience with that, but she'd never run from a challenge. If that's what it took to put that drowsy, hot look back in Abby's eyes again, she'd give it her best.

"You look pretty comfortable there," Abby said from the doorway.

"I am." Flann glanced over her shoulder and her mouth went dry.

The pale yellow sundress scooped just low enough to make it abundantly clear Abby had absolutely perfect breasts. Her hair was a golden tangle on her smooth shoulders, her bare arms sleek and bronzed. The flowing skirt hinted at slender thighs, and strappy sandals called attention to her equally elegant calves. Incongruously, each toe was tipped in pale coral.

"You paint your toenails," Flann said like an idiot.

Abby laughed. "I do. Frivolous, isn't it?"

"Sexy."

Abby blushed. "I'll take note of that."

"You look fabulous." Flann rose, chagrined. At least her jeans and white T-shirt were clean, but Abby was beautiful. Elegant, breathtaking. "I'm not fit to be seen with you. I should change."

"Don't be silly. I love the way you look in jeans and a T-shirt."

"You deserve better." Flann knew it was true, and she wasn't thinking about clothes.

Abby slipped her arm through Flann's. She had a day off, she'd just been kissed by the sexiest woman she'd ever met, and she was feeling sexier than she ever had in her life. For the next few hours, she didn't want to think of anything else. "As a matter of fact, I like you exactly the way you are."

Coming from anyone else, Flann would have discounted the statement as flirtatious, just one more move in the game. When Abby said it, she hoped it was true. More than she'd ever imagined.

CHAPTER TWENTY-THREE

I'm going to take you at your word about my clothes," Flann said as she started driving north away from town. "But next time we go somewhere, I promise I won't be wearing a T-shirt."

Laughing, Abby rolled down her window and let the brisk morning air blow through her hair. She didn't even care if it tangled, the breeze felt so good. The countryside stretched out on either side of the mostly empty road, rolling hills in more shades of green than she'd ever imagined. Flann swept around a bend and the river appeared, shimmering in the sun.

"God, it's beautiful up here," Abby said.

"You know what else?" Flann said. "You never get used to it."

"I believe it."

"Do you miss the city?"

"No." Abby turned in the seat to watch Flann drive. She drove as she did everything else, a little bit fast, competently, easily. Her window was open too, and the air rushing in pressed her T-shirt tightly to her chest. Her arms and shoulders were muscular, but sculpted rather than bulky, her breasts small and neat. Abby had an urge to slide her hand underneath the hem of her T-shirt and explore Flann's abdomen, suspecting it was flat and firm. As if reading her thoughts, Flann glanced over and her mouth quirked up at the corner. Abby almost expected her to ask if she saw something she liked, because she was certain her expression gave her away. Mercifully, Flann didn't comment.

"So you don't even miss the restaurants?" Flann said.

Abby grinned. "Okay, maybe the ready access to something besides pizza. Although the pizza at Clark's is damn good."

"We've got some good locally sourced restaurants a half-hour drive from town. Next time—"

"You seem pretty certain there'll be a next time."

"I hope there will be."

"Flann," Abby said, needing to be clear for her own sake as much as Flann's, "I'm not thinking about this as a date. We work together, my son and your sister are getting to be best friends, and one of *my* best friends is marrying your sister. We're going to be seeing a lot of each other."

"Like I said, I hope so."

Abby had forgotten how exasperating Flann could be when she'd made up her mind about something. Maybe those kisses had some amnesiac side effect, because they'd certainly affected her memory and her sanity. Grumpily, she said, "You're being purposely obtuse."

Flann grinned. "That sounds kinda sexy."

Abby considered punching her in her beautifully muscled arm, just to touch her. She was such an infuriatingly gorgeous animal. "Now you're purposefully being difficult."

Flann looked from the road to Abby again, and she wasn't grinning. She was smoky eyed and oh-so-tantalizing. "I'm not trying to be. I do think we're friends, but I don't usually kiss my friends, not the way I kissed you."

"I suppose I should say I'm sorry I let that second kiss happen, but—"

"Let it happen?" Flann snorted. "You mean it was all me?"

"No, you're right," Abby said, forcing herself to say the truth. "I didn't let it happen—I wanted it to happen, and that kiss was every bit as much my doing as yours."

"I want to kiss you again."

Abby sighed. "Why can't we just keep things simple."

"Why can't we just let what is, be? See what happens."

"I can't," Abby said. "I don't work that way. I'm not—casual. Spontaneous. I've never had the luxury of just doing what I wanted."

"So try it now," Flann said.

"Part of me wants to, that's why I'm sitting here in this Jeep with you right now. But I know myself, Flann. Really, I do. And I'm not the right kind of woman for you."

Flann's brow twitched. "You mean the kind that kisses me until my brains feel like they're gonna leak out of my ears? Because I have to tell you, I liked it."

Abby flushed. She liked knowing she could make Flann's brain melt. She liked knowing she wasn't the only one set ablaze by their kisses. The power was exciting, heady, a little addictive. "I like kissing you. But I'm not going to sleep with you."

"All right," Flann said easily, watching the road.

Surprised, Abby said nothing. And she ignored the surge of disappointment.

"So how do you feel about venison, because one of these places makes the most amazing grilled venison with fresh squa—"

Abby stared. "Did we not just have a long conversation about how we're not—"

"I got it, every word."

Flann slouched slightly behind the wheel, controlling the car with the fingers of one hand loosely curled around the wheel, her other hand resting on her thigh. With her tawny hair and sun-kissed skin, she resembled a big cat, deceptively somnolent when Abby knew for a fact she was dangerous. Flann had the power to strip away every last shred of her good sense.

"Somehow I don't think so."

"We're not going to date and"—Flann sent her a mildly infuriating grin, making her look even more attractive—"you're not going to sleep with me. Right?"

"More or less, yes."

Flann nodded. "Thought so."

"Just so we're clear."

"Crystal."

Flann's sudden acceptance left Abby deflated when she should have been exultant. Determined to enjoy the day, Abby concentrated on the river running alongside the road, marveling at how wide it still was so far north of the inlet in New York City, admiring the fields and farms dotting its shores, all the while refusing to think about the danger signals blaring in her head. Flann was so appealingly stubborn, pretending she didn't understand or care what Abby was saying. Refusing to be refused.

"Hey, Abby?"

"Hmm?"

"What if we agreed, just kisses."

Abby laughed, she couldn't help it. Flann was so outrageously attractive. If the kiss happened again, she knew she'd enjoy it. How could she not?

"If...and I mean if," Abby said, trying to sound stern but knowing she was failing by the little smile curling Flann's gorgeous mouth, "that does *not* mean I'll be tearing off my clothes and jumping into the nearest bed."

"Absolutely clear."

Fine. She could control herself, after all. And if Flann wanted to torment them both with kisses, why not? In fact, she could do a little tormenting of her own. Feeling slightly wild and not caring, she reached for Flann's free hand and pulled it into her lap. Flann tensed for the barest second and then relaxed, letting Abby intertwine their fingers. They rode along in silence, Abby slowly stroking her thumb over the top of Flann's hand. The contact was as erotic as if they lay naked together.

Abby needed all her willpower not to let that image fill her mind.

❖

The farmers' market was a ring of tents set up in a big pasture along the river on the outskirts of Saratoga, an historic village known for its racetrack, medicinal spas, and fine restaurants. Flann pulled behind a line of cars parked on the shoulder of the road, and they walked up the highway toward the fluttering canvases and the rumble of voices. Flann took her hand as they walked and caught Abby off guard by how much she enjoyed the simple proprietary gesture. The last time she'd been on a date with someone who was so easily physical and effortlessly possessive had been...never. She never would have thought she'd enjoy being so publicly involved with anyone, but she liked being seen with Flann, being her...date. Well, really. She was the one wearing blinders, and that was just plain embarrassing.

"Thanks for bringing me here. It's a fabulous day."

"And it's just beginning."

Her seductive croon sent a warm wave rushing through Abby's core. Searching for a safe topic, Abby blurted, "Do you cook?"

Flann grinned, not looking at her. Her face in profile was sculpted and bold. "I grill."

"Does your apartment have a yard?"

"My apartment doesn't have anything except three serviceable rooms, a little bit of furniture, and a television set."

Flann stopped at a card table set up under a multicolored umbrella and bought two paper cups filled with real lemonade from a smiling preteen with braces and beautiful sea-green eyes.

"Harper lives in a house on the farm, doesn't she?"

"That's right," Flann said nonchalantly.

"The place Carrie is moving into?"

"Yep."

"You didn't want to live there?"

Flann stopped again, bought two homemade chocolate chip cookies, and handed her one. "Nope."

"I'm sorry. I'm being nosy."

Flann stopped and met her gaze. "No, you're not. I'm being a jerk."

"No, you're—"

"Harper is the oldest, but that's not why she's my father's successor. She's always been the brightest and the best. I always wanted to be her, but I never quite made it. I don't want to step into her shoes now."

"I don't blame you." Abby frowned. "But you do realize you're an accomplished surgeon and a genuinely good person, don't you?"

Flann blushed. "Thanks."

"And I would add extremely attractive, but I doubt that matters to your parents."

Flann grinned. "Matters to me if you think so."

"Oh, I think so," Abby murmured.

"We should go somewhere so I can kiss you."

"Absolutely not. I want to see the rest of this place," Abby said, glad to see the light spark in Flann's eyes again. She started walking and Flann grabbed her hand, falling into step with her. "So if you don't grill at your place, where do you grill?"

"I'm the official chef at all the summer softball league barbecues—usually at least once a month. I help out at the pig roast, and every now and then my father lets me assist at family get-togethers."

At the mention of softball, Abby thought about Carrie again. "There's another game this week, isn't there?"

"A couple. Usually Wednesday, Friday, and Sunday."

"You can't play with your leg."

"Thought I'd try it on Sunday, but there's a game Friday. Are you going to come?"

"I don't play."

"How about cheering? I could use a bigger fan section."

Abby laughed as they crossed the grass and began walking along the rows of tables. Signs announced local farms and other businesses. Tables were heaped with fresh fruit, vegetables, breads, cheeses, and even meats in coolers.

"I can't believe you're lacking in fans."

Flann shook her head. "Harper and Carrie are the stars of our team."

"How is that?"

"Carrie is a phenomenal pitcher—pitched in college. Harper is a home-run star."

"And you? What's your claim to fame? And don't tell me you don't have one." Abby purchased a cardboard box of raspberries and almost groaned at the sweet burst of flavor. She held one out to Flann, who dipped her head and caught it between her lips. Abby's fingers tingled. "Could you try to behave for five minutes?"

Flann grinned. "I almost always get on base, and I hold the record for bases stolen."

"Now why doesn't that surprise me?" Abby shook her head. Stolen bases, stolen hearts.

"I'm fast and I'm wily."

"And you're interested in seeing the star pitcher." As soon as Abby said it, she regretted it. It was none of her business who Flann was dating. "And that is totally none of my business. Sorry."

Flann slowed in front of the table, picked up a peach, and handed the buxom blonde behind the table two dollars. She took a bite, and then held the golden fruit, juices dripping onto her fingers, out to Abby. "Try this. I guarantee you've never tasted anything like it."

Abby was about to refuse and then, on a whim, covered Flann's hand with hers, drew the peach closer, and slowly took a bite, sucking the sweet, meaty flesh into her mouth. Juice ran down her chin. She couldn't believe she was making such a mess of herself in public. As she chewed and swallowed, she watched Flann watch her. Then Flann's thumb was on her mouth, slowly wiping away the juice. Abby's breath caught as Flann brought her thumb to her mouth, her tongue flicked out, and she licked it with a slow swirl of her tongue. Abby's thighs weakened and her stomach fluttered.

"I'm not seeing anyone except you," Flann said. "I did ask Carrie to go out with me a while ago, but she hasn't taken me up on it. I intend to let her know we'd make better friends. She won't mind."

"You don't have to because of me," Abby said just a little breathlessly.

Flann lifted their hands, the peach still dripping, and took another bite. She licked some of the juice from Abby's fingers. "Not doing it for you. For me. You're the only woman I want to think about."

"You're right about the peach," Abby said. If Flann touched her now, anywhere, she'd go up in flames.

Flann grinned and held it up for Abby to take another bite. "Told you."

They passed the peach back and forth until it was gone and then found a portable water station and washed their hands. By the time they'd slowly made the circuit of the tents, Abby had picked up fresh fruits and vegetables and a package of steaks.

"There's a grill on the back porch at my place," Abby said. "Why don't you stay for supper?"

"Yeah?"

Flann's pleasure was so plain Abby's heart warmed. "Yes."

"I'd like that. Do you drink wine?"

"A red would work with the steak."

"Excellent." Flann slipped her arm around Abby's waist. "We'll pick some up on the way back."

Abby hesitated. "You know Blake will be there…"

"I figured." Flann's mouth brushed her ear. "He's your son. I know you're a family."

Abby stopped, turned her head, and kissed her, right there by the side of the road with pickup trucks and people passing by. "You are remarkable."

"I'll remind you of that the next time we're alone."

Abby settled into the passenger seat, the taste of peaches lingering on her lips. She reached for Flann's hand and tried to think if she'd ever had an afternoon quite so perfect. She knew she hadn't.

CHAPTER TWENTY-FOUR

Flann pulled over in front of the old schoolhouse that was Abby and Blake's home now. Two bikes leaned against the white picket fence. "Damn," she muttered.

Abby's brows furrowed "What?"

"Blake and Margie are here."

"I thought you said you didn't mind—"

"It's not them." Flann slid an arm around her shoulders and pulled her toward the center of the front seat. "I was hoping for more kisses. I seem to be suffering from a lack of them."

Abby's eyes cleared and she smiled, a satisfied, very feline kind of smile. "Oh. I see."

Flann pretended to be offended. "If I didn't know better, I'd think you were enjoying my discomfort."

Abby ran her fingers down the center of Flann's T-shirt, avoiding her breasts, but the way Flann's skin ignited, she might as well have been naked. Her hips lifted, and she growled. "Come on, Abby. That's no fair."

"Why not? After all, a kiss is more intimate than a little touch."

"That's not a little touch." Flann grasped Abby's wrist, turned her hand over, and kissed her palm. She flicked her tongue over the soft swelling at the base of Abby's thumb and bit down gently. Abby gasped. Flann glanced up at her, her mouth still pressed to her palm. "And there are all kinds of kisses."

Color flared in Abby's face and her eyes took on that dark, sultry haze again. "I suppose we should clarify exactly what kind of kisses we'll be sharing."

Flann shook her head. "Too late. Kisses, no qualifiers. Anywhere we want."

Abby's heart beat so rapidly she could feel it in her throat. Trying to set limits with Flann was like trying to stop the sun from rising in the morning, a force of nature far too powerful for human restraints. Especially when she didn't really want to restrain her. Heat swirled in her belly, and if she didn't have two teenagers waiting inside, she would have forgotten all about why getting involved with Flann was a bad idea. She couldn't look away from her mouth, couldn't stop thinking about how her soft, warm lips would feel on her skin—possessive and demanding. When had she developed the desire to be pleasured, to take, to want? She brushed Flann's lips with the thumb Flann had bitten. "You have a beautiful mouth. I'm going to enjoy your kisses."

"Jeez, Abby," Flann groaned. "Have a little mercy."

"Mmm. I don't think so." Abby laughed, popped the door behind her, and jumped out. "Come on, you promised me dinner. You're due at the grill."

Flann wasn't even sure she could walk. Her thighs were loose with desire while other parts of her were tight and swollen and hot. Somehow she had to get through dinner without looking like she wanted to jump on Abby, which she didn't want to do—yet. But damn, it was hard to hold back. She'd never been obsessed with wanting a woman before. Oh sure, maybe when she was thirteen or fourteen and every girl was an object of endless, sleepless fascination, but that was more about wanting sex than wanting sex with *some*body. After that insanity had passed, no woman had occupied her thoughts the way Abby did. No one fired her imagination or made her want things she'd sworn she'd never want. Not just kisses, not just being naked with her, not just making love to her until she screamed, which she wanted as much as she wanted her next breath, but more. She wanted more—she wanted the welcome in Abby's eyes when she walked into a room, she wanted to hear Abby's laugh when she teased her, she wanted to confess her sins and know Abby would help her to forgive herself. She wanted Abby's light in the dark night of her world.

Abby stood on the porch looking back at her, a question in her eyes. "You can't get out of it now."

"Don't want to," Flann yelled, and she knew in her heart she meant it. She jumped out of the Jeep and jogged up the flagstone path.

"Take it easy with that leg," Abby said.

"I'm good. Great." Flann stood a step below her looking up. "I had a fabulous day."

Abby held her gaze and slowly leaned down. Her kiss lingered, questing, a gentle demand.

Flann groaned. And then Abby was gone.

"How about I open that red," Abby said with a teasing smile from the doorway.

"Sure." Flann's voice was sandpaper rough.

"Great. Grill's on the porch."

Flann followed through the neat open-concept living room-kitchen area and out the back door. Margie and Blake sat on the porch steps with lemonade and a box of cold pizza between them.

"Don't eat too much of that," Flann said, "I'm cooking."

Margie craned her neck and looked up at her. "You are? Awesome."

Blake closed the box. "Breakfast."

Grinning, Flann said, "You two want to help me muscle this grill off the porch so I can get it started?"

Both teens jumped up. Margie and Blake grabbed one end and the three of them hoisted the grill down to the grass. Flann rocked the tank to be sure it had enough gas to get them through dinner and started up the grill. A breeze blew up from the river and cooled the sweat on the back of her neck. The sun was an hour away from dropping behind the hills on the other side of the valley. Beautiful night. Incredible day. Flann couldn't remember being so relaxed or so bone-deep content in her life.

Abby came to the back door. "Blake, Margie. Want to give me a hand cutting vegetables?"

"Sure."

"Okay."

Flann watched Blake and Margie troop inside, thinking they seemed at once young and a whole lot more mature than she'd been at their age. She wondered what was going on between the two of them, but didn't see as it was really any of her business. And whatever it was, she trusted them not to hurt each other.

A few minutes later, Abby came out with the steaks on a platter and a tray of sliced vegetables. "Salad's done. I think we're ready for you."

"Good." Flann checked the back porch and couldn't see either of the kids inside. Abby's hands were full. Perfect opportunity. She slid her hand behind Abby's neck and kissed her. Abby gave a little moue of surprise and then kissed her back, meeting Flann's subtle demand with some of her own. Flann felt a tiny nip on her lower lip before Abby pulled away. The kiss was even more satisfying for its briefness, a teasing hint of all to come when they were alone. Flann drew back, surprised at how short her breath had gotten, how fast her pulse. "I'll put those vegetables on now."

Abby stared, her gaze holding Flann's as she held out the tray. "Good idea."

Grinning, Flann laid out the vegetables, put on the steaks, and checked her watch. Five minutes later, Abby returned with two glasses of the red and handed her one. "How are they coming?"

"Everything looks good. Do you want to eat out on the porch?"

"There's no table."

"Doesn't matter. We can sit on the steps. It's a beautiful night and the sun will set right across the river in not too long."

"It sounds perfect," Abby said.

And it was. The four of them spread out on the porch steps and ate with their plates balanced on their knees, Margie and Blake regaling them with tales of the chicks and Rooster.

"He knows they're in the pen," Margie said. "He doesn't go very far away like he used to. He just scratches around in a big circle and every once in a while he hops over and tries to look inside."

"He's claimed them already," Blake said.

"You'll have to wait until they're about three months old to let them out," Flann said. "He'll want to make sure they know they belong to him when they start free ranging."

"Once the barn is rebuilt, we can get them in the coop, right?" Blake said.

"That's the plan."

"You're coming on Saturday, aren't you?" Margie said to Flann. "To the barn raising?"

"As long as I'm not at the hospital." Flann turned to Abby. "You know about it, don't you?"

"Presley mentioned it," Abby said. "It sounds like fun. I'll be there, but I can't promise I'll be much help. I think Carrie is planning on a wedding summit meeting."

"Oh, man," Flann moaned. "This is turning into a big show."

Abby laughed. "Of course! But don't worry—you can busy yourself with hammering and whatnot."

"Thank God," Flann muttered.

"So, Mom," Blake said, finishing off the last of the grilled zucchini, "I've changed my mind about school."

Abby set her wineglass down carefully, a jolt of fear running through her. If something had happened to make him want to change schools, he would have told her by now, wouldn't he? "How's that?"

Blake glanced at Margie. "I'm not going to study creative writing. I'm going to be a vet. Margie and I are going into practice together."

Flann laughed. "That's a great idea. Are you both going to do large animals or what?"

"Oh," Abby said, trying to switch mental gears. Not a problem. Just teenagers being teenagers. "You'll set up around here?"

"Oh, sure," Margie said. "I'll do the large animal work, mostly. Blake will specialize in small animals and domestic pets, but we'll cross-cover."

"Where are you planning to go to school?" Flann asked.

"We're thinking Penn for vet school," Blake said.

"And what about undergraduate school?" Abby said, running numbers in her head. Blake was smart and liked to study, but even a scholarship wouldn't cover the cost of eight years of college and vet school.

"That's to be determined." Margie smiled at Blake. "But we're thinking we'll try for the same place."

"Or at least close enough to see each other more than on holidays," Blake qualified. "Maybe Dartmouth or Yale."

"Okay," Abby said brightly. God, she needed to start budgeting a little bit differently. "Sounds like there's going to be a lot of serious studying going on the next year or two."

"Margie says we might be able to get part-time work or an internship at the vet hospital in Saratoga."

"You know Doc Valentine pretty well, don't you, Flann?" Margie asked innocently.

Flann shot her a cautionary look. She and Sydney Valentine had dated for a while in college, but they'd gone their separate ways when Flann went off to medical school and Syd to vet school. Syd was still single, and they'd had one brief weekend reunion a few years back before deciding the passion of youth was not to be recaptured.

"I know her well enough to give her a call and see if there's anything she could use you two for."

Margie grinned. "Awesome."

"Thanks, Flann." Blake stood. "We're gonna meet Terry and Phil at Clark's. I'll be home later."

"Uh-huh," Abby said. "Why don't you two carry in those dishes, rinse them off, and *then* you can go. If you're riding your bikes, you need to be back by dark."

"We'll walk," Blake said. "Then we don't have to be back—"

"Until ten," Abby said.

Blake grinned. "Right."

"I'll give you a ride home, Margie," Flann called as the two teens hustled into the house. She glanced at Abby. "That is, if you don't mind having me around for a few more hours."

"I don't mind at all," Abby said. Earlier that day, she hadn't wanted to be alone with Flann in the empty house. She'd thought at the time she hadn't wanted to be tempted, and worse, hadn't wanted to give in. What a difference the day had made. Flann's kisses were addictive, but it was more than kisses or the way Flann's possessive gaze made Abby feel sexy and sensuous and daring. *Flann* was addictive, with her intensity, her unexpected tenderness, her humor, and her hidden vulnerabilities. Now the idea of a few hours alone with her was anything but worrisome. No way would Blake and Margie return early, and her bedroom had a nice breeze at night…if needed. "Let's—"

"Let's sit out front and finish this wine." Flann picked up the half-empty bottle of Bordeaux and caught their glasses up by the stems in the other hand. "The sun's about down now, but the moon will be out soon."

"All right." Abby led the way to the front porch. What had happened to Flann's request for more kisses?

They sat side by side in the rockers and slowly sipped the dark, fruity wine as the moon rose beyond the town and the traffic noise faded away to be replaced by the near silence of a sleeping village.

Abby's house was at the far edge of town where Main Street drifted off into countryside, and soon even the lights from the village faded away.

"I used to think the night was empty because it was so quiet, but now I can hear the train whistle in the distance," Abby said, "and the river lapping over the rocks, and the owls. It's not empty, it's alive."

"Have you heard the coyotes?"

Abby laughed. "The first time I had goose bumps the size of thimbles all over my body. So eerie, yet so beautiful. It was after midnight, and I jumped up and rushed to the window, but I couldn't see them."

"Look along the river next time, they'll be running there. You might catch a glimpse of ghost shadows in the moonlight."

"You love it here as much as Harper, don't you?"

Flann studied her wine. "I can't imagine being anywhere else."

"I think I could easily come to feel that way too," Abby said. The clouds drifted across the moon, turning purple as the moonlight shone through, pulling at some place deep inside her, reminding her of how insignificant one life was and how precious each passing moment. "It's pretty obvious Blake already has."

Flann laughed. "Margie's pretty persuasive."

"Margie is an incredibly kind and generous and extraordinarily intelligent young woman."

"She's all of that." Flann stretched and sighed. "I haven't spent this much time just sitting outside in a long time."

"You don't belong in an apartment," Abby said. "You belong in a place with a porch and some land to walk around on and—"

"A picket fence, a dog, and a few kids?" Flann said slowly.

"I don't know about the last part." Abby's heart beat faster. "What do you think?"

"I would've said *no way* not that long ago. Now I'm not so sure."

"Any reason?"

Flann smiled at her in the moonlight, the bold planes of her face highlighted in silver. "I can think of one or two."

"I thought you said you wanted to kiss me earlier," Abby said softly.

Flann put her wineglass on the floor and leaned over, brushing a kiss gently across Abby's mouth, a tender, wistful kiss that had every bit as much power as her demanding, possessive kisses had earlier.

Abby found herself holding her breath, waiting for the spell to break, but even when Flann eased back, the wonder remained.

Voice just a little shaky, Abby said, "I don't know about you, but I think this is a dangerous game we're playing."

"No, it isn't," Flann said. "It's no game at all."

"What if I said I wanted more than kisses," Abby said, feeling reckless and not caring. She wanted kisses and more, and wondered why Flann had stopped.

"I'd say that could definitely be dangerous." Flann smiled. "And there's no rush."

Abby frowned. When had she become the one who wanted more, right now? Since when did Flann want slow? "I—"

The front gate banged open and Margie and Blake ambled up the walk, talking in animated tones about something someone had said about a concert. Abby steadied her breath, tried to still the pounding of her heart.

Flann rose. "Thanks for inviting me to dinner. I enjoyed it more than I can say."

Abby stood too, conscious of Blake and Margie on the walk a few feet away. "It was wonderful. Thank you for the day."

"Good night," Flann murmured.

"Good night."

Flann was already down the steps and slung an arm around Margie's shoulders. "Come on, we'll get your bike in the back of the Jeep, and I'll take you home."

Margie called, "See you at the barn raising."

"I'll call you," Blake said.

Abby waited until Flann drove away, leaning on the porch post and thinking about all the things she hadn't realized she wanted until now. She picked up the empty wine bottle and Flann's empty glass, found hers, and swallowed the last few drops.

"I saw the two of you kissing, out by the grill," Blake said quietly.

"Did it bother you?" Abby laughed softly. "More than the usual embarrassment when you come face-to-face with the fact that your parent has a romantic life?"

Blake snorted. "I think that was more than romance."

"Don't be a smart-ass."

"No, it didn't bother me. I like Flann a lot. I guess you do too."

"I do like her. I'm glad you feel the same." Abby hesitated. "What about you and Margie? Are you…romantically interested too?"

Even in the dim moonlight, Blake's chagrin was clear. "No, Mom. Jeez. We're friends."

"Well, okay. I was just wondering. I can tell you're really close friends, and I'm glad about that. I just wasn't sure if it was…more."

"I'm not ready to have a girlfriend," Blake said. "Or a boyfriend, or whatever."

"Right," Abby said, "or whatever." She slid her arm around his shoulders and hugged him. "Whenever you want to talk about it, let me know."

"Same goes," Blake said.

Abby gave him a little push toward the house. "Smart-ass."

But she was very glad that Blake liked Flann. Very, very glad.

CHAPTER TWENTY-FIVE

The homestead was dark when Flann pulled down the drive a little before ten thirty to drop Margie home. She smiled to herself. Early to bed, early to rise…et cetera, et cetera. Her mother would be up at four as she had been Flann's whole life, even though she didn't have a houseful to get off to school with only Margie living at home now. The kitchen would still smell like fresh coffee, bacon, and hot biscuits, and the table would still be set and waiting for whoever showed up. Sometimes she or Harper would roll in with the sun after a late-night call. Her father would be up shortly after her mother if he hadn't been out all night working, and then they'd all be out of the house again by six for early morning rounds.

The routine was a constant she'd come to think would never change, but as she looked back over the last few years, she realized life had been slowly changing for a long time. Carson was the first to leave when she'd married Bill while still in college. Harper moved into the caretaker's house when she and Flann returned from residency to start practice at the Rivers, but that had seemed almost like she still lived at home. Harper was gone now, having pretty much vacated the little house to live with Presley in their new home.

Flann hadn't spent a night sitting on the back porch with Harper and her father, talking about cases, in weeks. Margie was getting ready to drive soon, and it wouldn't be long before she'd be off to college. While Flann had been focused on avoiding any kind of personal ties, everyone else had been making their own lives. Oh, she could always come home—they all could and would, she knew that in her heart. But her life wasn't here anymore—it was somewhere else, waiting for her to be brave enough to grab it. The idea no longer seemed impossible.

"I'll see you at the game tomorrow night," Flann said as she helped Margie get her bike out of the back of the Jeep.

"You playing?"

"Not a whole game yet," Flann said. "I'm giving my leg a rest."

"You'll be there, though, right?"

"Wouldn't miss it." Flann ruffled her hair. She wanted to tell her to hold on to these summer nights, to imprint them in her bones, because the time would come when the memories would remind her of what really mattered the most.

"Okay, that's good."

Margie looked younger in the moonlight, younger and innocent and maybe just a little worried. Margie rarely if ever looked uncertain, and warning bells went off. "Is everything going okay with you?"

"Oh, sure."

She didn't sound so sure, and Flann wasn't much for subtlety anyhow. "How are things with Blake?"

Margie leaned against the Jeep. "You mean with him and the other kids?"

"Yeah. Or with you."

"Him being trans, you mean."

Flann reined herself in to go at Margie's pace. "If that's part of it, sure."

"Pretty much okay."

Margie wasn't one for noncommittal statements either. Flann leaned next to her and slid her hands into her pockets. This could take some time, and she had nowhere else to be that mattered more. "Does that mean sometimes yes but sometimes no?"

"Everybody I've introduced him to has been cool. But you know, all my friends are cool."

Flann laughed and bumped her shoulder. "Of course."

"Richie West is an ass," Margie said emphatically.

Richie West. Flann snorted. Richie West was one of those aimless guys a few years out of high school with no particular ambition who never really wanted to grow up—longing for the glory days of adolescence and resenting anyone who broke away from the pack. Flann saw him now and then, hanging around with a bunch of similar going-nowhere guys tinkering with motorcycles, drinking too much, and basically waiting for their big break to come along unaided by anything they might do. "He's giving you trouble?"

"Not really," Margie said. "Just the usual bullshit."

"What kind of bullshit do you mean?" Flann tried to keep her temper out of her voice so Margie would keep talking. If an older guy was after Margie, she was going to put a stop to that right quick. "He's been bothering you?"

Margie hunched a shoulder. "He's tried to get me to go for a ride with him a couple of times."

"A ride." Flann gritted her teeth. God, she wanted to kill him. "And what did you say?"

Margie grinned, her straight white teeth gleaming in the moonlight. She was a young lioness, and one day, she would rule her own pride. "I told him I wasn't interested."

"And he let it drop?"

"Sort of. Yeah, I guess."

"Come on, Margie. Why didn't you tell me about this before?"

"Because I didn't want you to hunt him down and kick his ass." She was laughing, knowing Flann didn't choose physical violence as a first resort.

"What's the rest of it?"

"He just makes comments when he sees me sometimes, and then Blake and I were walking home tonight and…" She shrugged again. "I told you, he's an ass."

"What did he say?"

"He just followed us awhile on his motorcycle, saying how Blake was a freak and if I wanted a dick he had one for me." Margie huffed. "He *is* a dick, but I didn't say it."

"Smart move," Flann said, a cold wave of fury rolling through her. "What did the two of you do?"

"Nothing. It's better not to engage."

Flann stroked her hair. "You're pretty damn smart, you know that?"

"Yeah." Margie leaned against her, and Flann slid an arm around her shoulders. "Blake is really brave, you know?"

Flann kissed the top of her head. "Yep. And so are you. If West bothers you again, you let me or Harper know."

"Okay."

Margie made no move to move away and Flann kept her close. They might not have too many moments like this.

"So, you and Dr. Remy have a thing?" Margie said finally.

"Margie," Flann groaned. "Personal. Remember?"

"Well, how come you can ask me about my personal stuff, then?"

"That's different."

"Why, because you're older?"

"Partly." Margie snorted, and Flann laughed. "I like her, okay?"

"Me too. Blake says she's been really cool with everything."

"They're both pretty awesome."

"Yeah, I think so too. So," Margie said, "you do have a thing?"

Flann sighed. "Maybe."

"Good. So—"

"That's all you get. Go to bed." Flann gave her a little shove toward the house. "Good night!"

Margie loped off, calling, "You too."

Flann started the Jeep. She was ready for bed, and she'd probably even be able to sleep now. Talking about Abby and Blake, thinking about them, settled her in a way she hadn't imagined possible. They mattered, and she hadn't known she'd wanted that, but she did. She wanted a life where love mattered.

Flann kept watching the parking lot as game time drew closer. Blake and Margie sat with Presley in the stands, but Abby hadn't come. The disappointment was a sharp pain in Flann's chest. She hadn't seen Abby all day, but every second when she wasn't busy, she thought of her. She replayed the kisses, how could she not? But mostly she came back to the moments they'd shared strolling through the market and sharing a bottle of wine while the sun went down. Moments far more intimate than anything she'd experienced naked in bed with near strangers. She wanted Abby naked in bed—she'd awakened with a craving for her that left her out of sorts and aching all day—but she wanted the quiet connections too. She wanted it all.

She tried to distract herself by watching the warm-ups. Carrie was loosening up, pitching to Harper. Usually Glenn would be hitting fly balls to the outfielders, but Glenn was missing in action too. Glenn never missed a game and was never late unless she and Flann were held up in the OR. A sliver of heat raced down Flann's spine. Glenn and Abby were missing. Together.

No, that was just coincidence. Abby wasn't a player, and Abby wouldn't have kissed her the way she'd kissed her if she was interested in anyone else. Still, a little niggle of doubt ate at her. She didn't want Abby kissing anyone else. But then how was Abby supposed to know that?

"God damn it."

"You're talking to yourself. You don't want to scare the horses."

Flann frowned at Harper, belatedly noticing Carrie had left the field to get some water. "There are no horses."

"All the same." Harper scanned the stands and grinned in Presley's direction. "You're not playing tonight, are you?"

"I thought maybe I could DH," Flann said, "if things get tight later on."

"Probably better if you give that leg a little more time to heal."

"Geez, when did you start channeling Mama?"

"Abby's admitting a patient with a rule-out MI, in case you were wondering," Harper said casually.

Flann crossed her arms and pretended not to be relieved. "One of yours?"

"No, Lorraine Peterson's. But I was seeing one of my patients in the ER when Lorraine's patient came in. Abby'll probably be along soon."

"Uh-huh."

"I just thought you might want to know that. Seeing as how you've been glued to the stands for the last half hour."

"No, I haven't."

"Oh, okay." Harper shrugged. "'Cause, you know, I thought the two of you had a thing."

"Jesus, is everybody interested in my love life now?"

"Is there one?"

Flann stomped over to the bench and sorted through the equipment bag to find her glove. "I'm gonna catch fly balls for a while."

"Don't do much running." Harper looked around as if to check who was nearby. They were alone. "Hold on."

"What?"

"Maybe you shouldn't do any running at all, Flann."

Flann tucked her glove under her arm. "Is that supposed to mean something?"

"Abby is special. So is Blake."

"You think I don't know that?"

"I think what you don't know is that you are too. Always have been."

"For fuck sake," Flann muttered. "Falling in love has really made you go soft."

"And it's just made you harder to live with," Harper shot back.

"I'm not falling in love."

"Aren't you?" Harper's brow raised. "Then you probably don't care that Hank Anderson asked me if Abby was available. And he's not the only one. Marsha—"

Flann growled. "Abby's not available."

"I didn't think so. Maybe you should tell *her* that." Harper grinned. "Don't push that leg tonight. We've got a barn to raise tomorrow."

Flann dropped onto the bench and scanned the bleachers one more time. No Abby. Hank Anderson was an ass, and Marsha Fitzroy was a player. She wondered how many other people were going to come sniffing around. God damn it. Abby was hers. *Hers.*

Glenn and Abby showed up together a few minutes before game time. Flann watched Abby climb into the stands and settle next to Presley. She looked at home, she looked perfect. The pain in Flann's chest eased.

Glenn hustled over and grabbed the equipment bag, nodding to Flann. "Hey."

"I didn't think you were going to make it."

Glenn grabbed her glove and sat to lace up her spikes. "Abby and I were looking at a patient with a diabetic foot ulcer. I cleaned it up a little bit but didn't think he needed to be admitted."

"I didn't get a consult."

"Oh, I stopped by on my way out. Just to check."

"You always stop in the ER before you leave at the end of the day?"

"Usually," Glenn said, tying her shoe. "That way I can catch anything that might need to be seen later at night." She straightened and glanced at Flann. "Cuts down on the calls for the night person."

"Right," Flann said, blowing out a breath. "I appreciate that. We all do."

Glenn grinned. "Besides, I'm trying to get Abby to go out to dinner with me—"

"You might want to back off there."

"Yeah, that's what I thought," Glenn said, a grin sliding free. "Just wanted to be sure, though."

"You set me up for that," Flann said in wonderment.

"Couldn't help myself." A rare spark of amusement flared in Glenn's usually unreadable eyes.

"Damn," Flann muttered. "You are a woman of hidden depths."

"Not so much," Glenn said. "You ready to play some ball?"

Flann grinned, checked the stands, and caught Abby's eye. She waved, and Abby waved back. "Yeah, I'm ready."

Chapter Twenty-six

Abby waved to Blake a few rows below her and settled next to Presley.

"Hi," she said, opening a bottle of water, her attention riveted to the field. The game was about to start and Flann was pacing by her team's bench, alternately watching the field and glancing over at Abby. "Not playing is driving her crazy."

"Who?" Presley's attention was riveted on Harper at second base.

"Flann. The other gorgeous Rivers sister. Hello, Presley."

"Oh hey, Abby." Presley smiled, sounding as if awakening from a daydream. "Oh!" Presley grabbed Abby's hand and pointed to the woman beside her who sat with a toddler in her lap. "This is Carson—Flann's sister."

Abby straightened and leaned around Presley. Of course Carson was a Rivers sister. She was striking, just like the rest of them. With her ivory skin, clear green eyes, and lightly feathered auburn hair, she didn't look much older than Margie. The toddler was probably a little over a year, his toothy smile and blue eyes filled with joy. She held out her hand. "Hi. I'm Abby Remy."

Carson smiled. "Great to meet you. I'm sorry I missed you until now. It's been so crazy lately, with the storm and everything."

"I know. I hope you didn't get much damage."

"Just a little on the roof and a lot of yard damage. We've been in cleanup mode, but nothing serious." The baby chortled and Carson bounced him. "This would be Davey."

"He's gorgeous."

Carson's smile widened. "Thanks."

Abby pointed to Blake. "The one next to Margie would be mine."

"Margie introduced us. He's gorgeous too."

"Thanks."

A cheer rose and Abby glanced over to watch the players take the field. Flann's team was up to bat. Abby slowly relaxed in the early evening sun, the tension in her shoulders easing as she let the constant demands of the ER fade away. Flann had finally settled onto the bench, but it was clear being a spectator did not agree with her. She alternately yelled advice and silently muttered to herself. Every now and then she glanced Abby's way and grinned, a grin Abby was certain anyone watching could read. Flann's heated gaze spoke of sinful things, of dark kisses and secret caresses, and more. The more was becoming a disturbingly constant distraction, physically and mentally.

She'd slept fitfully the night before, and she couldn't really blame it on the heat. Her windows had been open and a breeze had cooled her bare skin, but still she'd twisted and turned, her body blazing not from the summer air, but from the memory of Flann's hands, her mouth, and the way Flann's caresses made her ache. The arousal pulsing in her depths had kept her just on the brink of awakening, and when she'd finally given up on sleep and opened her eyes, she'd been swollen and heavy with urgency. Even her breasts had been tender and full. When she'd cupped her breast and caught her nipple between her thumb and fingers, the answering beat between her thighs had grown more insistent.

She could have come quickly if she'd wanted, but perversely, she hadn't wanted to rush. She'd wanted to tease herself the way Flann's kisses had teased her. Lying naked atop the sheets, she'd slowly stroked while recalling the heat in Flann's eyes and the way Flann's mouth had claimed hers and the possessive grip of her hands. She'd finally let herself orgasm when she couldn't stand the pressure anymore, and Flann's face had flickered before her eyes as her back arched and she bit down on a cry.

She smiled to herself now, imagining how much more potent the reality would be. When her gaze turned outward from the memory, she found Flann staring at her across the field, the look on her face one that suggested she knew exactly what Abby was thinking.

Abby pointedly looked away. Anyone watching them would see the desire. She'd already exposed her need to Flann, she could at least keep some dignity in public.

"They're hard to resist, aren't they," Presley said.

"Is it that obvious?" Abby murmured.

"Only to someone who knows both of you," Presley said with laughter in her voice. "Is it serious or just serious lust?"

"I'm not sure." Abby pushed her hair off her neck in hopes the breeze would cool some of the heat in her face. "I'm serious about the lust, I mean. That's very serious. Possibly terminal."

Presley choked on her laugh.

"But the rest of it, I'm a little afraid to think about. Sometimes it feels too—"

"Big?" Presley finished.

"Yes."

Presley nodded. "I know exactly what you mean. Wonderful and absolutely terrifying at the same time."

"Yes." Some of Abby's uncertainty dissipated, knowing Presley understood. "Is that normal, do you think? Because I'm not usually reduced to words of one syllable just from looking at a woman."

"I think so, when you love all the way."

Love. Abby wasn't sure. She understood love. She loved Blake with every atom of her being. She loved her mother. She loved her work. None of those things kept her awake at night or had her second-guessing every action. Only the fear of failing Blake frightened her, but not of loving him. Whatever she felt for Flann was different from all of those feelings. The want, the desire, the need left her open and vulnerable and raw. As if she might break. "I don't know if I even *want* to know."

Presley squeezed her knee. "You'll know when the time is right, and you'll know what to do."

Abby hoped so.

At the beginning of the fifth inning, the right fielder, a nurse Abby recognized from the ICU, motioned to Flann, spoke to her for a minute, and then slumped on the bench. Flann grabbed her glove and ran out to right field.

"Looks like Flann is going to sub for Mary Ellen," Presley said.

"Damn it," Abby said. "She wasn't going to play tonight."

Carson must have heard her. "You didn't really think so, did you? I gave her until the fourth inning."

"If she breaks open that incision—"

"She'll be careful," Carson said. "She's not nearly as wild as she looks."

Abby wasn't sure she agreed. She watched Flann field a ball on the run, her stomach a twisting mess. She couldn't bear to see her hurt again.

When the team came up to bat, Flann of course took her turn. She laid a solid line drive to left field, and Harper scored. Flann made it to first, and Abby let out a breath. Flann signaled to her bench and a pinch runner came in to take her place. Flann threw Abby a cocky smile back to the sidelines as if to say, *What, were you worried?*

Abby just shook her head and Flann laughed. Oh, she was wild, all right. Wild and sexy and driving Abby crazy. When the game ended with a win for their team, Abby was a little disappointed the evening was almost over. She wasn't usually a spectator, but she'd enjoyed the camaraderie of the cheering section, and she'd definitely loved watching Flann.

As Abby stood to make her way down the bleachers, Presley said, "Don't forget Carrie's planning a wedding summit tomorrow morning."

"I'll be there," Abby said.

"Carson?" Presley asked.

"Absolutely." Carson hiked Davey onto her hip. "Bill is planning on helping with the barn raising too."

"Good, I'll see you both then." Presley headed in the direction of the team and Harper.

Abby waved to Carson and met Blake and Margie on the field. "You two need a ride?"

"Yeah, but we're gonna get hot dogs from the stand first," Blake said. "You want one?"

"None for me. I'll meet you at the car. I'm parked in the middle of the second row."

"Okay. See you," Blake called. He grabbed Margie's hand and they disappeared into the crowd.

Abby walked behind the bleachers toward the parking lot. A hand snaked out, caught her wrist, and pulled her into the shade beneath the bleachers.

"Flann!" Abby laughed. "What are you doing?"

"Collecting my kiss." Flann pulled her close with an arm around her waist and kissed her, a kiss that blanked her mind and flooded her body with fire. Flann's kiss wasn't the gentle brush of lips like the last time—more a promise then than a joining. Now her mouth was hot and hard and demanding.

Abby opened to her, taking her in, drinking her in. She drove her fingers into Flann's hair and held her in place. She wanted more than a promise—she wanted an answer for the tension and wanting that had kept her awake all night. Flann slipped into her mouth and Abby moaned softly. Deeper—she wanted her deeper everywhere.

Flann tugged Abby's shirt from her shorts and slid her hand onto her lower back, fingers spread, molding their bodies even closer together. "I missed you."

Abby's mind was a whirl of sensation, the scent of summer grass, the heat of summer sun, the taste of lust. "Oh God, Flann. We can't do this under the bleachers."

"No one's looking," Flann growled.

"Not right this minute," she gasped. "Mmm, you feel so good. I can't stand it."

"Good. I've been going crazy thinking about this." Flann kissed her way down Abby's throat. Her hand closed on Abby's breast, and she moaned again. "You're going to have to stand it for a while longer, because I want you. Abby, I want you."

Gathering every shred of her tattered willpower, Abby pushed away. The wild hunger on Flann's face almost made her not care where they were or who might see them. But she wanted more than a kiss. More than almost. She wanted all.

"Blake and Margie are waiting," Abby said. "And one more kiss like that, and I'm going to want a lot more than kisses."

"You're right," Flann said, breathing hard. "What I want to do I can't do here. When—"

The roar of motorcycles drowned out Flann's words, and a strange look passed over Flann's face.

"What?" Abby asked, recognizing Flann's focus shift to risk assessment.

"Where are Blake and Margie?"

"They were getting something to eat and heading for the parking lot to meet me. Why?"

Flann took her hand. "Probably nothing. Come on. Let's go find them."

"What aren't you telling me?"

"Some guy's been bothering Margie," Flann muttered. "It's probably nothing, I just want to—"

Blake and Margie stood next to Abby's car. Four young men on motorcycles ringed them, the engines rumbling like threatening predators. Abby's pulse raced and her mind sharpened. The threat had materialized.

"Stay here." Flann strode quickly toward the group. Abby followed on her heels and edged over toward Blake and Margie.

Flann halted inches from a scruffy bearded boy in a nondescript T-shirt and grimy jeans. About twenty, he was hollow-cheeked, his eyes narrow and small. He looked like an angry rodent of some kind, the type that bit when cornered. Abby's chest tightened.

"You're gonna want to stay away from my sister and her friends, Richie," Flann said.

"No law says I can't talk to her," Richie said.

"When you're fifteen, you can get away with being a bully unless somebody puts a stop to it. Somebody should have set you to rights then." Richie smirked. Flann's stony expression never changed. "Now what you're doing is called stalking. If I see you around Margie again, or she tells me you're following her, or verbally accosting her, you'll get a visit from the sheriff."

Richie snorted, but his gaze shifted away from Flann's solid one.

Harper eased up beside Abby. "What's going on?"

"Not sure, something about Margie and that boy on the motorcycle. He's been following her, it sounds like."

Harper stepped up next to Flann. "Hey, sis. Need help swatting flies?"

"Not just yet."

"Fucking dykes," Richie said, but his voice was thin and shaky. He glanced at Blake. "Freaks. Figures."

"You're gonna want to back off now, Richie," Flann said softly, but loud enough for everyone who had gathered around to hear. "And you'll want to stay away from my sister and her friend Blake."

"You see, Richie," Harper added, "Blake's family."

"Yeah. Whole family's freaks," Richie muttered, but he was pushing his motorcycle back away from Flann and Harper. His friends silently followed suit and the crowd parted, disdainful glances following the group as they turned and rode away.

Abby wanted to grab Blake but knew he would be embarrassed. Instead, she said as casually as she could manage, "Everybody doing okay?"

Blake nodded. "Yeah. They're just jerks."

"I agree. Not a particularly scientific assessment," Abby said lightly, "but accurate."

Presley cut through the crowd to Harper and took her hand. "Everything all right?"

Harper kissed her. "Fine." She slid an arm around her shoulders. "Let's go home."

Presley wrapped an arm around her waist. "Good idea."

The crowd broke up, and Flann watched until Richie West and his friends pulled onto the highway and roared away. "Morons."

She turned, took in Margie and Blake. "They come near you again, you call me. Or Abby or Harper. Day or night. Right there on the spot. If you can't get us, you call 9-1-1."

"They won't bother us again." Margie glanced at Blake. "They're cowards."

"Bullies usually are," he said quietly.

"Just remember," Flann said, "you don't ever have to take it. Either of you. That's why we're here. All of us."

Blake looked at Flann, then his mother. "We know."

"I'll be with you two in a minute." Abby took Flann's hand and drew her away. "Thank you."

Flann cupped her cheek and kissed her. "No thanks necessary. I really wanted to tear his mean little head off, but I didn't want you to think I was uncivilized."

"You can be as uncivilized as you want when we're alone."

Flann grinned. "Be careful, I might take you at your word."

Abby walked toward the car. After a few steps, she glanced over her shoulder, liking that Flann was watching her. "I expect you to."

CHAPTER TWENTY-SEVEN

I knew we should've gotten here earlier," Blake said, practically vibrating in the front seat.

Abby pulled in behind a long line of pickups, Subarus, and an occasional minivan in the drive leading up to Presley's farmhouse. Construction equipment in vivid yellow, green, and orange crowded the slope behind the house. She thought the big prehistoric-looking things were backhoes, but she hadn't quite gotten the nomenclature straight yet. "It's seven o'clock in the morning. I don't think it's polite to show up before people actually get out of bed."

"Mom," Blake said in an aggrieved voice, "this is the *country*," as if she didn't know that, "and everyone gets up at sunrise."

Abby gave him a look. "This coming from the guy who used to complain about getting up before nine."

He jumped out of the car as soon as she put it in park, peered in at her, and grinned. "That was before. Margie and Flann and everybody are probably already here. I don't want to miss anything."

Laughing, Abby climbed out and waved him on. "Go, then. And be careful with the tools."

Blake gave her the aggrieved expression reserved for parents who clearly didn't get it, and jogged off down the drive. Abby took her time following, wending her way between cornfields, basking in the cool air that would give way in a few hours to heat and humidity. It was July, after all, but she found she didn't mind the weather. How could she mind when surrounded by clear skies and the smell of growing things everywhere? No, she definitely didn't miss summer in the city.

No wonder so many city dwellers had historically escaped north into the mountains and countryside every summer.

She smiled. She'd never have to escape again. She was already home. She was as sure of that now as Blake had been almost from the beginning. All she needed was to be sure the job worked out and Blake adjusted to his new school. No small tasks for either of them, but they'd both made great progress so far. Thanks to Margie, Blake had a growing circle of friends who would help him when school started, and she had made solid inroads to getting the ER residency program up and running. And then there was Flann.

Flann was a very definite reason to want to stay right where she was.

As if reading Abby's thoughts, Flann appeared at the top of the drive. "Hey! You made it."

"According to Blake, we're already late."

"Not to worry. People will be drifting in and out all day." Flann wore her usual nonhospital attire of work boots, jeans, and a T-shirt, this time with her sleeves cut off and a raggedy V slashed at the neck. The shirt was tight enough to show the curves of her breasts if you were looking, and Abby was looking. She shaded her eyes, the better to take in every inch of her, and Flann slowed as if knowing exactly what she was doing. The easy grin Abby was coming to love spread across her face.

"Sleep okay?" Flann slid her hands into her pockets and rocked a little on her heels, waiting for Abby to draw next to her.

Abby wanted to say *How could I, considering the state you left me in*, but she decided to be more subtle for the moment. "Great. How about you?"

Flann leaned close, her breath warm against Abby's cheek. "Had a hard time getting to sleep, thinking about all the things I wanted to do with you and didn't get a chance."

Abby drew a long breath, savoring the earthy freshness of her. She'd know Flann's scent anywhere. "Really? I fell asleep the second I lay down."

"And here I thought you never exaggerated." Flann chuckled and slipped an arm around her waist. "Didn't you think about me just a little?"

Abby slid her hand onto Flann's back, tracing the edge of muscle running from her shoulder down her spine, hungry for the touch of her solid, sexy body. She pressed into her just a little, not caring they were standing in the middle of the drive. "I'm still waiting for the wild part."

"Glad to hear it."

Abby was about to invite her to get as wild as she wanted when Harper yelled down, "Hey, Flann, you gonna work today or what?"

Flann sighed. "You're not going anywhere, are you?"

"No," Abby said, meaning it. "I'm second call, so as long as it stays quiet, I'll be here."

"Good. I'll find you." Flann turned as if to go, turned quickly back, and kissed her. "I'm feeling a lot more than a little wild."

Abby laughed and gave her a push. "Don't be thinking about anything except what you're doing out there."

"Promise."

"Thank you." Abby grabbed her hand. "Would you keep an eye on Blake for me?"

"Of course. You never have to worry about that." Flann ran a finger along the angle of Abby's jaw. "I want to kiss you but if I do, I'll never get to work."

"Go," Abby said, already so aroused she ached. "I'll see you in a little while."

Flann jogged away and Abby slowly followed, giving her body a chance to calm down while enjoying the view of Flann from the back. She had a great ass. Finally she rounded the corner to the back porch, which, along with the kitchen, she'd quickly come to realize was the center of all activity.

Carson occupied one of the rocking chairs with a cup of coffee and an amazing-looking biscuit balanced on a plate on her knee. The scent of something marvelous—yeasty and sweet—emanated from the kitchen on a wave of strong coffee fumes.

Abby's mouth instantly watered. "What is it?"

"Buttermilk biscuits with fresh blueberries. Lila and Mama are making breakfast."

Abby tried not to moan on her way inside. Carrie and Presley were filling their coffee cups from an industrial-sized coffee urn. The table was laden with baskets of biscuits, slabs of butter, syrup, and fruit. A few dozen plates and piles of silverware filled one end.

"Oh my God, this is heaven," Abby murmured.

Ida Rivers ladled mountains of scrambled eggs from a cast-iron skillet the size of a satellite dish onto a platter. She smiled at Abby over her shoulder. "I hope you came hungry."

Abby blushed, instantly shy, a sensation she wasn't usually prone to experiencing. But this was Flann's mother, and a woman she greatly admired. And she'd just been hungering for her daughter. "Famished. Anything I can do?"

"Lila and I have the food situation under control. I understand Carrie is handling the important business of the morning." Ida shook her head. "We could have used her when Carson got married. Harper and Flann were about as useful as tits on a bull as far as the planning end of things went."

Abby's mouth dropped and she couldn't hold back a laugh. "Oh my God. I'm going to have a hard time getting that image out of my mind anytime I look at either of them."

Ida smiled, set the eggs aside, and forked slices of ham onto another platter. "Well, we all have our strengths."

"Flannery certainly does," Abby said quietly.

Ida nodded and continued spearing ham with a practiced flip of her wrist. "She does, but she's never been willing to see it."

"She just needs to slow down long enough to notice."

"You seem to have noticed, though," Ida said.

"It's not hard to see, when you look. She's wonderful." Abby paused. "She's kind and brave and tender."

Ida handed her the platter of eggs. "I'm glad you know that. Put this on the table for me?"

"Of course."

"And don't let her fool you," Ida said conversationally as she deposited the ham beside the biscuits. "She's just been waiting for someone to catch her. Even if she doesn't know it."

"This looks delicious," Abby said. "And I'll remember that."

Ida hummed and went back to laying out bacon into a skillet.

Flann wasn't the only one who'd been running. Abby'd been running from her own needs in the race to take care of everyone else's for fifteen years. But she'd stopped running now, and the thought wasn't the least bit scary.

Now she had all the time in the world. She grabbed her coffee, piled more food than she usually ate in three meals onto a white porcelain plate, and traipsed out to the porch to join the others. She took the last rocker. "Okay, what's the plan?"

Carrie flipped open a loose-leaf binder that was sectioned with colored tabs and turned to the first section. "Okay—location and setup." She pointed a matching colored pencil at Carson. "Since you know the homestead and the local vendors, you're in charge of that. Tents, tables, chair rental, all that kind of thing. Okay?"

"Got it," Carson said. "We can just use the same people we did for my wedding. In fact, I still have the old lists." She rummaged in a voluminous bag at her side and pulled out a stack of spreadsheets. "It's been a few years, but it's a starting place."

Carrie waggled her fingers. "Gimme."

For the next two hours, they divided up phone calls to vendors, discussed floral arrangements, menus, musicians, guest lists, childcare facilities, and the need for Porta-Potties versus comfort vans, all the time accompanied by a cacophony of power tools, pounding, shouts, and laughter coming from the direction of the barn. Men, women, girls, and boys drifted in and out of the kitchen, filling plates, and discussing weather, crops, sports, and opinions on the latest books and movies. Blake and Margie rushed in with a scrum of teens who acted as if they hadn't seen food in a millennium. Abby noted Blake's jubilant expression and avoided embarrassing him by calling out hello.

By midday, the skeleton of the damaged portion of the barn had been erected and people swarmed over the roof, laying down new slate and tin. Abby kept an eye out for Flann but couldn't find her until almost one when Flann walked over to an outdoor hose across the yard, turned it on, and doused her head and shoulders with water. Her wet T-shirt clung to her torso as she shook her head vigorously like a dog coming out of the lake after a particularly wonderful swim. When she brushed both hands through her soaked hair, she glanced at the back porch, caught Abby watching, and sent her an if-you-like-it-come-and-get-it smirk. Abby's mouth went dry.

She was about to take Flann up on her obvious invitation when a woman cut across Abby's line of sight, moving like an arrow with

Flann as her target. The svelte blonde sauntered as if on a New York runway and looked distinctly out of place among the cotton and denim crowd. Her jade capri pants and sleeveless raw silk shirt clung to her in a way that accentuated the curve of her shapely hips and full breasts. Her high-heeled sandals were definitely not meant for tramping around the barnyard.

"Who's that?" Abby said, hearing the edge in her voice and not caring.

"Oh," Carson said, "that's Dr. Love."

"I'm sorry?"

"Sydney Valentine. She's a local vet. She got the nickname in high school, because—well, because all the boys and quite a few of the girls wanted to sleep with her, and the rest of us just wanted to *be* her." Carson smiled wryly. "You know the type? Top of the class, captain of the tennis team, homecoming queen—everything every girl wanted to be. She broke the hearts of half the football team when she wouldn't sleep with any of them and ran through most of the interested girls like a threshing machine too."

"I'm assuming Flannery was one of them," Abby said, the desire to grab the blonde by her elegant neck and drag her away from Flann making her palms itch. She'd never had a physically violent thought in her life but decided she'd worry about what it meant later. When the vet put her hand on Flann's upper arm, Abby rose. "Excuse me."

She strode across the yard, dodging children playing a pickup game of catch, and stepped up to Flann. "Are you ready for a break?"

"Pretty quick," Flann said. "Abby, this is Sydney Valentine. She runs the big vet clinic in Battenkill."

Up close, Sydney's eyes were a chocolate brown, intelligent and appraising. She was stunning. Abby held out her hand and resisted the urge to pluck Sydney's fingers from Flann's arm. She did, however, make a point of staring at the offending appendage. "Abigail Remy. Nice to meet you."

Sydney laughed lightly and held out her hand. "Nice to meet you too. I was just telling Flann I would've been here earlier, but one of my clients had a mare who was having trouble foaling." She smiled at Flann. "Thanks for calling and letting me know about today. I would have hated to miss the party."

"No problem," Flann said easily.

"It's so nice to see everyone again." Sydney looked pointedly at Flann. "It's been too long."

Abby gritted her teeth and took Flann's hand. "Your mother was looking for you."

"Sure," Flann said, her brows quirked quizzically. "I'll see you later, Syd."

"Of course."

Abby pulled Flann through the gaggle of kids toward the front of the house and away from the center of activity.

"Really," Flann said, laughing. "My mother?"

"Never mind." Abby strode across the porch and inside to the deserted foyer. The hallway beyond was dim and cool. They were alone. Abby, Flann in tow, marched toward the staircase.

"Abs?" Flann asked.

"You invited her?"

Flann took the stairs two at a time to keep up with Abby's rapid pace. "Yeah, I thought—"

Abby stopped at the bedroom she'd stayed in the first time Flann had kissed her, pulled her inside, and shut the door. She turned and pressed Flann back against it. "Be careful what you say right now."

Flann's eyes widened. "I thought I could introduce her to the kids. Help them get an in at the clinic."

Abby caught Flann's chin in her hand and kissed her until Flann groaned and gripped her hips. She pulled back, breathless. "Good answer."

"Abby," Flann said hoarsely. "What are you doing?"

Abby smiled. "I'm staking my claim."

"I—"

Abby pressed her fingers to Flann's mouth. "I think you'll get my meaning in a minute."

"You do realize where we are?"

Abby laughed. "Do you think anyone's paying any attention? In case you haven't noticed, you can't hear yourself think around this place for all the hammering and whatnot." She skimmed her mouth down Flann's neck and licked the hollow at the base of her throat. "Unless, of course, you'd rather leave."

"Hell no," Flann whispered, tilting her head back against the door.

She'd never been claimed before, never been taken, and suddenly she wanted that more than she'd ever wanted anything. She wanted to belong to Abby. "I don't want to go anywhere at all."

"Good," Abby whispered, tugging Flann's T-shirt from her jeans. "Because you're not going to."

CHAPTER TWENTY-EIGHT

The door," Flann said hoarsely, words deserting her.

"I'll take care of that." Abby reached back and turned the old-fashioned brass key in the lock. A clunk signaled the outside world was shut away.

Nothing mattered now except the desire that bound them.

Flann pressed her hands flat against the door. Abby wanted to be in charge. She couldn't remember a time when a woman had made demands of her, other than that she satisfy her. She'd never minded, but this…this was something completely different. Something she hadn't realized she wanted until just this moment, and now she wanted Abby's hands on her more than she wanted her heart to keep beating.

Abby grabbed the bottom of her T-shirt and yanked it up over her breasts. Flann automatically raised her arms and Abby stripped it off, dropping it behind them.

Abby smiled. "I've been wanting to see you without your shirt on since the first moment I saw you."

"You could have asked and I would—"

Abby pressed her fingers to Flann's mouth. "I don't want you to say anything. I don't want you to think about anything. The only thing I want is for you to feel what I'm doing to you."

Silently, Flann nodded. Her heart pounded so hard it had to be visible through her skin. Abby pressed both hands to her chest, splaying her fingers over Flann's muscles, moving slowly back and forth as if taking her measure. Flann was never so happy in her life that she spent her spare time working around the farm. She had trouble catching her breath. She had trouble focusing. She blinked, searched for some place to hold on, and met Abby's eyes. They weren't hazy the way they got when they kissed. They were sharp and intent, glittering with hunger. Hunger for her. She couldn't keep quiet. "Okay?"

"Oh, honey. More than okay," Abby murmured. "I love the way you look." She slid her hands down Flann's chest and cupped her breasts, lifting slightly so their weight fell into her palms. She brushed her thumbs over the tight tan nipples. "Look at you. So damn sexy."

"God," Flann choked out. Everything was too slow, too soft, too perfect. Already blood was pounding between her legs, the beat like a frantic creature racing from a soaring hawk. She'd embarrass herself if she got much more excited. "Abby—"

"I know," Abby said gently, lowering her head and closing her lips around Flann's nipple.

The shock arrowed straight down her spine. Flann's legs trembled and she locked her knees to keep upright. Her breasts tingled. Lightning coiled in her belly, a storm brewing, about to explode. Flann cupped Abby's head, pressed her mouth harder to her breast. "Feels so good."

Lips curving in a triumphant smile, Abby took her time. She had all the time in the world now. This was where she belonged—this place, this world, this woman. She'd been searching and hadn't even known it. She moved from one breast to the other, kissing the firm curves, nipping at the tender nipples, reveling in the rasp of Flann's breath and the soft whimpers she doubted Flann even knew she was making. She brushed her mouth over the soft skin, a pirate claiming her treasure. Flann was hers and she intended to mark her in some deep, indelible place, in her body and her heart. "You're mine."

"Yes," Flann gasped.

Abby kissed her way back to Flann's mouth, delved inside, and slid a hand between their bodies. She flicked open the button on Flann's pants.

Flann muttered softly, "Need you, Abby. Please."

"I'm here." But Abby had no intention of releasing her just yet. She dropped to her knees, gripped Flann's waistband, and pulled her jeans down her legs. Of course she'd gone commando. Nothing ever reined Flann in, not clothes or convention. Only her. Only here, where all their secrets were exposed, where every need was celebrated, and every want satisfied. "Kick off those boots."

"I don't think I can move. I want to come so bad."

"Mmm, I like that." Abby kissed the base of Flann's belly and reached down until she found the laces on Flann's boots. She pulled them free. "Now, off."

Flann managed to kick free of her boots, and Abby pushed the jeans after them. Abby's vision hazed. Flann was naked, arms spread against the door, waiting, ready. Her arms and legs were bronzed and sculpted, her breasts proudly lifting, her abdomen a tight plain of smooth skin and muscle. She was glorious.

The sight of her, the taste of her, the scent of her desire stirred a madness Abby embraced with joy. Never in her life had she felt so powerful, or so blessed. She skimmed her fingers up the inside of Flann's thighs, urging her to open. Flann's body followed her commands, and Abby dipped her head and kissed her.

"Damn!" Flann's hips thrust forward, and she drove her fingers into Abby's hair.

Abby pressed her cheek to Flann's thigh, struggling for enough control to continue. Flann's need enflamed hers. She wanted to take her in, swallow her, drive her over the edge. But not yet. Not this first time. She raised her head, met Flann's hooded gaze. "You're gorgeous."

"Take what you want." Flann's face was stark with need and something more. Trust.

Abby's heart filled. "I want you. You, Flann. All of you."

Flann's fingers trembled in Abby's hair. "I'm yours. All of me."

"Here?" Abby stroked one finger between Flann's thighs.

"Yes. Yes, please."

"Mmm. Wait." Abby followed the path of her finger with her mouth, traced the folds and valleys, closed her lips around Flann's clitoris, circled her feather-light.

Flann groaned. "Close, close."

Abby slid her arms around Flann's hips and caressed her ass, held her firmly against her mouth, and sucked.

Flann's head banged back against the door. A hoarse cry wrenched from her throat, and her fingers convulsed on Abby's neck. She came hard in Abby's mouth, pumping once, twice, a third frantic thrust of her hips. Abby kept up the long easy strokes until Flann sagged with a tortured groan.

Abby rose quickly, cinched an arm around Flann's waist, and

kissed her. Not done yet. She wanted more. She cupped her, eased inside. "Again."

Flann moaned and tightened around her. Abby stroked, slowly at first until she felt Flann tense and grip her harder. She kissed her, increasing her tempo and swallowing her moans. Flann grabbed her shoulders so tightly she'd probably leave marks. Abby didn't care. She reveled in the feel of Flann coming apart in her arms. When Flann came again, Abby pressed her mouth to the wild pulse in Flann's neck. *Mine.*

"Done," Flann finally gasped. "I think you fucking killed me."

Abby laughed, the triumphant sound of a warrior trumpeting her victory. "I certainly hope not. I'm not done with you."

"I don't ever want you to be done," Flann said fervently.

Abby leaned back, cupped Flann's face in both hands. "I never will be. I love you, Flann."

"I need you Abby." Flann kissed her. "I love you, if you'll have me. I swear—"

"You're already mine, Flann," Abby whispered and kissed her back.

Flann caught her second wind midway through the kiss. Abby loved her. Abby wanted her. Abby was hers, as she was Abby's. She slipped an arm behind Abby's shoulders, the other under her knees, and picked her up.

"Flann! What—"

Laughing, Flann strode four paces to the bed and dumped Abby in the center. Abby shrieked and Flann straddled her hips, already unbuttoning the sexy shirt she was wearing.

Abby raised up so Flann could get it off and her underwear followed. Then the shorts and Abby was naked, spread out before her and so beautiful Flann forgot to breathe.

"You'll forgive me," Flann muttered, sliding between Abby's legs, "if I don't go slow the first time."

Abby laughed, wild and reckless. "Who wants slow? Hurry."

Flann's mouth came to Abby's breast at the same time as her hand slid between her legs. The fire that had been burning in Abby's depths for days roared to life and she arched, pushing against Flann's fingers. She grabbed her wrist, pushed her deeper. "I want you to make me come. Right now."

Flann's teeth closed on Abby's nipple just hard enough to send a jolt burning through her clitoris. She arched her hips, rode Flann's hand, and closed her eyes as everything inside her unraveled. She lost count of how many times she crested, lost awareness, lost everything except the sensation of Flann above her, inside her, owning her. At last she lay boneless with Flann stretched out on top of her. She had just enough energy to kiss her neck.

"That is unequivocally the best sex I've ever had," Abby murmured in a voice she didn't recognize. Throaty and obscenely satisfied.

Flann chuckled against her throat. "Wait till the next time."

Abby stroked her hair. "Will that be soon?"

"I sincerely hope so."

"You do realize it's a package deal?" Abby wasn't so far gone not to know she couldn't be so exposed without being sure. For once in her life, she wanted to be selfish. She wanted it all.

Flann marshaled her strength and pushed herself up on her elbow. Her face was loose and relaxed and she looked years younger. And supremely satisfied. Such an arrogant, gorgeous woman. Abby's heart clenched. *Please.*

"If you mean Blake, of course I know that. If you'd let me be part of his life, I would be honored."

"You know you already are part of his life. And mine." Abby caught her lip between her teeth and waited until her voice was steady. "I'm going to want the whole deal, you know. That means you and only you for me. And same for you. The three of us, together."

Flann's brows drew together. "That works for me, for now."

Abby's throat closed. "For now?"

Flann kissed her throat, the valley between her breasts, the place where her heart beat. "I know it's asking a lot of you, but I was thinking we might work on a sister or brother for Blake."

"I'm almost thirty-five years old." Abby stroked Flann's face. "So I suppose we should get started fairly soon."

Flann grinned. "Let's find a house and get Blake settled at school. Then you say when."

"We should probably tell Blake about us first. He'll be so happy."

"Then that makes three of us."

Abby pulled Flann down beside her and curled up with her head on Flann's shoulder. "I'm afraid he'll want a farm."

"Plenty of those around. Maybe we can compromise and get a reasonable-sized spread closer to town." Flann stroked her arm, her talented surgeon's fingers tracing light patterns on her skin that set Abby ablaze again. "A barn, some pastureland, but not so big we can't handle it ourselves."

Abby nuzzled her neck. "I want to see the river. I love the sound of the water at night."

"Anything." Flann tilted her chin and kissed her. "Anything you want."

Abby smiled. "You're what I want."

"Done," Flann murmured. "And if we stay here much longer I'm going to want you again. Sooner or later we'll be missed."

"I know." Abby sighed. "We should get back." She laughed. "But I'm showering first."

"Good idea. I'll help."

Abby sat up, pressed her palm to Flann's belly. Muscles jumped, and her blood heated. "Not the recommended course of action, Dr. Rivers."

"Do you have a better treatment plan in mind, Dr. Remy?" Flann stretched under Abby's caresses, indolent and satisfied.

"Mmm, I do." Abby leaned down, kissed her, and quickly rose before her willpower deserted her. "Much more of that as often as possible."

Flann grinned. "Sounds like the perfect prescription."

EPILOGUE

Three Weeks Later

Thunder pulled Flann from a deep sleep. Rain pelted the tin roof of the old schoolhouse, filling the bedroom with a melody as familiar as her own heartbeat. Beyond the window, the faint gray light heralded the dawn. She listened to the sounds of the world awakening—a tree frog's rumbling croak, the first trill of birdsong, the distant whistle of a freight train chugging along the river. Nature's symphony washed over her like a soothing caress, but what warmed her most of all was Abby's slow, steady breathing—her presence still new and already achingly central to Flann's life. Abby slept on her side with her back to Flann, her hips pressed into the curve of Flann's body as if they had been sculpted to fit together. Flann slid her hand around Abby's middle and gently brushed her palm over the curve of her belly. Abby murmured, arched under her touch, and edged closer. Flann rested her cheek in the curve of Abby's neck, breathing in the pure, clean scent of her hair and skin. The night was warm and they'd gone to sleep naked beneath the sheet. The sensation of Abby's soft, warm skin against her nipples made her loins tighten.

"Mmm." Flann kissed her neck.

"Again?" Abby murmured sleepily.

Flann chuckled. "What's the matter, are you worn out already?"

"Three hundred times in three weeks? Not a chance."

"That's good. As I think we've got a few thousand more times to go." Smiling, Flann cupped Abby's breast and swept her thumb lightly over her nipple, inflamed as always by the quick indrawn breath, the tightening surge of Abby's hips.

Abby turned onto her back, curved one arm around Flann's neck, and drew her down for a kiss. "At least, but who's counting."

Flann kissed her again slowly, savoring the softness of her mouth, exulting in starting another day beside her. "I love you."

Abby purred. "I love you too." Another wave of thunder rolled through and Abby frowned. "Do you think they're all right out in this?"

"Sure. Part of the fun of these weekend camping trips is getting caught in a rainstorm. They'll be muddy and wet, but fine." Flann rubbed her cheek on Abby's breast and circled a tight nipple with her tongue. "He'll love it."

"It's his first time with kids he doesn't know. Who don't know him."

"Margie's there, and Bill runs these outdoor work weekends like boot camp—everybody works, everybody contributes, no favorites. Bill will keep an eye on them, and they'll have the pond cleared and be canoeing by noon." Flann looked up, smoothed her thumb over the crease in Abby's forehead. "And I asked Bill to keep an eye on him. He would anyhow, but I just wanted to be sure. It was Blake's idea to go with the mountain club—we have to be as brave as he is."

"I love you for loving him," Abby said quietly, "but I fell in love with you for myself. I need you."

Flann's heart swelled. How had she gotten so lucky? "We need to do this every day."

"Which part?" Abby teased, running her fingertips down Flann's spine, caressing her ass. "Waking up together, having sex before the sun comes up, or sharing the joys and terror of raising a teen?"

"All of the above. I want to come home to you every night, wake up to you every morning, plan every day of my life with you and Blake."

Abby's eyes gleamed as she caressed Flann's face. "Is that a proposal?"

"Damn right. I don't just want us to live together. I want us to get married."

"*Married* married, like married?" Abby's voice trembled.

Flann laughed. "Dr. Remy, words seem to fail you this morning."

"Oh no, I got that word just right. The whole deal, you mean."

"I've never meant it more." For just a second, Flann panicked. Hadn't she been clear before that she wanted Abby to be hers, Abby and Blake? Granted, they'd spent just about every spare second since the barn raising in bed or figuring out how to get there, what with the way their schedules sometimes rarely lined up, but she'd thought she'd said everything she was feeling out loud. How could Abby not know? "I love you. I don't want a life without you and Blake in it. Yes, hell yes, I want the whole deal. You said you wanted—"

"I know what I said. I want exactly the same thing. You are the one I want. Today, tomorrow, every day." Abby kissed her, a firm, fiery, undeniable kiss of ownership. "The answer is yes, Flann. Always, yes."

The tension in Flann's chest eased, and she rested her forehead on Abby's. "We've still got Harper and Presley's wedding to get through, and—"

Abby laughed. "The wedding planning is not exactly a chore, but it is going to take everyone's free time for the next little while. And then there's Blake…"

"We should probably let him get settled in school first," Flann said, "but I want to house hunt, okay?"

"Absolutely. If the three of us are going to be cohabitating, which it looks as if we are, we need a little more room."

"Good. I saw a place just at the edge of town that looks perfect. Close enough so Blake can easily see his friends, but there's good land, Abby. The house needs a little work, but—"

"Let's go see it."

"Until I met you," Flann murmured, easing on top of Abby and framing her face so their eyes met, "I didn't want to be needed. I was afraid I would fail somehow. That I might not be enough. You make me strong, Abby."

Abby slid her leg behind Flann's and pulled her into the cradle of her hips. "You have always been strong. And you're everything I need."

"God, Abby," Flann whispered, feeling the hunger flare to life along with the joy. "You're everything. I'll never get enough of you."

Abby smiled. "I'm glad to hear it, but I don't mind if you try."

About the Author

Radclyffe has written over forty-five romance and romantic intrigue novels, dozens of short stories, and, writing as L.L. Raand, has authored a paranormal romance series, The Midnight Hunters.

She is an eight-time Lambda Literary Award finalist in romance, mystery, and erotica—winning in both romance (*Distant Shores, Silent Thunder*) and erotica (*Erotic Interludes 2: Stolen Moments* edited with Stacia Seaman and *In Deep Waters 2: Cruising the Strip* written with Karin Kallmaker). A member of the Saints and Sinners Literary Hall of Fame, she is also an RWA/FF&P Prism Award winner for *Secrets in the Stone*, an RWA FTHRW Lories and RWA HODRW winner for *Firestorm*, an RWA Bean Pot winner for *Crossroads*, and an RWA Laurel Wreath winner for *Blood Hunt*. In 2014 she was awarded the Dr. James Duggins Outstanding Mid-Career Novelist Award by the Lambda Literary Foundation.

She is also the president of Bold Strokes Books, one of the world's largest independent LGBTQ publishing companies.

Find her at facebook.com/Radclyffe.BSB, follow her on Twitter @RadclyffeBSB, and visit her website at Radfic.com.

Books Available From Bold Strokes Books

Illicit Artifacts by Stevie Mikayne. Her foster mother's death cracked open a secret world Jil never wanted to see...and now she has to pick up the stolen pieces. (978-1-62639-472-8)

Pathfinder by Gun Brooke. Heading for their new homeworld, Exodus's chief engineer Adina Vantressa and nurse Briar Lindemay carry game-changing secrets that may well cause them to lose everything when disaster strikes. (978-1-62639-444-5)

Prescription for Love by Radclyffe. Dr. Flannery Rivers finds herself attracted to the new ER chief, city girl Abigail Remy, and the incendiary mix of city and country, fire and ice, tradition and change is combustible. (978-1-62639-570-1)

Ready or Not by Melissa Brayden. Uptight Mallory Spencer finds relinquishing control to bartender Hope Sanders too tall an order in fast-paced New York City. (978-1-62639-443-8)

Summer Passion by MJ Williamz. Women loving women is forbidden in 1946 Hollywood, yet Jean and Maggie strive to keep their love alive and away from prying eyes. (978-1-62639-540-4)

The Princess and the Prix by Nell Stark. "Ugly duckling" Princess Alix of Monaco was resigned to loneliness until she met racecar driver Thalia d'Angelis. (978-1-62639-474-2)

Winter's Harbor by Aurora Rey. Lia Brooks isn't looking for love in Provincetown, but when she discovers chocolate croissants and pastry chef Alex McKinnon, her winter retreat quickly starts heating up. (978-1-62639-498-8)

The Time Before Now by Missouri Vaun. Vivian flees a disastrous affair, embarking on an epic, transformative journey to escape her past, until destiny introduces her to Ida, who helps her rediscover trust, love, and hope. (978-1-62639-446-9)

Twisted Whispers by Sheri Lewis Wohl. Betrayal, lies, and secrets—whispers of a friend lost to darkness. Can a reluctant psychic set things right or will an evil soul destroy those she loves? (978-1-62639-439-1)

The Courage to Try by C.A. Popovich. Finding love is worth getting past the fear of trying. (978-1-62639-528-2)

Break Point by Yolanda Wallace. In a world readying for war, can love find a way? (978-1-62639-568-8)

Countdown by Julie Cannon. Can two strong-willed, powerful women overcome their differences to save the lives of seven others and begin a life they never imagined together? (978-1-62639-471-1)

Keep Hold by Michelle Grubb. Claire knew some things should be left alone and some rules should never be broken, but the most forbidden, well, they are the most tempting. (978-1-62639-502-2)

Deadly Medicine by Jaime Maddox. Dr. Ward Thrasher's life is in turmoil. Her partner Jess left her, and her job puts her in the path of a murderous physician who has Jess in his sights. (978-1-62639-424-7)

New Beginnings by KC Richardson. Can the connection and attraction between Jordan Roberts and Kirsten Murphy be enough for Jordan to trust Kirsten with her heart? (978-1-62639-450-6)

Officer Down by Erin Dutton. Can two women who've made careers out of being there for others in crisis find the strength to need each other? (978-1-62639-423-0)

Reasonable Doubt by Carsen Taite. Just when Sarah and Ellery think they've left dangerous careers behind, a new case sets them—and their hearts—on a collision course. (978-1-62639-442-1)

Tarnished Gold by Ann Aptaker. Cantor Gold must outsmart the Law, outrun New York's dockside gangsters, outplay a shady art dealer, his lover, and a beautiful curator, and stay out of a killer's gun sights. (978-1-62639-426-1)

White Horse in Winter by Franci McMahon. Love between two women collides with the inner poison of a closeted horse trainer in the green hills of Vermont. (978-1-62639-429-2)

Autumn Spring by Shelley Thrasher. Can Bree and Linda, two women in the autumn of their lives, put their hearts first and find the love they've never dared seize? (978-1-62639-365-3)

The Renegade by Amy Dunne. Post-apocalyptic survivors Alex and Evelyn secretly find love while held captive by a deranged cult, but when their relationship is discovered, they must fight for their freedom—or die trying. (978-1-62639-427-8)

Thrall by Barbara Ann Wright. Four women in a warrior society must work together to lift an insidious curse while caught between their own desires, the will of their peoples, and an ancient evil. (978-1-62639-437-7)

The Chameleon's Tale by Andrea Bramhall. Two old friends must work through a web of lies and deceit to find themselves again, but in the search they discover far more than they ever went looking for. (978-1-62639-363-9)

Side Effects by VK Powell. Detective Jordan Bishop and Dr. Neela Sahjani must decide if it's easier to trust someone with your heart or your life as they face threatening protestors, corrupt politicians, and their increasing attraction. (978-1-62639-364-6)

Warm November by Kathleen Knowles. What do you do if the one woman you want is the only one you can't have? (978-1-62639-366-0)

In Every Cloud by Tina Michele. When Bree finally leaves her shattered life behind, is she strong enough to salvage the remaining pieces of her heart and find the place where it truly fits? (978-1-62639-413-1)

Rise of the Gorgon by Tanai Walker. When independent Internet journalist Elle Pharell goes to Kuwait to investigate a veteran's mysterious suicide, she hires Cassandra Hunt, an interpreter with a covert agenda. (978-1-62639-367-7)

Crossed by Meredith Doench. Agent Luce Hansen returns home to catch a killer and risks everything to revisit the unsolved murder of her first girlfriend and confront the demons of her youth. (978-1-62639-361-5)

Making a Comeback by Julie Blair. Music and love take center stage when jazz pianist Liz Randall tries to make a comeback with the help of her reclusive, blind neighbor, Jac Winters. (978-1-62639-357-8)

Soul Unique by Gun Brooke. Self-proclaimed cynic Greer Landon falls for Hayden Rowe's paintings and the young woman shortly after, but will Hayden, who lives with Asperger syndrome, trust her and reciprocate her feelings? (978-1-62639-358-5)

The Price of Honor by Radclyffe. Honor and duty are not always black and white—and when self-styled patriots take up arms against the government, the price of honor may be a life. (978-1-62639-359-2)

Mounting Evidence by Karis Walsh. Lieutenant Abigail Hargrove and her mounted police unit need to solve a murder and protect wetland biologist Kira Lovell during the Washington State Fair. (978-1-62639-343-1)

Threads of the Heart by Jeannie Levig. Maggie and Addison Rae-McInnis share a love and a life, but are the threads that bind them together strong enough to withstand Addison's restlessness and the seductive Victoria Fontaine? (978-1-62639-410-0)

Sheltered Love by MJ Williamz. Boone Fairway and Grey Dawson—two women touched by abuse—overcome their pasts to find happiness in each other. (978-1-62639-362-2)

Death's Doorway by Crin Claxton. Helping the dead can be deadly: Tony may be listening to the dead, but she needs to learn to listen to the living. (978-1-62639-354-7)

Searching for Celia by Elizabeth Ridley. As American spy novelist Dayle Salvesen investigates the mysterious disappearance of her ex-lover, Celia, in London, she begins questioning how well she knew Celia—and how well she knows herself. (978-1-62639-356-1).

Hardwired by C.P. Rowlands. Award-winning teacher Clary Stone and Leefe Ellis, manager of the homeless shelter for small children, stand together in a part of Clary's hometown that she never knew existed. (978-1-62639-351-6)

The Muse by Meghan O'Brien. Erotica author Kate McMannis struggles with writer's block until a gorgeous muse entices her into a world of fantasy sex and inadvertent romance. (978-1-62639-223-6)